BOOK 2 OF EUPHORIA ONLINE

NIGHTMARE KEEP

PHIL TUCKER

NIGHTMARE KEEP
Book 2 of Euphoria Online

Copyright © 2018 Phil Tucker

All rights reserved.

ISBN-13:9781727025347
ISBN-10:172705342

Table of Contents

NIGHTMARE KEEP

Philip Tucker

1

I T WAS IRONIC. I was being escorted by necromancer and a
dozen skeletal champions along the escarpment that led from
Castle Winter to the highland meadow, and I'd never felt safer. I
stumbled along, the toes of my boots catching on every rock, my
mind a churning well of thoughts and regrets. My friends and
I had striven for the impossible: to liberate the castle of ridiculously challenging foes – and won. Yet despite our heroic success,
everything had immediately gone horribly wrong.

Michaela, on the other hand, was in high spirits. She strode
with a vigor that belied her undead state, her long, muscled legs
extending from her thigh-slit skirt with each stride, her staff
resting across her shoulders, hands dangling over it as if she were
in a stockade. Skull mask tipped back over her head, she whis-
tled under her breath. If it hadn't been for the gaping holes in
her neck and side, you could have been forgiven for thinking she
was a regular lady out on a Sunday stroll.

Movement caught my eye. Someone was climbing up along the ridge toward us, clad in a simple white tunic and tan breeches, jogging along the path with easy athleticism. He stumbled to a stop upon spotting us, and turned as if to flee.

"Falkon!" I waved both arms. "It's me, Chris! Don't run!"

My friend hesitated. I didn't blame him. Nobody liked to be approached by skeletal champions, much less twelve of them. Invigorated by the sight of my friend, I hurried past Michaela and ran along the path that hugged the rocky slope, heart thudding in my chest. The very thought of him running away and leaving me to face this madness alone was terrifying.

"Chris?" Falkon's usually confident tone was decidedly shaken. "What's going on?"

"Nothing good," I said, coming to a stop. Michaela, rather diplomatically, hadn't approached any closer. I gestured at her with my thumb over my shoulder. "She showed up just after we killed the wyvern—"

"You killed the *wyvern*?"

"—and saved me from Lotharia."

"Saved you from—what?"

"Yeah. She used the spider staff at the end to save me. But she used it too much, and she…" A sickening feeling roiled through me as I thought of those last moments once more. "I don't know what's the right word. Turned?"

"Oh, damn," said Falkon, running his hand over his hair. "And she attacked you?"

I nodded. "Turned out trying to take her staff away was a bad move. But then Michaela there showed up and saved my life with a green forcefield. Lotharia fled into the keep, and Michaela insisted rather forcefully on accompanying me to meet you."

Falkon closed his eyes and rubbed his brow with a wince. "Wait. You're hurting my head. The undead chick saved you and then demanded to meet me?"

"That's not all. She said her boss has been trying to arrange an audience for some time now, and when they saw the smoke from the blown-up stables they came running."

Falkon opened his eyes. "I feel like I'm being beaten around the neck and shoulders with an information overload stick here. Her boss?"

"Yeah." I hesitated. There was no slick way of saying this part. "Um. Dread Lord Guthorios the Forlorn? He's the guy in charge of Feldgrau."

Falkon stared at me, wide-eyed, then clapped me on the shoulder and gave a strained laugh. "Haha! You had me going there. You're a freaking riot, you know that, Chris? Now, seriously. What's up with the undead lady and her skeletal champions?"

Michaela chose that moment to interrupt. "They are called Servitors," she said, striding down the path toward us. "And Chris' account is accurate. My master desires to speak with you both. Your friend Lotharia removed herself from my sphere of influence by entering the keep, but you two shall suffice."

She stopped before us, one hand on her hip, the other leaning her staff over her shoulder, and gave us a lazy, feline smile. "C'mon. Surely the brave warriors who killed four ogres and a wyvern aren't afraid of meeting one little Dread Lord?"

Falkon choked so I chose that moment to extend his bastard sword to him. The sight of his weapon gave him strength; he took hold of it with a sharp inhalation. "The rest of my gear?"

Michaela snapped her fingers without looking back and a skeletal champion came running up, all of Falkon's chain and plate mail jangling in his arms. "You'll find you get only the best customer service from the undead."

"Sure, sure," said Falkon, gingerly taking his gear from the skeleton's arms. "And this Guthorios, what's he want?"

"Don't bother," I said. "Michaela takes an unusually cruel delight in answering all questions as cryptically as she can."

"Damn," said Falkon, struggling into his chain shirt. "As if dying weren't enough of a bummer." He tugged the shirt down, then grabbed his belt and buckled it over the shining links.

"On the plus side," I said, "she's confirmed that we're not to be killed and recruited. Like she was, apparently."

"Oh yeah?" Falkon eyed her as he slid his scabbard onto his belt. "Only the best customer service, hey?"

Michaela rolled her eyes. "It's a short, sordid story filled with screams, futile pleas for mercy and unhallowed rites. I'm sure you don't want to hear it, and even if you did, tough luck."

"Fair enough," said Falkon. He stared at the pommel of his sword. "Hey, my mana's all gone."

"Sorry," I said. "That was me."

"You really killed the wyvern?" Falkon's eyes glowed green. "Holy crap. Level ten?"

"What?" Michaela sounded outraged. "You're only level ten?"

"Yeah," I said to Falkon, ignoring her but feeling a little smug. "Killing level thirty ogres is apparently a great way to earn XP." I paused. "Wait, what? Level ten? No. Level eight."

"Nope. You're level ten, you lucky bastard. I got nothing because I died. Haven't you checked your XP since you killed the wyvern?"

"I've… I've not checked, to be honest."

He raised his eyebrows. "Not checked. You killed a wyvern and you weren't even curious?"

"It's been an intense past half-hour. I'm really at level ten? Wait a second." I summoned my character sheet and studied the first window.

 You have gained 160 experience (160 for defeating a wyvern). You have 172 unused XP. Your total XP is 922.

Congratulations! You are Level 9!
Congratulations! You are Level 10!

"Holy crap is right," I said, swiping the window away. "That one encounter overall raised me five levels."

Michaela was staring at Falkon. "You can see people's stats?"

"Oh, you a player, then?" Falkon eyed her with renewed interest. "Yeah, it's a perk I've got." His eyes flashed green as he stared at her. "Nice. Level fifteen."

I re-evaluated Michaela. "Huh. I thought you'd be higher level."

She flushed, which was impressive for an undead lady to pull off, and raised her chin. "I don't care what you thought. Lord Guthorios will be even happier to meet you now. If you're *quite* ready?"

"Wait," said Falkon, staring more closely. "You're in Death March mode, too?"

"None of your concern," she said, voice harsh. "We march."

Falkon sighed and threaded a strap through his breast plate, back plate, and pauldrons, then heaved them over his shoulder. "I'll put these on later. Lead the way."

Michaela gave a signal and half of the skeletal champions moved back up the ridge toward the first switchback that headed down to Feldgrau, with the other six following us from behind. She took the lead, clearly miffed and no longer interested in chatting.

"What the hell?" asked Falkon in a low whisper. "She's undead and in Death March? That means she's going to actually die when her six months are up."

"That's fucked up," I whispered back. I stared at Michaela's back in horrified fascination. "No wonder she said she was 'forcefully recruited'. Man. I feel awful for her."

"And what do you think this Guthorios wants with us?" asked Falkon. "I've never heard of the undead wanting to chill, you know?"

I hesitated, eager to move to my next character advancement window. "She said they need us alive. And that we'll be working together. Beyond that, just smug smiles and half answers. My guess is that they plan to force us to help them with whatever they're trying to accomplish down in Feldgrau. I mean, Guthorios was left behind by the guy who ran the original attack on Castle Winter?"

Falkon shifted the weight of his plate armor over his shoulder. "Could be. Looks like we'll find out soon enough. Go on." He grinned at me. "Check your upgrades."

It felt weird to be excited about anything with Lotharia lost to us in the keep, but then again, life had taught me to enjoy myself whenever I could. Like how I'd been excited to hang out with Brianna even after Justin had been arrested back home. You couldn't stop living your life, not even while you were living with tragedy. Moments would creep up on you, and suddenly you'd catch yourself laughing, enjoying yourself, having forgotten all about the heavy stuff you were dealing with. You'd feel a flash of guilt, of unease... and maybe that would ruin the moment.

And maybe it wouldn't.

I sighed, thinking about Justin, thinking about Lotharia, and then opened the next window. One thing I'd learned after experiencing so much tragedy in my life already was that feeling guilty and holding back didn't help anybody.

 Your attributes have increased!

```
Mana +2
Strength +1
Dexterity +1
Charisma +1
```

You have learned new skills!

```
Melee: Basic (III)
Backstab: Basic (IV)
```

Hmm. Not as much as I'd hoped. Then again, I'd been ridiculously spoiled by my previous jump in levels. Still, I'd take a boost to my melee and backstab skills any day. Also, I surreptitiously ran a hand over my other arm – there was a definite swell there now of defined muscle over my bicep and triceps. Much more than I'd ever had back home. Trying to look casual, I tucked my hand under my spider silk shirt and felt a faint hint of ridged abs up my core, along with actual pec muscles.

Dang. I was getting ripped.

Falkon eyed me and then laughed. "Want help with that examination?"

"I, uh – what? No! Thank you. I've got it under control." Most of the time I just thought of Falkon as a guy, but every now and then he reminded me that his player was a girl. A straight girl, at that. It was easiest to just accept him as he or she was, and not think about it too much. Which worked fine until he offered to feel up my abs for me.

I swiped to the next window.

 There are new talent advancements available to you:

No kidding. I'd devoured two of them during the fight with the wyvern. What remained were Darkvision, Wall Climber (I), and Cat's Fall. The two new talents were:

Mute Presence

XP Cost: 75
- Allows you to mute your presence in Euphoria, making it harder for monsters and characters to notice you.
- Your stealth skill is boosted and even those with *Astute Observer (I)* find it harder to notice you.

Heads-Up

XP Cost: 75
- The tighter the bonds of friendship, the more a companion can sense what you've just seen.
- Allows an ally within fifty feet to notice whatever you've detected, even if they would normally be unable to do so.

Interesting. I mused over my options there for a while, only half seeing the steep path we were following down to ruined Feldgrau. *Darkvision* seemed like the most useful, but I wasn't ready to make any purchases just yet. I swiped the window away and opened the next.

 There are new spells available to you:

Evenfall: Your affinity with the shadows allows you to target natural sources of light, quenching flames within 100 feet through mere application of will.
- Mana Drain: scales up with the size of the flame
- Cost: 75 XP

Ebon Tendrils (II): Animate two lengths of shadow so that they obey your will, growing up to a length of 7 yards and with two-thirds your physical stats.
- Mana Drain: 2 to summon, 2 to maintain for every additional 10 seconds
- Cost: 75 XP

Grasping Shadows: The darkness hungers for your foes, and will seek to bind and constrain any targets you designate when they move through sufficient areas of darkness.
- Mana Drain: 3
- Cost: 100 XP

I let out a low whistle. "Very nice. Man, I love leveling."

"You and the rest of the world," said Falkon. "It's all about the dopamine."

"Yeah, yeah, I know. But brain chemistry aside, these are some great powers. Want to take a look?"

Falkon opened my sheet and spent a few minutes reading through my options, then swiped it away and gave me a grin. "Hard to believe you're now a level higher than I am. God damn it. If I'd managed to hang in there for the ogre and wyvern XP, I'd be level twelve or something now."

"Yeah. Thank you, by the way." My serious tone caused Falkon to give me a sharp look. "For stepping in there against Mogr and saving my life. Literally saving my life. Thank you."

I extended my hand, and after a moment's hesitation he grasped me by the wrist in a warrior's clasp and squeezed. "You're welcome, Chris." Then he laughed. "I mean, are you kidding me? You in Death March and all, and you think I'm going to hang back and be selective? I lost a couple of levels. That's nothing compared to what you've got on the line."

"Still—"

Michaela had turned to look at me over her shoulder. Damn. Just how sharp was her hearing? She considered me with lowered brows then looked away.

"Still, thanks. It's why I insisted on picking you up before heading to see Guthorios. I wanted – no, needed – someone who I trust to watch my back."

"Yeah, see, that sounds sweet, but then I step back and realize it means you're dragging me to Feldgrau's Broken Tower, and suddenly it doesn't sound quite as great." He paused then gave my shoulder a shove. "Kidding. I can't wait to meet the guy. I mean, 'the Forlorn'? He sounds like he's going to be a blast. Now. What're you going to buy?"

"I'm thinking Darkvision," I said. "I can see inside my own Night Shroud, but given that I'm supposed to operate all the time in the dark and shadows, being able to see what I'm doing would be a huge plus."

"I can't argue with that reasoning. And just a little more XP will tip you over the seventy-five mark again, meaning you can then buy another spell or talent in quick succession."

"Yeah. Too bad my rat killing days are over." I opened my sheet again, gazed over my options, then tapped Darkvision. The letters glowed gold, and the new talent appeared below the others. It being mid-morning, I didn't have a way to test it, but I couldn't wait to check out what it would do to my vision.

The path had just about leveled out now and Feldgrau loomed ahead, a graveyard of half-toppled buildings, circling crows, ashen ground and torn earth. I realized with a distinct sense of unease that Michaela's rather jocular style had lowered my guard, making it easier to not really appreciate just what we were walking into. Seeing the decayed village right ahead of me, however, brought it home – hard.

"Easy," said Falkon. "Like you said, they want us alive. That means we've got something they need. Neither of us are particularly diplomatic or charismatic, so let's not try anything fancy. Just hear them out, and then see where we go from there."

I thought of Lotharia with her Diplomacy: Basic (IV) and charisma fourteen. This was precisely the situation in which she'd shine. What was she doing at this very moment? With what manner of monsters was she dealing or conversing? For all I knew she could be fighting for her life, or forging new alliances with terrible beings. And here I was getting a kick out of spending XP.

Life goes on, I reminded myself. *Don't feel guilty for being alive.*

I sighed, rubbed at my face, and then pushed my shoulders back and raised my chin. We'd reached the outer edge of Feldgrau.

Michaela stopped and turned to us. "You're safe, of course, as long as you remain by my side. It feels a little demeaning to have to say this, but if you choose to bolt you'll not only have me after you, but all of Feldgrau. I can't guarantee your safety if that happens." She gave an apologetic shrug. "Clear?"

"You're really good at this," said Falkon. "What's your diplomacy at? Intermediate?"

Michaela flashed a perfect smile at him. "Intermediate two."

He snorted. "Charisma fifteen?"

Michaela's smile grew wry. "Close. Sixteen."

"Makes sense," said Falkon. "The apologetic note there was just perfect. Making us feel like you're secretly on our side. Like you're a victim yourself in this whole situation. Which—" He paused, eyes widening. "Oh, wow. This is all underscored by your 'forced recruitment' story." A smile of appreciation spread slowly across his face. "Of course, you couldn't know I'd suss out that you were in Death March mode, but even that only makes your tale more persuasive. Seriously. Good job. I thought I was onto how much you were manipulating us, but I didn't realize just how much I was still scooping what you were pooping."

"Scooping what she was pooping?" I asked.

Michaela's smile faded away. "Not everything here is a ploy, Squire Alastoroi, nor everything I say a lie. But if you want to be suspicious of everything, then I shall attempt nothing beyond the bare necessities."

"Nice," said Falkon. "You don't stop! You kidnap us and force us to meet a Dread Lord, and now somehow you're actually making me feel guilty by playing the wounded sincerity card? That's some seriously advanced shit."

Emotion flickered in Michaela's dark eyes – could that have been pain? And then she turned and led the way into Feldgrau.

"Ease up," I whispered to Falkon as we fell in.

"What? C'mon, Intermediate Diplomacy two and charisma sixteen? Don't tell me it's working on you?"

"No, I see what you're saying. But she's a player as well. And if she was really playing in Death March mode when she was converted then she's in the worst situation ever." I tried to separate manipulation from truth, to tease out diplomacy from honesty, and realized I didn't know where to draw the line. "Lotharia explained how regular players, once raised, have to decide whether to play as undead or log out and forfeit the rest of their Euphoria session, which is bad enough. But Michaela? She's screwed. So even if she's playing us, there's a chance we could befriend her in truth. And given how few allies we have in here? That might not be a bad move."

Falkon stared at the ground for a bit, making frustrated faces, and then blew out his cheeks. "Fine. You're right. Maybe I was a little harsh there. Or maybe not. Regardless, you've got a point. When you're drowning, you might as well clutch at straws."

"Your metaphors are sucking right now," I said. "Can we can them till you cheer up?"

He gave a hollow laugh. "Yeah. I'll let you know when that happens."

The ashen ground crunched beneath our boots. Whether it was slender branches or hollow bones I couldn't tell. The buildings rose up around us, gaunt, faded, windows like hollow eyes. Decaying forms slowed their passage and turned to stare at us. The silence grew powerful, with only the cawing of the crows overhead to break it.

"It sickens me to see Feldgrau like this," said Falkon under his breath. "The color gone. The people dead. The life sucked from its core. No matter what comes, I won't forgive Guthorios this travesty."

I wanted a weapon on which to rest my hand, a bastard sword like Falkon's. To make a gesture to reassure myself, no matter how futile. Skeletons stood swaying as they stared at us, strips of dried flesh still hanging from their bones, skin stretched taut as old parchment over their skulls, wisps of hair hanging like flax. Zombies were even worse, their old features discernible. Sunken eyes, lips pulled back to show dark gums and elongated teeth, hands curled into wretched claws, weeping sores and torn flesh.

On the skeletal champions strode, led by Michaela, and I noticed a subtle change come over her as we drew deeper into the town. She moved in a more stately manner, placing her feet with elegant care so that she never stumbled, shoulders swept back, chin raised, not looking to either side. Whomever she was, whatever her level, she moved through Feldgrau as if it were beneath her. I didn't know how that made me feel.

The Broken Tower rose into view over the last line of sagging and sunken rooftops, a perpetual vortex of buzzards circling slowly counterclockwise over its jagged peak. Only the first three floors remained, but the tower was wide enough to have once supported ten or more; it gave me the impression of Aragorn's shattered blade from *The Lord of the Rings*, a shard, a remnant of its former glory.

We rounded the last corner and stepped out into Feldgrau's main square, and there I beheld the charnel pit. The stench assaulted me so that I thrust my face into the crook of my elbow, and Falkon hawked and spat in an attempt to get the greasy, disgusting taste out of his mouth. The pit was as large as two tennis courts shoved together, its banks shallow at first then growing ever steeper till they sank into darkness. A darkness in which I could make out rubble and body parts, arms and legs and heads emerging from the dark earth, some unmoving, others twitching as if coming to life.

I could have used Darkvision right then to get a better look. I didn't want that to be my first use of my new power, however.

Didn't really want to see what was taking place in the depths of that hellhole.

The undead had congregated here, as if gathered to witness our entrance into the tower. Their ranks were easily five or six deep, and they had to number in the upper hundreds, if not thousands. My throat grew tight as I followed Michaela around the edge of the pit, trying not to look around wildly at the deadly forces arrayed in every direction. Banshees, lumbering hulks the size of small hills made of dozens of bodies, draugrs slinking everywhere I looked, and worse.

Six massive steps like lead coffins led up to the tower entrance, which was recessed under a once-glorious archway. Huge rotting doors of black wood banded with iron stood open at their top, and from that doorway came a cool and moldering breeze, like the exhalation of a grave.

Falkon and I both stopped at the bottom step, held back by some nameless dread. Michaela climbed the steps slowly, then turned, her foot on the highest, to gaze down at us with pensive sympathy. "You've come this far. Don't balk now."

I was sweating, I realized. A cold sweat that made me want to shiver under my spider silk shirt. Falkon's jaw was clenched, his brow lowered. This wasn't natural. The tower exuded some fear effect. Even gazing at its stones made my stomach churn.

"All right," I said, my voice a rasp. "We've come this far. Lead on, Michaela. I'll follow." And with that, I placed my foot on the first step.

2

O UR FOOTSTEPS RANG out in the stairwell that led to the second floor, our breaths pluming in the gloom. We'd turned away from the great chamber that filled the ground floor, seen only hints of death and depravity before Michaela had led us up into the dark. This was the first time I didn't welcome the presence of shadows, so with a breath I activated Darkvision so as to better see where we were being led.

The darkness swirled as if a stone had been dropped into a pool of ink, and then grew lighter, the edges and shapes hidden within its depths emerging. No color, however; everything appeared in tones of gray, with only faint hints of purple and green. I turned to look down and behind us: the natural light of the morning, filtered as it was in the beginning of the stairwell, looked normal. Interesting.

Michaela led us around the final curve of the stairs and we emerged onto the second floor. It was one massive chamber, circular and with a high ceiling, the rafters blackened by smoke and fire. Faded war banners hung down the walls between tattered tapestries, and the torn and moldy remains of rugs were laid out over the wooden floor. My eyes, however, were riveted to the figure in the center of the room.

I wasn't sure what I'd expected. An imposing throne, perhaps, made from melted swords, or carved from a massive black rock. Something terrible and awesome. Instead, the man sat on a large wooden chair – imposing, to be sure, but nothing a grandfather might not have relished by any inn's fireplace. He sat, straight-backed, chin sunk to his chest, eyes closed. Were it not for his lack of breath, I might have thought he slept.

A crown was bolted to his brow. There was no unifying circlet, but instead each black iron prong was nailed straight to his head, rising up like a forest of cruel knives. Faint tendrils of dried blood ran out from under each prong. He was a large man, or had been in life; his muscles had since wasted away, leaving his imposing frame withered beneath his torn and rusted black scale mail. Huge hands that looked to be all knuckles and sinew clutched at the arms of his chair nails long and dirty and broken.

His cheeks were sunken, his lips the color of liver, his skin spotted with lesions. Yet there was still something noble to his face, something of the faded glory he might once have wielded in life. And when he opened his chill blue eyes and raised his face to meet our gazes, I had the impression of the sun, seen on a misty morning just over the horizon, shorn of its beams but glorious still.

"Greetings," he said, and his voice was hoarse and worn as if from disuse. "Be welcome to the Broken Tower."

Michaela walked up to his side and there turned to face us, her expression sober and cold. We'd be getting no help from her.

I coughed into my fist and stepped forward. "Greetings, Dread Lord." Somehow, I couldn't help but be formal. "You wanted an audience?"

It was eerie how no part of him moved. His shoulders didn't rise and fall, his chest didn't expand, his hands and feet didn't so much as twitch. Everything but his jaw might have been a statue. "Indeed. I have yearned to speak with you since learning of your arrival. Your names?"

"Chris Meadows," I said, painfully aware how prosaic it sounded.

"Squire Falkon Alastoroi."

"There was another," said Guthorios.

Michaela stirred. "She was corrupted by necrotic energy and escaped into the keep shortly after I arrived."

"A pity," said Guthorios. "But such is fate. Falkon I recall from the original siege. Why have you come here, Chris Meadows?"

"I—uh—" How to explain a jealous and possibly mad ex to an undead lord? "I was tricked. By a former... lover? I joined the Cruel Winter faction without knowing what I was in for."

"Amusing," said Guthorios. "Did she trick you into your parlous state?"

"Parlous... state?" I didn't know what the word meant. Something to do with parlors?

Falkon leaned in. "He means your Death March status."

"Oh. No. That was all me. I'm taking the risk so as to benefit when I leave this place." Diplomacy: Basic (I) was doing me no favors. That and trying to translate real-world issues into fantasy-speak on the fly.

"Your soul glitters all the more brightly for it." Guthorios frowned as he studied me. "Undead created from the likes of you are as powerful as they are rare. Should you enter my service, I

promise that you would be raised as a Death Knight if not something greater."

"Um, no thanks." I gave him a sickly smile. "I'm kind of partial to being alive."

"So be it. And in truth, I need you living if you are to assist me. Both of you. For years I have sat here, tasked by my god to accomplish a task beyond my reach. But you. You are members of Cruel Winter, and within you burns the divine spark of life. You can help me." He leaned forward, old sinews creaking. "You *will* help me."

He was just an old dead man seated in a wooden chair, but waves of black magical power rolled off him like cold from a glacier. I fought as hard as I could to hold his gaze, and failed.

"Not so fast," said Falkon, and I admired him more than I could ever express for the bold tone in his voice. "We're not doing anything without a good explanation first."

"Of course." Guthorios sat back in his chair. "It was decreed by my god that Castle Winter must fall, and the treasure hidden in its depths delivered unto him. So we raised a mighty force, tore the dead from their graves by the thousands, and threw them against these mighty walls."

His voice sank into a whisper, and I listened, rapt.

"Our great foe was the archmagus. The treasure, we surmised, was of his creation. He repelled us, but our forces were inexhaustible. His power, great as it was, was not. We broke through, and were poised on the edge of victory when he cast his last and most terrible spell. He placed a ward upon the ground, preventing our kind from delving into the depths and securing his treasure. My god struck him down, but it was too late."

Guthorios' eyes glittered. "Since then, I have bided my time. Our enthusiasm led to our defeat; we slew and raised every person who could have passed his wards while alive. But now here you are. You can pass his wards, for you are members of Cruel Winter. So this I demand of you: to enter the dungeons below the castle and determine the nature of this treasure. Then, that accomplished, you shall bring it to me so that I may deliver it unto my god."

Falkon laughed. "Wait. You're the guy who attacked my home, killed my friends, and ruined everything. You expect me to help you finish the horrors you started? Why the hell would I do that? It would be the ultimate betrayal."

I could understand Falkon's passion. I was only nominally a member of Cruel Winter, and that more by accident than anything else, but to him this had been everything.

If Guthorios was impressed by my friend's outrage, he gave no sign. "Of course it is repellant for you to help your enemy complete the destruction of that which you once loved. But such is your fate. You have no choice. You must do this. My god wills it."

"Well, you can tell your god to shove—"

I stepped forward, hand extended to cut off my friend before he got us both killed. "Dread Lord. You're going to have to work with us here. Give us a reason to help you. If Jeramy thought it best to hide this treasure from your god, then I'm pretty sure he had a good reason for it. You had to know we wouldn't agree. So what were you planning to offer?"

Guthorios turned to consider me, his blue eyes burning. "I can end your life with but a thought. Your divine spark shall be quenched, and never again shall it burn. You must do as I say or you shall die forevermore."

"Persuasive," I said, throat tightening up. "Pretty persuasive. But that won't work on my friend here. He'll just respawn or, worst-case scenario, ditch his Falkon avatar and go play something else."

"Chris—" began Falkon, but I cut him off.

"Plus, you didn't know I was so committed to this life." I stared at Guthorios, hating how little I could read his undead face. "So you couldn't have counted on using that against me. What were you going to offer us?"

To my surprise, Michaela was the one who answered. "My lord can cleanse your friend of her necrotic corruption. You can save her by helping us."

I thought of Lotharia, hidden in the keep. "That's a step in the right direction."

"You are correct," said Guthorios, and now he stood, rising to his full height, joints creaking. He had to be nearly seven feet tall. His rusted black scale male glinted in the faint light coming through the windows, and in it he looked like nothing so much as the ghost of a departed black dragon. "This was my induce-ment: an appeal to your curiosity. I know you think me and mine the villains of this world, and I cannot fault you. Our essence is inimical to your kind. We are born from your death. But in this matter, we do not act along a moral line as you understand it. My god's goals here are not evil. We had cause to attack the archma-gus, for he in turn was not good. Not as you are prone to under-standing that term."

"Jeramy was one of ours," said Falkon. "He was hilarious, awesome, and yes, a good guy. Why should I take your word over my own experiences?"

"The archmagus was a complex man. He had many sides. Any who rise to such exalted levels of power must by definition be more profound than you comprehend. I tell you this, Squire Alastoroi: the archmagus harbored ambitions that imperiled all of Euphoria. We moved against him to stay his hand. He was not your true friend."

The Dread Lord's words hung in the air like the peals of a bell. I glanced sidelong at Falkon, who was clenching and unclench-ing his jaw.

"I do not expect your immediate faith. Instead, I expect you to agree to my request out of an immediate desire to live. No doubt you will ultimately lie to me so as to escape my clutches. Such is to be expected. However, I challenge you to conduct your own investigations. You must rescue your friend, must you not? The entrance to the dungeons lies within the keep. Explore. Investigate. Test my words. See if you do not uncover evidence to support my claims. Then, when you bring me your friend for cleansing, we shall visit this quest anew. Fair?"

He had our number. I had absolutely no intention of dying inside this chamber, and was completely prepared to lie to get out. However, Falkon's class was based on his being chivalrous; it was coded into his essence. Before he could put his foot in his mouth, I gave a tight smile.

"Fair. We agree at this point only to return with Lotharia for healing, at which point we'll revisit this conversation in light of anything new we've discovered. Right, Falkon?"

"Fine. I can agree to that much."

"Then we are agreed," said Guthorios. "I shall lend you Michae-la's aid for your endeavors within the keep. The perils you shall face therein are too great for you to assail alone."

"Told you," said Michaela.

"Sure, great," I said. "But if she's coming with us, she has to agree to do what we say. I don't want her going rogue or choosing to do stuff we'd never agree to."

"Wait a second," said Michaela.

"You wish to have command over her?" Guthorios didn't sound upset. "So be it. Michaela, you are to obey all reasonable orders pertaining to the infiltration of the keep and extraction of their friend."

Michaela steeled herself. "Yes, my lord. As you command."

"Very well. I would equip you with items to even the odds, but such items would be infused with the same necrotic energy that has corrupted your friend, and would be barred by the ward from being taken below. Instead, I offer you the full run of Feldgrau, and the amity of the dead who walk its streets."

"Joy," I said, then caught myself. "I mean, thank you, Dread Lord. Unless there's anything else…?"

"That is sufficient," said Guthorios. "For now. You have my leave to depart."

"Great," I said. "Michaela, want to meet us up at the castle this evening?"

She leveled a flat glare at me. "As you command, Chris."

"Good, good. Well. Great visit, very constructive, time to go. Bye!" I hurried out of the chamber, down the steps, then out of the Broken Tower into the town square. Falkon followed hard on my heels. I averted my eyes from the charnel pit, and in silence we jogged out of Feldgrau, heading toward the path that led up to Castle Winter. It was only when we were several hundred yards beyond the village's perimeter that we stopped.

"OK," said Falkon, turning to stare at the Broken Tower below us. "That was truly messed up."

"No kidding," I said, moving to sit on a rock. "Do you believe any of what he told us?"

Falkon scowled, hands on his hips. "I don't know. This is some serious stuff, though. His 'god' – the Dead King that Kreekit told us about – has to be Albertus Magnus the AI. The god is called Uxureus in Euphoria, but all the gods are just thin veneers for Albertus himself. Which means Albertus itself wanted Jeramy's treasure. Which… doesn't make any sense."

"Jeramy was an archmagus, right? Lotharia told me that meant he could weave magic outside of set spells. Create magical effects as he saw fit. Which… if spells are like running set programs in the Euphoria system, then archmagic would be like coding directly into the system, right?"

"Yeah," said Falkon. "Something like that. But to run with your metaphor, even an archmagus has to work within the coding language of Euphoria. That's the essence we see around us. So even if he wanted to, Jeramy couldn't create something completely outside of the Euphoria reality."

"Not true. Lotharia and I ran into his robot butler inside his tower. That's outside the Euphoria paradigm, right?"

"Yeah… true enough. Even if it was within his own sanctum. I don't know." He chewed his lip. "This is some weird shit, I'll tell you that. I mean, Guthorios said Albertus took out Jeramy. That's never supposed to happen. You can get killed by just about anything in this game, but by the god of the undead directly? I've never heard of that happening. Ever."

"And why would Albertus want Jeramy's 'treasure'?" I rubbed at the back of my head, trying to figure it out. "That makes no sense. What would Albertus want with in-game treasure of any kind?"

"I've no idea," said Falkon. "I mean, this is all assuming Guthorios told us the truth. But even if he's lying, these are really weird lies for an NPC to make. I'm suddenly really glad Michaela's going to be joining us. I've got a bunch of questions for her now."

"Yeah, I can imagine." I rubbed at the stubble on my jaw. "Either way, an NPC horde of undead came in incredible strength and wiped out a bastion of player activity. That happen elsewhere in Euphoria?"

"I mean, there are huge raids set up to test cities and the like, but they're not overwhelmingly powerful. They're designed to provide a really exciting battle, lots of moments of heroism, and are usually clearly signposted as to what levels should be where and when. I've taken part in a bunch, and they're a blast. Low-level guys run equipment and tackle minor infiltrations, mid-level players are usually on the walls, while the high-level guys are running super important missions to take out the enemy leadership." He gestured at Feldgrau. "But they've never resulted in anything like this. Hundreds of player avatars slaughtered and raised as the dead? An entire castle abandoned? An archmagus killed by the god of undeath slash Albertus himself? No way."

"Huh," I said. I turned to gaze up at the ruins of Castle Winter. "Well, here's a question for you. Why the hell was this castle built all the way out here in the middle of nowhere? Lotharia told me it'd take ages and ages to hike to the next closest civilization. Like, months. That normal?"

"Well, normal? No. But it's not all that weird, either." Falkon sighed and sat next to me, setting his pack of bundled plate armor on the grass. "I mean, Castle Winter is like first gen, built right at the beginning when Euphoria was starting up. Things didn't always make organic sense at the beginning. And Jeramy always said he picked this place because he was sick of being bothered by stupid people and wanted an amazing spot in which to party. Every morning, people who wanted to teleport out would gather in the bailey and he'd send them to Goldfall or Seven Crags or whatever. So… yeah. It wasn't a big deal to be isolated, and actually we kind of wore it as a badge of pride. Being Cruel Winter felt kind of like being part of a really cool club."

I nodded slowly. I remembered the reporting on Euphoria when it started out. It had been depicted as a wonderful kind of Wild West, where there were few rules and lots more craziness. That had all settled down over the following few months as Albertus got a grip on how he'd wanted to run the game, implementing more realistic systems and layouts and doing away with the HUD and crunchier aspects of the game.

"Still," I said, "there's no way Albertus or Uxureus or whatever took out Castle Winter just because people were partying too much in here. And what about that ward? That struck me as the weirdest part of all this. As powerful as Jeramy was, how could he create a ward to keep Albertus himself out?"

Falkon blew out his cheeks. "Damned if I know. Guthorios' story is so full of holes that I'd discount it as a pack of lies. But. He's a really, really powerful NPC. I'm sure Albertus has allotted enough processing power to him that Guthorios is smart enough to know how ridiculous his story must sound. Which means he's either deliberately trying to make us think he's lying, or actually believes what he's saying."

"OK, this is starting to hurt my head," I said. "One thing's clear, however: we don't have enough information to decide what's true or not."

Falkon snorted. "Which Guthorios knew. Hence his urging us to let our curiosity drive us forward. Sneaky. Because now I *do* want to know the truth of all this. I had real friends in Cruel Winter. It really hurt when I got trapped in that time bomb. I was upset in the real world for weeks. And I want to know what or who was responsible for that, and make them pay."

I nodded. "I'm curious, too. You know I'll help as much as I can."

"Yeah," said Falkon. He gave me a grin. "You're good people, Chris. I'm glad it was you who got me out of that trap."

"Any time." I stood, stretched, then clasped my hands to my stomach as it gurgled. "Oh, man. I'm hungry enough to eat a horse."

Falkon heaved his plate armor back up over his shoulder and rose. "Let's go see what Barfo's got cooking. I'm up for a big lunch, a long nap, and then a good chat with our new friend Michaela."

"Agreed."

Falkon started up the path, but I lingered a moment longer. Stared down at ruined Feldgrau, at the charnel pit and the Broken Tower. I hated to admit it, but I was excited. Excited to be caught up in these strange events, to be in the center of a mystery that defied my understanding. When I'd signed up for Death March I'd known this would be an intense experience, but I'd never guessed it would be this fascinating, this terrifying, this bizarre and fun.

If only Lotharia were here to enjoy it with me. My feeling became bittersweet, and I was filled instead with a sense of intense resolve. I turned and followed Falkon back up to the castle. I must have been mad, but in that moment I'd not have traded my place for anyone else's in the world.

3

W<small>E WALKED IN</small> through the main gate of the castle for the first time, no longer needing to bother with the siege bridge and crack in the tower. I intended to head right up to the keep and call for Lotharia, but my thoughts were dashed by a bizarre sight. Barfo stood atop the wyvern, a huge cleaver in hand, a leather apron tied around his neck, grinning and prancing as if he'd won the lottery. Dribbler had started a large fire, which frankly looked like it was rapidly growing out of control, while Kreekit sat to one side in a meditative pose, eyes closed, a faint nimbus of green light floating around her head.

"Guys?" I slowed to a stop. "What's going on here?"

"Feast!" Barfo slapped the flat of his cleaver down on the wyvern's flank. "Feasty times! The best of times, when hungry goblins eat and munch, blood goes spurt and bones go crunch—"

Dribbler cut in seamlessly, dancing around the fire now and bowing to it as if the flames were an eldritch god. "We dance and drool, we cut and slice! Hot sizzling wyvern taste very nice!"

Barfo held up his cleaver and sang to it, his voice charged with excitement. "So much fresh and yummy meat! More than we could ever eat! Slice and dice and cut it fine, then goblins eat for the rest of time!"

I grinned. "Wyvern tastes that good, huh? And what about Kreekit there? What's she doing?"

Dribbler stopped his mad prancing and assumed a sober look. "Kreekit commune with goblin shaman of the Big Burpie Tribe. She call them to come buy meat. We going be rich!"

My grin disappeared. "Wait. She's inviting a whole goblin tribe here? How many we talking about?"

Barfo scratched his chin. "Big. Big Burpie called Big Burpie because they big. They have seventeen goblins!"

"Only seventeen?" said Falkon. "That's not so bad."

"Well, no. That's the only number Barfo knows. Could mean anything."

Dribbler ran up to us, suddenly all solicitous and kind. He patted our knees then ran around us in a tight circle. "Fear not, big humans! This Green Liver land! We masters of the meat! Ogre meat, wyvern meat, rat meat – the Big Burpies will respect, will behave, and will give us much gold and silver for such rare and juicy food!"

"Yeah, sure," I said. "But how are we going to go about our business in here if this turns into a goblin meat market?"

"Oh, but you so smart, you must think better with that big head of yours," said Dribbler, caressing my knee. "You want all this meat to go bad? Stink up castle? Ratties and batties and flies and maggots, squirming and wiggling and making this very, very bad place? No! You need get rid of meat. Now. You have two options."

"Seventeen options," agreed Barfo.

"Best option first: you let us be helpful. Friendly goblins get rid of meat for you, and pay you gold! Or two: you cut up meat all by your sad lonesomes and throw in ravine. That would make the world sad, and everyone cry forever. Not a good choice."

I couldn't help myself. They were so earnest and excited. "All right, all right! You can sell the meat to the Big Burpies. But let's not have their whole tribe move in, right? Keep them on the lower slopes outside, and only have their important goblins come in to deal. OK?"

"Chris so wise!" Dribbler did a backflip and came up grinning. "He so smart he sharp like whip, his words go snicker-snacker bip bip bip!"

"Yeah, don't make fun of his charisma eleven," said Falkon. "And, if you think about it, Dribbler's right. We get these huge carcasses taken care of, and make some money in the process. First, though, you should claim the cleared portion of Castle Winter, allowing you to claim your commission of all trade done within its walls."

"Now we're talking," I said. "All this talk of Dread Lords and mysteries aside, that's my long-term goal here. Make as much money as I can, which I can convert to dollars to use alongside Albertus' pardon to help my brother and set us up with a new life. So. How do I go about claiming the castle?"

"Here, open your character sheet." I did so. An icon appeared that indicated he was looking at mine as well. "Now, see that top-level stat called 'Domains'? Tap it."

I did so, and a new window opened up before me.

 You currently claim no domains. You currently have four partial domains available to be claimed:

The goblin tower [broken, 2] (Castle Winter)
The Iron Throat tower [broken -4] (Castle Winter)
The bailey [broken -2] (Castle Winter)
The barbican [broken -4] (Castle Winter)

"All right," I said, fighting down a shiver of excitement. Claiming territory? Awesome. "I see the two towers, the bailey, and the barbican. But they all have the broken condition?"

"Right," said Falkon. "Until you direct resources to have them fixed, they won't generate any reputation for you. But in the meantime, go ahead and tap them. Since nobody else is claiming them right now, all you need do is claim them for yourself."

I did so, and each flared gold and then moved up to appear under my new header of 'claimed domains'. "Awesome. And how do I go about fixing them?"

Falkon frowned at his own sheet. "Looks like the crunch has changed on this like everything else. But basically, you need gold and workers. Here. Close out of that window and open 'Allies'."

I did so, and a new window opened up before me.

 You currently claim no allies. You have one potential ally to be claimed:

The Green Liver tribe [Level 1 goblin tribe, +1 labor] (Shaman Kreekit)

"Right. Now, you can't just claim the goblins as your allies until you officially ally with Kreekit. Once she's agreed to work for you, you can claim them and give them tasks."

"This is feeling more old school," I said. "More familiar to what I was used to. You said there was even more crunch back in the day?"

"Yeah," said Falkon. "It looks like Albertus has reduced the system to just labor and broken conditions. Once you claim all of the castle – including the keep – you can claim the title of Castellan, and that'll open up a host of new options for you. Until then, you can work on fixing your partial domains, which should confer a host of new benefits, like titles, income, reputation, and so forth. But with just three goblins under your command, that's going to take some time."

"Huh," I said, flicking back to my newly claimed domains. "Looks like the goblin tower and bailey should be relatively easy to fix."

"Sure. Now, try this: tap on any of those Castle Winters you see."

I did so, and a new window popped up:

 `Castle Winter is comprised of six partial`
`domains. You currently claim four:`

> `The goblin tower [broken -2] (Castle`
> `Winter - Chris Meadows)`
> `The Iron Throat tower [broken -4] (Castle`
> `Winter - Chris Meadows)`
> `The bailey [broken -2] (Castle Winter -`
> `Chris Meadows)`
> `The barbican [broken -4] (Castle Winter -`
> `Chris Meadows)`
>
> `The archmagus tower (Castle Winter -`
> `Archmagus Jeramy [uncontesting])`
> `The keep [broken -5] (Castle Winter -`
> `Xylagothoth [contested])`

"Xylagothoth?" I frowned at the name. "Who the heck is that?"

"The boss of whatever's occupying the keep. To be honest, I'm relieved we didn't see Lotharia's name there. Now, if we clear the keep you should ostensibly be able to claim it. See the 'uncontesting' and 'contested' tags there? That means you have to take the claim from Mr. Xyla, but once you do so you can claim all of Castle Winter as your full domain, as Jeramy set his ownership of his tower to 'uncontesting', meaning he'll fold his partial domain under your full domain. Make sense?"

"Yeah, mostly." I looked past the goblins and corpses to the keep. "What about the dungeons beneath the castle? Why aren't they listed?"

"My guess? They're simply not part of Castle Winter. That, or it's related to this whole ward thing Jeramy put up, and Albertus isn't able to list it in your sheet. I don't really know."

I nodded, rubbing my chin. Barfo was tracing his future cuts along the wyvern's shoulders and back. "Time to lock in some allies."

"Atta boy," said Falkon. "Have fun. I'm going to scrounge up some food."

I stepped over to where Kreekit was meditating, and sat cross-legged before her, resigned to waiting until she was done with her spell. To my surprise, her eyes opened, revealing just the whites, which then rolled down to show her irises. The green glow over her head faded away, and after blinking several times, she smiled toothily at me.

"Chris make Green Liver tribe very rich."

"Yeah, I think we all stand to benefit. Not least because we no longer have ogres and wyverns living right next to us."

"Yes, yes. New age! We turn meat into gold. Grow fat in belly, fat in money sacks."

"Yeah. About that. We've been working great together. Barfo's poison and super soup really made a difference in the fight, and

Dribbler's wiring of the barrels of pitch was great. I respect you and your wisdom, and think there's a lot more room for us to grow together."

"Mm-hmm?" She'd adopted her poker face, which meant she looked crafty and pleased with herself.

"Mm-hmm is right. So what do you think about formalizing our partnership? I've laid claim to most of Castle Winter at this point. I'd like to make the Green Liver tribe my allies, and work together so that we both get rich. And well fed. Sound good?"

"Wise," said Kreekit, and I let go of a breath I hadn't realized I'd been holding. "Many Big Burpie goblins coming. Good to stand united. To present power they must respect. I accept your offer of alliance. Green Liver tribe work for Chris, as long as Chris take care of Green Liver, treat us with respect."

"Deal," I said, and I extended my hand. Kreekit studied it in confusion for a moment then slapped it away.

"We no squeeze handies. We exchange blood." She drew a small dagger from her side and slit her palm open. "Now you."

"Right." I wasn't thrilled, but what could I do? I cut the meat of my thumb then pressed the wound to her own. A new chime sounded, and when I pulled back the cut had healed. "So. About the Big Burpie tribe. I don't want them inside the bailey in numbers. Have them camp on the slope below, and then invite their leaders in. How much gold do you think you'll make from them?"

"Shaman Lickit is very wise, very fat. Drive hard bargain. But we have wyvern meat. Lickit will drool too much to be sharp." She turned to consider the corpses. "We make much gold. Take all of Big Burpie gold. How we split it?"

What was fair? How greedy should I be? "You guys will be doing all the butchering. Plus you found the customers, and will be negotiating with them. You should get most of the gold. How about I get a quarter of whatever you make?"

Kreekit nodded. "Fair, fair. We hold gold for you till you come for it. Big bags! We getting rich. Lickit will lose many goblins to Green Liver. Soon, we grow."

"Great. When you do, I was hoping you could do something for me. Let's clean out the bailey once the corpses are taken care of, yeah? Remove the stakes, throw all the ruined parts of the stable into the ravine, wipe out the rat swarm, those kinds of things. You think you can do that?"

"Yes, Green Liver make bailey pretty again." She gave me her toothy smile once more. "Maybe we have Big Burpies do the work in exchange for some meat. Kreekit too important now to spend time carrying stones."

"Sure." I grinned. "Sounds good to me. Now, we're going to be having a visitor soon. Her name's Michaela, and she's undead. For the moment we're working with the Dread Lord from Feldgrau. Just investigating some stuff for him. When she arrives, don't attack her, all right?"

Kreekit lowered her brow. "You work for Dread Lord? You no tell me you his ally."

"I'm not. Absolutely not his ally. We didn't shake or anything. I just agreed to investigate the keep for him. Mostly because he'd have killed us if I didn't."

"Ah, Kreekit understand. Kreekit make many, many promises to save neck over time. Very wise of Chris."

"Yeah, I hope so. Oh – and Lotharia is in the keep. Can you have Dribbler keep an eye on the front door? If anything comes out, tell him to just start screaming. I've no idea what she's doing in there, but it can't be good."

"Yes," said Kreekit. "Dribbler very good at screaming. Much practice. Talented. I set him to watch."

"Great. Awesome! I'm glad we're allied, Kreekit." I reached forward in an excess of good will and patted her awkwardly on the shoulder. "We're going to achieve great things, you and I."

"Already have! Ogre steak wrapped in wyvern steak wrapped in more ogre steak!" She gulped down a mouthful of spit. "Crackling with Barfo's special seasoning. Bloody and raw in middle, crunchy and black on outside! Kreekit going to get fatter than Lickit. Going to get this fat!" And she extended both arms out wide.

"We all need dreams," I said, chuckling and rising to my feet. "I'll do my best to support yours."

I opened my sheet as I walked away and tapped through to Allies. The Green Liver was now listed as mine. Sure, a tribe comprised of just three exuberant goblins might not be all that impressive in the big scheme of things, but they were mine, and heck, I actually really liked them.

I made my way into the goblin tower, found a straw-stuffed pallet which I decided not to inspect too closely, and lay down to rest. Sure, my legs from the calves down stuck out on the stone floor, but I was tired and wrung out enough that I didn't care. Slinging an arm over my face, I allowed myself a long, slow exhalation. Progress. That was all that mattered. Slow or fast, incremental or in fell swoops, I was making progress.

Someone kicked my boots, startling me out of a nightmare where a corrupted Lotharia stalked me through endless twisting hallways. I sat up, nearly blowing mana on Adrenaline Surge by reflex, hand groping at my hip for a dagger that wasn't there.

Falkon stood over me in the gloom, and through the great crack in the side of the tower I saw that the sun had nearly set.

"C'mon," he said. "Michaela's here. First some questions, then we're going to get to work."

"Sure, sure," I said, rubbing grit from the corners of my eyes. I checked my character sheet as I got up: mana was back to full, including my marble, a delicious ten out of ten. Dusting some errant pieces of straw off my black spider silk shirt, I ran my fingers through my hair, wobbled my jaw from side to side and then followed Falkon out into the bailey.

Barfo had made a shocking amount of progress on the wyvern. He was still busy at work, wielding his cleaver with determination as he hummed loudly from within the corpse. Most of its hide had already been flayed and draped over a matrix of sticks, and the front half of its body had been expertly dressed down to the bone. A huge pile of liver-colored flesh, marbled with seams of fat and shot through with sinews, was laid out on a bed of what might have once been clean straw.

Dribbler was busy scraping fat or whatever from the inside of the scaled hide with a rock chisel, while Kreekit was stretching an expanse of hide tightly over a frame.

"Damn," said Michaela, standing to one side, arms crossed, bone mask pushed up over her hair. "Your goblins are ridiculously efficient."

"We've got another tribe incoming," I said, moving up to join her. "The Big Burpies. Kreekit plans to offload most of this meat onto them in exchange for a substantial amount of gold."

"And what do goblins need gold for?" asked Michaela. "I thought they worked along some primitive barter system."

"I don't actually know." It was a good question. "But since I'm getting a twenty-five percent cut, I don't mind too much. Plus, as they explained, we need to shift these corpses before they start to rot and make the castle uninhabitable. So. Everybody wins."

We stood in silence, watching as Barfo got to work on prizing the wyvern's left wing free of its joint, working the tip of his cleaver deeper into the socket and then hauling back on it. After a moment of strenuous effort, he was rewarded with a cracking, tearing sound, and the whole wing popped free, held in place now only by a few skeins of hide.

"Wyvern wing!" he called over to the other two. "I got good sauce for it! Spicy hot like succubus booty!"

Dribbler cheered while Kreekit only gave a pleased nod.

"I can honestly say that I never imagined I'd witness anything like this when I entered Euphoria," I said. "Amazing."

"Barfo's Spicy-Hot Succubus Booty Sauce," said Falkon, shaking his head slowly. "Genius. I'm going to market that in the real world when I get out."

"As impressed as I am," said Michaela, "and I am impressed, I'm not sure Guthorios wanted me to come up here to witness acts of culinary genius."

"I don't know," said Falkon. "Maybe we should send him some Succubus Booty Sauce. He might decide that's all the treasure he needs to please his god."

Michaela smirked. "Unlikely, but feel free to bring some the next time you're summoned."

"So, Michaela." I turned my back to the butchering so I could focus. "Falkon and I have some questions."

"I'm sure you do," she said. "This whole situation is weird as hell. But I can't promise I'll have the answers. I've only been in

Guthorios' employ for about three weeks now. I'm more of a useful tool than a trusted confidant."

"Sure." I considered her. "Are there other players in his employ down below? And if not, why'd he recruit you?"

She sighed. "You want to hear about my 'recruitment'."

"Yeah. Sorry. Amongst other things. I'll tell you this much, however: I want to trust you and work with you like a real team. But I can't do that unless I know more. And given that I'm in Death March mode here? I don't have much leeway for messing up."

"Fine. It's not like my past contains any huge secrets, after all." She hugged herself and watched something over my shoulder in a distracted manner. "Not too long ago I was Michaela Firion, an Emerald-level wizard in the town of Kravasse, perhaps a day's journey up the coast from Goldfall."

Falkon nodded as if that meant something.

"Word had been spreading of undead raids on the local villages. Weird raids. People couldn't figure out what was up. The undead were trying to capture folks, carry them away, but their numbers were too few and inevitably they'd either be destroyed mid-raid or chased down and eradicated. Anyways, about a month ago in-game a large force attacked Kravasse. As one of the town's main defenders I was ready, even excited for the fight. We repelled the first two waves pretty easily, but then wraiths descended upon me from the sky. I was alone atop one of the guard towers – nothing fancy like this castle, just platforms raised above our wooden palisade – and was paralyzed by their enervation attack."

Her expression curdled in distaste. "It was stupid of me, thinking the attacks would only come from the far side of the wall. They carried me up into the sky, and I saw the attack being called off. They kept me paralyzed and flew me through a portal. We emerged in Feldgrau, and I was taken into the Broken Tower."

Michaela's lips thinned. "I'll skip what happened inside, but Guthorios raised me as a necromancer, converting my essence and spells. Given that I'm in Death March mode, that was it for me. I've got a couple of months left before my six in-game months are up, then I'm going to flatline."

She was trembling as she said this, hugging herself extra tight. I didn't know what to say. She was a dark mirror to my own situation. The fate that awaited me if I messed up even just a little.

"I'm… I'm so sorry," I said.

"Skip it." Her tone became harsh. "I've no desire for pity. I—I knew what I was getting into when I signed up. I tried, and I lost. That's all there is to it." She blinked a few times, as if pulling herself away from a memory or emotion, then focused on the pair of us. "So that's my happy tale. Satisfied?"

"No," I said. "I mean, your situation doesn't make us feel 'satisfied'."

Falkon's tone was grim. "Do you think Guthorios was sending out his undead raids to catch Death Marchers specifically?"

Michaela hesitated. "Maybe? He grabbed me." She looked distinctly uncomfortable for some reason. "I can't claim to know why he's doing what he's doing."

"It guarantees him you won't log out," I said. "Makes you his slave. Which, given how he needs pawns with the 'divine spark' he talked about, means perhaps he was hoping to send you down below into Jeramy's dungeon?"

"Maybe," said Michaela again.

Falkon tapped his chin. "And that would also explain why he's not had much luck recruiting other players. There aren't that

many Death Marchers around, and they're all universally para-
noid and good at playing it safe. He'd be hard-pressed to snatch
them up easily."

"Fair enough," I said. "What about this 'treasure'? Any clue
as to what it is?"

"None," she said firmly. "Guthorios has no idea either. He's
just after it because Uxureus demands it."

Falkon raised an eyebrow. "Uxureus. You mean Albertus
Magnus."

"Not quite. Uxureus is slightly more limited than Albertus,"
she said. "But… yeah."

"And how do you explain Uxureus killing Jeramy? Since when
do the gods of Euphoria take out players? And how did a player,
even an archmagus, create a ward so powerful it could keep Uxureus
out?"

"I don't know," she said. "I wish I did. It's been an infuriating
few weeks. It feels like I've fallen into a coding glitch in Euphoria,
where the normal rules have all been broken. Trust me. Nothing
about this is normal."

We stood in silence, each of us mulling over our own thoughts.
Finally, I gave myself a shake. "Well. You guys up for exploring
the keep?"

"That's why I'm here," said Michaela, forcing a smile.

"Cool." I hesitated. There was no smooth way to ask. "Listen.
We've no idea what we're in for in there. Might help if we all
had a sense of each other's abilities."

She gave me a sly smile. "You mean you want to check out
my sheet?"

Damn. Was the undead chick trying to get a rise out of me? "Sure," I said. "I'll show you mine if you show me yours." I could give as good as I got.

She laughed, genuinely amused, and punched up her sheet. "All right. Look all you want."

I opened mine in turn, shared it with her, and then pulled up her sheet.

 Michaela Firion

Species: Undead Human
Class: Wizard
Level: 15
Total XP: 1434
Unused XP: 59
Guild: None
Title(s): Dark Exarch
Domain(s): None
Allies: Dread Lord Guthorios
Cumulative Wealth: 3122gp

Attributes

Strength: 8
Dexterity: 13
*Constitution: 14
Intelligence: 14
Wisdom: 17
*Charisma: 16
Mana: 21/21

Skills

Survival: Basic (III)
Knowledge (Undead): Intermediate (II)

Diplomacy: Intermediate (I)
Stealth: Basic (III)
Melee: Basic (III)
Athletics: Basic (III)
Spellcraft: Basic (IV)
Intimidate (III)

 Talents

Spellcasting: Basic
Meditation: Intermediate (III)
Quick Reflexes: Basic
Astute Observer (II)
Minor Magic

 Spell List

Life Sight
Necrotic Bolt
Cause Fear
Bone Puppet
Command Undead
Sentry Skull
Osseous Fists
Animate Dead: Basic (II)
Wither: Intermediate (I)
Unholy Ward
Cantrips: Basic

"Dang," I said. "That's quite the spell collection."

"No kidding," said Falkon, scrolling through her list. "And they sound nasty, too."

"Yeah." Michaela sounded ambivalent about the praise. "Guthorios was… generous with his gifts. What do you wish to know?"

"How about a quick rundown of your main spells?" I closed her sheet so I could observe her directly. "Just to give us a sense of what to expect."

"Sure. I'll take it from the top." She then proceeded to name each spell and give us a quick summary of what it did. I glanced over at Falkon when she was done. He was struggling to not look overly impressed.

"Well, I'm glad you're on our team," I said. "And extra glad I didn't try to fight you off when we first met."

Michaela's full lips curled into a derisive smile. "I wouldn't have killed you. Just hurt you until you submitted."

"I'm sure. Bone Puppet was bad enough." I shuddered. That said, I turned to stare at the gaping entrance through which Lotharia had entered the keep that morning. "Looks like it's time to get some answers. Come on."

4

I LED THE WAY up to the keep's entrance, and there paused to study the darkness that filled the great doorway. I switched on Darkvision, but that made little difference; the darkness beyond was impenetrable. Thinking of Lotharia, I activated Detect Magic. The darkness was a cloud of necrotically-aligned mist. On the off chance that it might work, I created a ball of Light and sent it darting forward into the darkness, where it was devoured.

"Well, that's not reassuring," said Falkon.

"It's a moderately powerful obfuscation spell," said Michaela. "Impressive in that it seems to be permanent. It shouldn't affect us other than feeling unpleasant as we pass through it."

"Why place it there?" I stepped a little closer and extended my hand toward the shifting darkness. It was cool, like the air next to a waterfall.

"Hard to say." Michaela stepped up alongside me, searching the tapestry of necrotic magic as if for clues. "It serves various functions, not least being a psychological one. But I believe we can condense all the possibilities into a simple generalization: it's a warning. Stay away."

"Not much luck for that," said Falkon. He'd donned his plate armor, and gently pushed his way past us both. "I'll take point. Don't wait too long to follow, all right?"

"Such a gentleman," said Michaela.

Falkon snorted. "Right. Now, the ground floor of the keep used to be the servant quarters, kitchen, storerooms, guardroom and the like. Right through this door was a small hall with a stairwell to the hard left that led up to the second floor where the grand hall was, along with a few side rooms. Third floor was where the important bedrooms were located, along with a library and private meeting chamber. There was access to the keep roof, where four large catapults were kept along with other defensive gear."

"Any subterranean rooms?"

"Sure," said Falkon with a grim smile. "What castle is without its dungeons?"

"Lovely," said Michaela. "I can only imagine what the new residents have done with that decor."

"All right," I said. "Here's the game plan. I'm guessing Jeramy's ward is going to make the dungeons a separate realm for now. Let's just focus on what's above ground. Lotharia ran in there in a state of panic. It's likely she ran right past the stairwell. We'll clear the ground floor first, then work our way up."

"Ambitious," said Michaela. "And delightfully confident. What could go wrong?"

I ignored her. "Now, just a reminder: this is only a scouting trip. If things get hairy in there, we get out, fast. No heroics. Understood?"

They both nodded grimly, and then Falkon lit a torch and stepped through the undulating black curtain and into the keep. I fought to steady my breathing. This was it. My first real attempt to rescue Lotharia. I wasn't going to mess this up. I gave Falkon enough time to clear the doorway, and then stepped in right after.

It was unlike the shadows I had grown used to. Instead of a welcoming, velvety embrace, this darkness was cold, shockingly so, reminding me of nothing so much as the frigid depths of the lake I'd swum across in Australia once when I was young. It shocked my mind into a state of utter clarity while numbing my extremities, so that when I emerged on the far side into a short hallway, I felt at once clumsy and alert.

Darkvision was still in effect, and it allowed me to see past the radius of Falkon's torch into the large room beyond. No movement. As promised, the entrance to a stairwell opened up on my left, and a quick glance in and up showed that it, too, was empty. Falkon gave a small shrug as if easing his armor into a better fit, and stepped forward just as Michaela emerged, her staff raised, a nimbus of green light floating about its top.

None of us spoke. We listened, but all was still.

"Feels abandoned," I whispered.

"Let's find out." Falkon stepped to the entrance of the large room beyond and raised his torch. Warm, dancing tones of crimson and yellow lit up what had once been a kitchen; three large tables ran down its center, while others were set along the walls, broken up only by massive ovens, open grills, and copper-topped fireplaces on which empty pots now stood.

The withered remnants of bunched vegetables hung from the rafters, while more pots dangled from hooks along the walls. It was huge, and no doubt had once been able to feed hundreds, but now it was abandoned and covered in dust.

Where might danger lurk? Counting on my Astute Observer talent I studied the corners, peering into the darkest shadows, which revealed their secrets to me. I crouched to peer under the tables from where I stood, then cast Detect Magic once more. Nothing glowed.

"Looks suspiciously empty," I whispered.

"Agreed," said Michaela. "Shall we press on?"

Falkon gave a slow nod and stepped inside, then moved between two of the long tables, casting long, deliberate looks all around him as he went, fully expecting an ambush.

Michaela and I entered right after him. My breath puffed out before me in the gloom. The overlapping play of Michaela's green light, Falkon's rosy torchlight and my own Darkvision over the walls and furniture made for an eerie combination. I listened intently. Surely the keep wasn't actually abandoned? At the very least Lotharia had to be in here, right?

"Something's coming down the chimney," said Michaela, turning toward the massive flue. Her voice had gone taut with tension. "I hear claws."

Silence. Falkon cocked his head, face blank. Still, I immediately oriented on the large fireplace, summoning my Death Dagger as I did so. It coalesced in my palm, icy cold and reassuring, its blade undulating to an icicle-like point and edged in burning blue.

Falkon leapt up onto the table that separated him from the fireplace, boots crashing down on the wooden surface, then stepped down to land on the far side, blade held up before him. I slid Dukes of Hazard-style over the table before me and fell into a crouch. Michaela moved back, staff held high.

Something emerged from the chimney, but I couldn't tell what it was. It was plain to see, but it failed to resolve itself into an easy category like *goblin* or *spider* or *slime*. Instead, it was an amalgam of them all, its skin oily black and gleaming, its head bursting with eyes like a dollop of caviar, twin ant-like pincers bracketing its mouth, its back hunched, dozens of claw-tipped legs emerging to grasp the interior of the fireplace and hold the creature in place as it stared at us.

At first, I thought it the size of a small dog, but as more of it emerged from the chimney it swelled in size, growing to that of a small pony, filling the large fireplace completely. The iron pot on its tripod fell over with a clatter.

"Level twenty!" called Falkon. "Retreat!"

But it was too late.

Everything happened at once. Michaela sent a bolt of screaming green fire from the tip of her staff into the fireplace, but the creature was gone; shards of stone exploded from the now-empty fireplace as Falkon twisted violently, swinging to his left where the creature had just appeared, its pincers slicing deeply into his thigh.

I Shadow Stepped, sinking into the shadows all around me and emerging under the table behind Falkon, swiping out with my Death Dagger at where the monster had been moments ago. My blade cut through empty air, and then some sixth sense warned me to move and I threw myself forward just as claws swiped through where I'd been crouching. I rolled back out into Falkon's torchlight and came up and around to stare under the table – but it was gone.

Michaela screamed and a sphere of swirling green light slammed into existence around her, knocking the monster back. It retreated, stepping away and then sliding up onto the ceiling as if gravity had simply plucked it away. It crouched there, between the rafters, and its eyes were actually bubbling, rising and falling as if its head was a pot of soup. Foam emerged from between its pincers and dripped free, but instead of falling to the ground the foam floated away in the air.

"Come here, spawn of darkness!" Falkon's yell cut through the air. "I challenge you to a duel, to show what worth you have, be it none or less than none! Come meet my blade!"

The creature shook and emitted a high-pitched keening sound, which I realized to my horror was laughter. Then it vanished.

This time I was ready. When it appeared behind Falkon I threw myself at it, intercepting its lunge by slamming my shoulder into its goblinoid body and slashing with my dagger. To my horror, it wrapped its spider legs around me and sucked me into darkness just as Falkon wheeled to strike.

It was like Shadow Stepping, but infinitely worse. My mouth filled with bile, my stomach tried to turn itself inside out, and then I was inside an incredibly cramped space, arms pinned by my side, darkness above me, trapped and abandoned as the monster disappeared once more.

Darkvision revealed a shaft of dressed stone rising straight above and opening to other fireplaces on the higher floors; it had transported me into the chimney flue and left me firmly wedged.

Bastard. I immediately Double Stepped back down into the kitchen, where I appeared crouched beside the fireplace. Falkon had just tipped over one of the long tables to charge at where the monster was assailing Michaela's forcefield, so I used the second half of my Double Step to cross the room and appear beside the monster, where I stabbed my Death Dagger deep into its side.

It squealed as I tore it open, and a torrent of steaming blood burst free in ridiculous quantities to knock me to the floor, pouring over me like a firehose. *What the hell?* The blood scalded my skin then cooled far quicker than was possible, turning into a rigid substance like rubbery cement in seconds. Like that, I was locked in place, frozen in my attempt to climb to my feet.

Falkon slammed his blade into the monster with such force he lifted it clear off the ground and sent it flying against the far wall; it never hit, but disappeared into the darkness and then fell on him from above, driving him to the ground.

Once more I Shadow Stepped out of the binding goo, emerging under a table. The monster was savaging Falkon's armor with its pincers, scoring deep grooves in his breast plate as my friend sought to bring his pinned blade to bear. Green worms of electricity suddenly flickered into existence around the monster, dancing over its body and causing it to screech; it fell off Falkon, skittered away, and then disappeared.

I rose to my feet, breathing heavily, and stepped over to give Falkon a hand. "What was that?"

"Wither: Intermediate (I)," said Michaela, also panting. She let the forcefield fall as she turned to scan the room. "Should have killed it, but somehow I don't think it did."

"We should go," said Falkon. "Regroup."

I checked my mana. I'd already burned half my supply. I'd be in dire straits already were it not for my mana marble. "Good call. Let's—"

The monster burst through one of the far doors, leaping up onto one of the long tables and racing down its length toward us even as a second emerged above us to fall upon Falkon once more. A third emerged from the chimney, looking warped and desiccated, and then all hell broke loose.

I leapt forward, moving to intercept the first, and cast Ebon Tendrils, willing an arm of shadow to emerge from under the table and wrap around the beast, lifting it up into the air. It screeched in fury and I somehow felt it try to escape, only to be held in place by my spell. Shadow magic neutralizing shadow magic? I'd no idea, but I drew one of my daggers from my belt and hurled it at the monster's head, activating Uncanny Aim and Distracting Attack at the same time.

My blade sliced through a number of its eyes, causing them to pop and release puffs of black vapor into the air, and the monster ceased trying to escape and instead lunged at me, pulling at the tentacle that held it in place. I leapt up onto the table, then activated Expert Leaper at the last moment to somersault right over the creature, ordering my tentacle to drag it down just as it spat out a mass of hissing fluid. I lashed out with my Death Dagger as I passed over, cutting deep into its head, and the blue flame of the blade caused a dozen more eyes to pop.

I landed and was immediately knocked off the table as a second spider goblin launched into me out of nowhere. Before I could hit the ground I Double Stepped, appearing back on the table where I'd originally been, only for the same spider to slam into me again from the same angle, an exact repetition of what had just happened. Again I flew off the table, and this time I used the second half of Double Step to appear under the table beneath the trapped spider goblin. It fought my Ebon Tendril, seeking to tear itself free and into the shadows. I activated Adrenaline Surge and a terrible burst of power flowed through me, and with a cry I slammed my Death Dagger straight up even as I ordered my tendril to press the spider goblin to the table.

My Death Dagger cut cleanly through the wood and punched into the spider goblin's gut. Again that boiling blood came bursting out, but this time I was ready. I leapt out from under the table, backpedaling as I took in the rest of the room.

Crap. Michaela's forcefield was flickering as she fought off two more of the monsters, both vaulting toward her over and over again and then disappearing moments before her Necrotic Bolts or Wither blasts could catch them. Falkon had been backed up against the wall, his left arm pinned to his side by the blood cement, numerous wounds cut through his chain.

"Retreat!" I screamed. "Michaela! Drop your forcefield! Kill your light! Falkon! Charge your way out!"

Michaela snapped her head around to stare at me wide-eyed, and for a second I thought she'd refuse, but then her forcefield dropped, her green light extinguished, and I Double Stepped to her side. I immediately summoned another Ebon Tendril, which I swung so it batted away the spider goblins. Then I grabbed hold of Michaela.

Taking a deep breath, I used Shared Darkness to drag her with me through the second half of my Double Step, through the shadows and out of the kitchen altogether. We emerged stumbling beside the stairwell just as Falkon let out a roar of anger.

"For justice! For glory! *For the king!*"

My skin prickled with awe at the sheer ferocity of his yell, then he was charging our way, blasting right through the last standing table in a cloud of splinters. Headlong Charge, maybe? A spider goblin phased into existence right above him, but Michaela was ready: she threw a Necrotic Blast at it at the same time I hurled my last remaining dagger. I'd activated Uncanny Aim, but the monster flicked away into the shadows mid-dive just before either of our attacks could hit.

Falkon burst into the small hallway, literally scooped us both up in his right arm, and carried us through the swirling portal and back out into the evening calm of the bailey.

We fell with a crash to the ground and just lay there, tangled up and panting, our limbs intertwined and our minds spinning, Falkon's armored weight pinning us in place. After a moment he rolled off with a groan and I sat up, only for Adrenaline Rush to expire. I fell back with a convulsive shudder.

"That… that was insane," said Michaela. "Five level twenty monsters at once?"

"No wonder Mogr boarded up the doors and windows," said Falkon. He tried to sit up and then let his head sink back down.

"Not like boards would stop them if they wanted out," I groaned, turning onto my side. I fucking hated Adrenaline Surge. I felt like an old man, muscles all cramped up, joints aching, stomach filled with acid and my head pounding. "And that was just the kitchen?"

"We're going to have to come up with a better strategy," said Michaela, climbing stiffly to her feet. She brushed at her crimson dress, tugged it into place, then knelt by Falkon's side. "How badly are you hurt?"

"It's not good," he said. "But with Barfo's special soup I'll be fine." He hissed. "Mind grabbing it for me? My left arm's kinda trapped."

I watched as Michaela scowled and cut through the black rubbery blood till she could reach his belt and pull free the small wineskin. She unstoppered it and held it to Falkon's lips, raising his head with her other hand. He gulped it down eagerly and then laid his head back with a sigh. "Ah. Damn, that's good soup."

The worst of my Adrenaline Surge faded away. I sat up and rubbed the back of my head. My pulse was only now starting to slow. "You guys ever heard of anything like those things in there?"

"No," said Michaela.

"Nope," said Falkon. "I couldn't even get a good look at them. They wouldn't stand still long enough."

"I did," I said. "Darkvision for the win. They were pretty ghastly. Like, take a black goblin, explode its head into a mass of bubbling eyes with wicked pincers, then add twenty or so spider legs coming out of its back."

"Did we even kill any of them?" asked Michaela. "I believe I hit one square on with my Wither spell, but I'm not sure I killed it."

"I don't think so," I said. "I hurt one badly at the end there with my Ebon Tendrils and Death Dagger combo, but even then… no XP."

"Shit," said Falkon, sitting up and wrapping his arms around his knees. "This is going to be much tougher than I thought."

"Let's list their powers," I said, refusing to give in to despondency. "They can Shadow Step, and unlike me, I don't know if there's a limit to how many times they can do it. If you cut them, they eject a black superglue blood."

"They spit some kind of acid," said Michaela.

"And their jaws can almost cut through plate armor." Falkon rubbed at the deep grooves in his breastplate. "And they make short work of chain."

"Worse, they can transport you when they Shadow Step," I said. "One of them tried to trap me high up inside the chimney.

If I hadn't been able to Shadow Step right back out, I'd have been screwed."

Michaela and Falkon stared at me, eyes wide.

"I know. Not fun. But I did discover that my Ebon Tendrils can nullify their Shadow Step ability. Maybe my Night Shroud would have the same effect? But if I cast it, you guys would be blinded."

"True, but if that works maybe you could function as crowd control," said Falkon. "Use your spells to trap them and hold them back while Michaela and I focus on killing them one at a time."

"Yes," said Michaela, leaning forward. "My Wither spell definitely had an effect. Perhaps you could trap one with your Tendrils, and then I'd hit it with Wither while Falkon attacks it with his blade."

"Yeah, that might work. Falkon, maybe you could even lure one into the hallway with your Challenge Foe ability, and I could block the kitchen with Night Shroud. We could use that natural bottleneck to control their ability to rush us."

"Smart," said Falkon. "That way, if things get dicey we can simply back out into the bailey again."

Michaela smiled at us both. "I like the way you guys think. Spending time with you might not be quite as painful as I'd feared."

I grinned and rubbed my palms on my thighs. "So here's the plan. We'll step inside. Michaela, you and Falkon stay by the doorway. I'll enter the kitchen, get the attention of one of them, then retreat to you both. We all stand inside your forcefield – that seemed to work at keeping them out – and Falkon, you use Challenge Foe to bring it at us. I'll snag it with my Ebon Tendrils, then you both lay into it while I keep the others out with Night Shroud and more Tendrils."

Falkon grinned at me. "How did I go from super bummed out to cautiously optimistic so quickly?"

I grinned right back. "It's gaming 101. When you're underpowered, you never go toe-to-toe. You retreat, think up a new strategy, and try to work the terrain to your advantage. Bottlenecks, pinning – even a level twenty sucker's dead to rights if he can't get away, attack, or get reinforcements."

For a moment we simply smiled at each other, and then I stood with a sigh. "For now, we just need to focus on recovering our mana and healing up. Let's grab some dinner and crash. Michaela, we both sleep in the goblin tower – they've got this funky tent city going on in there that allows you to easily make a private little room of your own. Want in?"

"It's a long trek down to Feldgrau," she said, "and I'd rather not return until I have something positive to report. Sure."

"Great." I grasped Falkon by the forearm and hauled him up. "Then let's go see what wyvern steak tastes like."

I WAS AWOKEN BY a chorus of shouts and yips and trumpeting from outside. Startled, I leapt to my feet, pulling my tent compartment apart around me, and then ran to the goblin tower door to stare out into the bailey.

Bedlam.

What looked like a hundred goblins had invaded the castle and were engaged in an all-out riot. Everywhere there was chaos: small, wiry green bodies tumbling and leaping, wrestling and humping each other in the morning sunlight. The greatest fervor was centered around the wyvern's mostly butchered corpse, where Kreekit and an incredibly obese goblin with a deer skull over his head were glaring at each other, both of them standing high upon the wyvern's bony shoulders.

"What the hell?" Falkon stepped up next to me, pulling straw from his hair. "Is it a carnival or an attack?"

The new goblins all wore a slash of purple cloth diagonally across their chests, but otherwise were dressed in everything from rusted chain to loincloths. A band by the main gate was the source of most of the noise, where a dozen of them banged on drums and blew on crude trumpets, stirring up the crowd before them which heaved and danced and brawled.

With a heaving cry, a dozen goblins tore free one of the long arm bones from the wyvern. Holding it overhead, they took off at a drunken run, screaming with excitement, only to slam the end of the bone into the back of a goblin's head, knocking him down and causing the rest to trip and collapse beneath the bone itself.

"What do we do?" I asked, equal measures overwhelmed and amused.

Falkon grinned, crossed his arms, and leaned against the doorway. "You're the one trying to claim Castle Winter. It's your call."

Not how I'd imagined starting my morning. Still, if I didn't control this chaos, who knew where events might lead? I took a deep breath as if about to dive into a swimming pool and stepped out into the sunlight.

The closest goblins caught sight of me and let out screams as if I were a horror from the abyss. Several fell over themselves in shock, while others grabbed hold of each other and cringed.

"Human!"

"Death! Death comes for us all!"

"Humans! Humans! Humans!"

Man. They didn't have a high opinion of people. Then again, every game I'd ever played used goblins as early leveling fodder. No wonder. I raised my empty hands and strode toward the wyvern's corpse. The cries of outrage and shock spread out across the crowd, and more and more of the Big Burpie tribe stopped their antics to stare at me, eyes glittering like those of small birds, their humor disappearing to be replaced with a growing sense of menace.

What had started out as comical was rapidly starting to feel threatening. There were easily hundreds of goblins in here. If they decided to tear me apart, there'd be little I could do.

"Kreekit!" My yell cut through what was left of the revelry. "Hey! Kreekit!"

My shaman tore her gaze away from the obese goblin and blinked at me. "There! There is master of the castle! He tell you the law! All Big Burpies go outside!"

I reached the wyvern's corpse and stared up at the pair. "That's right. Only chieftains and shamans are allowed inside."

The corpulent goblin was nearly as broad as he was tall, and he wore an impressive array of glittering junk in a massive necklace that hung down to his bellybutton. Shiny scraps of metal, bright feathers, bones, shards of crystal – it all gleamed and glittered in the morning light. He studied me with a look of open appraisal and cunning, then threw his hands up and turned to the crowd.

"Who here a Big Burpie goblin?"

Several hundred voices were immediately raised in eager shouts.

"Who here do whatever Big Lickit say?"

Again, the massive shout of agreement.

The shaman was starting to get into it. He didn't have much room to pace, but he swung back and forth, bobbing his head and waving his arms. "If Lickit say kill, what you do?"

"Kill kill kill till our faces turn blue!"

"If Lickit say break it, what do you do?"

"Snap it and shake it and break it in two!"

The shaman pointed at me. "If Lickit say eat it, what do you do?"

The horde of goblins turned to stare at me as one. "Cut it and cook it and put it in stew!"

"I am Shaman Lickit!" He jabbed his chest with his thumb. "Shaman of Big Burpie tribe! We are many, you are few. We hungry, you good barbeque!"

Well, shit.

I was right out in the open under the morning sun. No shadows to speak of. Any attack on Lickit would no doubt provoke the others to swarm me. I could summon my Night Shroud and then Shadow Step away, but that would effectively be admitting the castle was Lickit's and force me to have to fight the entire tribe to earn it back.

There was nothing for it.

I grabbed hold of a ridge of bone high up the wyvern's leg and hauled myself up. Lickit gave way grudgingly, and in a matter of moments I was perched up alongside him on the wyvern's back, gazing out over the sea of upturned goblin faces.

"Welcome to my castle, Big Burpie tribe!" Curse my charisma eleven and Diplomacy: Basic (I). They weren't going to do me any favors. "My name is Chris, lord of this land, killer of wyverns and ogres!"

The goblins frowned up at me and suddenly I understood why – I wasn't rhyming.

I coughed. "The meat is fresh, it's cut up good, and when it cooks will make good food!"

This at least they could agree on. The goblins turned to each other and nodded.

"But not long ago, the meat was alive! Wyvern flew, and ogre strived! My friends and I, we snuck in by night, and when the monsters saw us, we started a fight!"

The goblins cheered, and a number of them sat cross-legged, clearly eager for the story. I froze. Nothing came to me. Several hundred or so goblins waited, eyebrows raised. My mouth was dry. Michaela stepped up next to Falkon in the tower doorway, eyebrow raised.

Desperate, my mind called up a song of truth and power, a childhood favorite I'd spent hours memorizing so that I could amaze my friends in the playground.

"On the half shell, we were the heroes four,
And in Euphoria who could ask for more?
The ogres were mighty, the wyvern mysterious,
All the guards and humans were furious!"

The goblins were digging it, nodding their heads in time with my words. I grinned and kept going.

"They needed help like quick on the double,
Have pity on the castle 'cause man it was in trouble.
They needed heroes just like the Lone Ranger,
When Tonto came pronto when there was danger.
We didn't say 'We'll be there in half an hour.'
'Cause we displayed… Euphoria Power!"

Shaman Lickit tried to elbow his way forward. "Me big Shaman, me know what's right. When I say 'kill him', you say 'fight!'"
I raised my voice, shouting him down.

"That was the last straw. We sprang into action!
We fought the ogres and you saw what happened.

We cut them down and butchered them all
Cause the bigger they are, the harder they fall!"

This elicited a big cheer from the crowd.

"Then from out of the sky came an awesome sound!
Screamed like a hurricane as it came on down.
Our backs to the wall, swords in our hands,
This was for real, we made our last stand!
The wyvern was bad, but we were much badder,
And its every attack only made us much madder!
With fury and power we cut it real deep,
And now here it lies, cold and dead at my feet!"

There was a moment of silence, and then the goblins burst into applause and screamed their approval. I placed my hands on my hips and grinned, one foot resting on the wyvern's head.

Kreekit raised her arms, waved them around until the cheering died down, and then moved to stand precariously before me. "This is Castle Winter! It belong to Master Chris! He say all Big Burpie goblins wait outside! Now go! Or he summon his big magic, he pull out his big sword, and he cutty you up!"

The goblins grumbled and shoved at each other and looked to Shaman Lickit, but even I knew the tide had changed. The fat shaman scowled then gave a nod. "Shaman Kreekit speaks true. All Big Burpie goblins wait outside. Soon we feast! Prepare big fire. Much meat to cook!"

The goblins gave a cheer and began shoving at each other as they slowly made their way out the main gate, over the drawbridge and to the grassy slopes beyond.

"Master Chris very impressive," said Kreekit. "Teach me your song? What it called?"

"Sure," I said. I had to work hard not to grin like a fool. "It's called, er, *Euphoria Power*. I'll teach it to you later, yeah?"

"Yes," said Kreekit. "Now we talk gold! Shaman Lickit. You start very bad, very naughty. I had good terms for you, but now am angry."

The large shaman gave her a placating little bow. "No angry, Kreekit. You looking bigger than last time I saw you. Nice and plumpy. You eating well?"

"Very well," said Kreekit with a sniff. "So much steak I vomit."

"Oooh," said Lickit. "Very nice. But Green Liver, Big Burpie, we always good friends. No need for anger."

"Hmph," said Kreekit, crossing her arms. "Such good friends you not come when humans kill Green Liver."

"Big Burpie busy!" Lickit sounded outraged. "We cry big tears, roll around in sadness, compose many songs in your honor. Very sad time. But that long gone. New day! Time for big feast. How much gold you want?"

Kreekit sniffed. "One gold per plate of meat."

"What?" Lickit staggered as if struck by a blow. "We no have so much gold!"

"Then," I said, inserting myself smoothly into the conversation, "how about this? For every gold you don't want to pay, one of your goblins has to work for me for a week. I'll feed them while they work, but they must do as I say."

Lickit didn't hesitate. "Deal!"

Kreekit gave me a disapproving look. "We lose much gold."

"But we gain in labor. There's lots of work and clearing to be done. Now, I'll let you figure out the details, Kreekit, but I want the goblins who decide to work to focus first on emptying out the bailey, removing the broken buildings, clearing out the rubble, and then to work on the spider tower, cutting down all the webbing and so forth inside. Once that's done, let's topple the siege bridges that are still crossing the ravine. All right?"

"You the boss," said Kreekit. "We make it happen."

"Great. Good meeting you, Shaman Lickit."

He bowed as low as his prodigious gut allowed, and my XP chime sounded.

That done, I scrambled down off the wyvern's corpse and crossed back to where my companions waited by the tower doorway.

"On the half shell?" asked Falkon, grinning widely. "Really? *Really?* You just defeated a tribe of goblins with the Turtle Power song?"

I laughed. "Do or die, man."

"I'm not familiar with this song," said Michaela. "Regardless, I'm impressed. Falkon and I were trying to figure out how to save you if things went sour."

"And?" I looked from one to the other. "What did you guys come up with?"

"We didn't," said Falkon. "Several hundred goblins, all at once? Tricky."

I gave a weak laugh. "Glad I didn't know that at the time. How about we give it an hour or so to make sure Kreekit has things well in hand, then try the keep again?"

"Sounds good," said Falkon. "I hate to have things hanging over my head."

"That, and I want a taste of revenge," said Michaela.

"All righty then. But first, breakfast."

Falkon nodded toward where Barfo was already turning the spit over hungry flames. "With all this steak I'm starting to forget the difference between breakfast and dinner."

Michaela gave a predatory smile. "Meat is meat. Let's eat."

Falkon elbowed her as they both walked toward the fire. "You're starting to sound like a goblin. And I didn't know undead ate food."

"This one does," said Michael. "I don't need to, but the taste, the act of eating – it reminds me of my former self." She forced a smile. "So. Chris, you coming?"

"Yeah, give me a sec." I pulled up my character screen, and a few windows popped open with it.

You have gained 25 experience (25 for surviving the Big Burpie tribe encounter). Your have 97 unused XP. Your total XP is 947.

Your attributes have increased!

Charisma +1

You have learned new skills! *Diplomacy: Basic (II), Goblin Rhyme Fighting (I).*

Goblin Rhyme Fighting, huh? Now that was a skill I was sure I'd be using all the time.

There are new talent advancements available to you:

Besides Wall Climber (I), Cat's Fall, Mute Presence, and Heads-Up, there was a new entry: Adrenaline Surge (II). Huh. That'd cost me seventy-five XP, and would both extend the duration and increase the severity of the cooldown period's nausea. Great. Still, I was right at ninety-seven XP. Just a little more would give me Grasping Shadows, which sounded like awesome battlefield control. I closed my screen and jogged after the others, stomach rumbling in anticipation.

"FALKON, DUCK!" I hurled my Death Dagger right at his head. He spun toward me, eyes going wide, then dropped just before my dagger flashed by to sink deep into leaping spider goblin. It screeched and then bounced off Michaela's green force shield, disappearing before it hit the ground.

Sweat ran down my face as I stumbled back, panting for breath. Six of my Ebon Tendrils wavered in the hallway ahead, the corpses of three spider goblins caught in their grasp like dead fish in the strands of a jellyfish. Beyond lay my Shroud, filling the kitchen with its enervating darkness.

"How many more?" asked Michaela, voice taut with effort. "My shield's about to go down."

"We've killed three," said Falkon, flicking blood off his blade as he rose to his feet. "One for the road?"

"Let's—" I never got to finish.

Three shadow goblins dropped from the darkness above, and immediately Michaela's shield flared a virulent green, trapping them against the hallway's stone ceiling. Sparks of green magic rained down on us as they fought the shield, digging talons and fangs into its curvature.

"Run!" screamed Michaela. "I can't—"

I took a deep breath. "Drop the shield!"

She didn't hesitate. The green glow vanished. I burned through six mana and a forest of tendrils erupted around us, surging up to encircle the spider goblins as they fell.

Falkon roared and swept his blade through the closest, causing it to erupt in a shower of blood; before Michaela could be soaked I tackled her around the waist, forcing her to fall back and out through the keep's doorway.

We rolled apart on the bailey floor and a moment later Falkon back pedaled after us, only to turn and let out a roar of delight and pump his fist into the air. My XP chime sounded and I sat up with a grin. Our plan had worked!

"Drop my shield?" Michaela's smile was as broad as my own. "Are you insane?"

"Four of them!" Falkon sighted down the length of his blade for notches. "Like clockwork. Snicker snack went my vorpal blade! Well, right up till the very end."

I bounded to my feet. "We can rest up and then rinse and repeat. Unless they're respawning, we'll mow them down eventually. And even if they are, we'll gain some amazing XP." I wanted to run right back inside and get to work. "At this rate, we'll be able to rescue Lotharia in no time at all."

Falkon wiped his blade clean and sheathed it. "No time at all, eh? I like your confidence. Those spider goblins never—Hey. Who are they?"

I turned. Five strangers stood just inside the main gate, and the variety in their appearance immediately told me they were players. The rest of the bailey was empty, the skewer and fire pit abandoned, the butchering implements dropped or left half buried in the ogre and wyvern corpses.

"No idea," I said, turning so I stood shoulder to shoulder with the other two. "Michaela? You know 'em?"

The strangers stepped out into the afternoon sunlight. Each one was completely distinct from the other. The man in the lead was clad in a coat of the purest white, which extended from his buttoned high collar all the way down to his shins. A broad copper sash wrapped around his waist held a large, curved knife. A cloak of snowy whiteness hung behind him, and large gloves of the same coppery hue as the sash rose nearly to his elbows. His head was completely shaved, but instead of giving him a thuggish look it imparted upon his striking features an air of distinction and severity, like that of a monk.

"Greetings," he called out with mock cheerfulness. "This would be Castle Winter?"

"Depends who's asking," I replied. I had meant it to sound defiant, but his expression of arch amusement left me feeling like a kid who'd watched too many movies.

He took his time looking about the bailey, eyeing it much as a potential buyer might a new property, and from his thinned lips it was clear he wasn't too impressed.

"Falkon?" I whispered. "Level?"

"Twenty-seven," he whispered.

The man to the leader's left was, if anything, even more imposing. He wore a severe outfit of black trimmed in bronze over his powerful frame, with a stylized bronze skull over his head that left his lower jaw uncovered; a black silk hood under the helm meant I couldn't even make out his eyes. At over six feet in height and with the build of a linebacker, I'd have expected him to be the group's bruiser, but instead the artistry of his mask and complex suit of black leather gave him a more refined air, much like Doctor

Doom or Thanos from the comics. A heavy hexagonal rod of bronze and black metal hung at his hip, and even from this distance I could make out the faint tracery of runes down its length.

"Vanatos," he said, voice a bass rumble, "shall we remove them?"

"Not yet," said the man in white. "We are, after all, but guests. Let us question them first."

"Guy in black is level twenty-five," said Falkon.

I forced myself not to gulp. Those two alone could have taken us, especially in our current mana-depleted state, but the three others with them solidified my sense of doom.

"Wyvern," said the orc woman at the back of the group, pointing at the corpse with a brutal-looking stone falchion. "What's left of it."

She was as large as the man in black, and wore an assortment of furs bound with leather straps and random oddments of plate armor over her powerfully athletic form. Her thighs were so muscled as to almost appear deformed, while her shoulders and arms were corded with muscle so I had no doubt as to her ability to swing her twin falchions. Her thick black hair was gathered into a topknot and spilled down her back, her face at once brutal and handsome, feminine and savage.

"And four ogres," said Vanatos. He came to a stop and considered us. "Your work?"

A quick calculation: play it low-level and prevent them from thinking us a threat, or claim the kills and seek to bluff them?

"Orc's level thirty-one," whispered Falkon.

"Perhaps," I said. "Who are you? What do you want here?"

Vanatos' smile never reached his eyes, which had the flat, cold stare of a killer. "We're known by several names, most of them less than flattering. Of all our monikers, however, I'm partial to the Beggars of Solomon."

"Shit," hissed Michaela.

Some stubborn core prevented me from turning to flee. Instead, I placed my hands on my hips. "And we three are of the Cruel Winter guild. This is our home. What is it you want here?"

The fourth member of their group stepped forward, laying an elegant hand on Vanatos' spotless white shoulder. "How bold. How foolish. Come, let's play with them." She was an elf, her skin ashen, her body wiry and lean like that of a professional ballet dancer and clad in a suit of beautifully worked metal that revealed her pale form as much as protected it. Ivory hair fell like coils of mist down past her shoulders to her high breasts, and her face was over-refined, complete with harsh, high cheekbones, an aquiline nose and full, red lips.

"We've come to fulfill a contract," Vanatos called out, slipping an arm around the elf's narrow waist. "Cede the castle to me and quit its grounds till we're done, and there shall be no need for violence."

"Elf's level twenty-five," said Falkon. "And the battlemage is level twenty-seven."

The battlemage stood in the center of the group, wearing a leather jacket whose hue gradated from dark crimson at the hems to black at the cowl that hung over his face. The jacket hung open, and I could see leather belts crossing his bare, muscled chest, which was completely covered in tattooed words like the page of a book.

"We can't take them," continued Falkon. "There's nothing to decide here."

"I won't abandon the castle," said Michaela, voice shaking. "It's not an option."

"We can't fight them off," said Falkon. "Cede the castle, Chris. We'll think up a new strategy."

"Who hired you?" I asked.

"That's none of your concern," said Vanatos. "My patience wears thin. Transfer the domains under your control to me. Now."

I've always hated bullies. But what could I hope to achieve here through a futile act of resistance?

The large man in black and bronze turned his head slightly to one side, as if examining us from a fresh angle. "The one in the center is in Death March mode."

The elf's mouth curled into a wicked smile. "He is? How delicious. Let's keep him. It's been too long since I turned one into a soul stone."

Her words sent a chill through me. Soul stone? I summoned my character sheet and checked my mana: down to five. Not good.

"First, we question them," said Vanatos. "Then you can have your fun, Delphina." He turned to make eye contact with the other Beggars. "Understood?"

"I'll take them alone," said Delphina, eyes shifting to burning vermillion. "Make them talk. Nobody interfere."

"Get out of here, Chris," said Falkon. "We'll hold them."

I didn't have enough mana to transport us all away with Shared Darkness and Double Step. A split second to think. No way we could defeat them. Fight our way free?

Vanatos crossed his arms and rocked back onto his heels. "Are you sure? You've nothing to prove, my dear. But very well."

"Hold tight, Falkon," I said, and taking Michaela's hand in mine I pulled her back into the shadowed doorway of the keep.

All hell broke loose.

Falkon sank into a defensive crouch, bastard sword held before him. Delphina strode forward, the air before her face beginning to shimmer and warp as if growing superheated, and then the darkness claimed Michaela and me, sucking us into oblivion and spitting us out atop the curtain wall. We appeared beside the wyvern's tower, and I immediately released Michaela's hand.

"Supporting fire!" I said, then stepped back into the darkness.

The swirling, velvety embrace of the shadows, and I stepped out of the base of the goblin tower behind the Beggars. Delphina was still striding toward Falkon, who had inexplicably frozen up. He was struggling to free himself, his whole body shaking, sweat running down his brow, but he was paralyzed.

A bolt of screaming green fire came arcing down from above. Delphina threw herself aside at the last moment, soaring high into the air, knees to her chest, but in doing so whatever spell she'd cast on Falkon broke. His Avalanche Roar burst from his throat, reverberating across the bailey, and he charged forward, cleaving his blade at Delphina where she landed nimbly in a crouch.

The elf did a backflip, avoiding the swing that would have lopped off her head, and kept flipping away from Falkon as he charged after her.

I activated Uncanny Aim and took a bead on Delphina, drew one of my daggers and hurled it with Pin Down high overhead. The dagger spun through the air just as Michaela called out a harsh spell from above, causing flickers of green lightning to envelop Delphina, who cursed and quit flipping just as my dagger fell from directly above her to sink into her boot.

The battlemage let out a croak of laughter.

Delphina ducked beneath Falkon's slash, then kicked his feet out from under him. He fell with a crash of armor. The elf plucked my dagger free, came up into a handstand then flipped to her feet, launching my dagger right back at me.

Shit.

I burst forward into the sunlight in a full sprint, swinging wide around the other four Beggars. My dagger curved through the air, orienting on me. I ran, watching incredulously as it corrected its flight path to swing in and slam into the back of my thigh like some kind of impossible heat-seeking missile.

I fell into a roll and came up awkwardly. Delphina screamed as her body suddenly went rigid. Green bolts of electricity played over her ashen skin once more, then sank into her body.

"I've got her!" yelled Michaela. "Now, Falkon! Now!"

He sprang to his feet and brought his blade up so it gleamed in the sunlight, but just before he could swing, the black and bronze Beggar raised his hand. A complex circle of golden light sprang into being over Delphina's head then dropped over her, driving Michaela's green magic before it till it impacted the ground and burst with a flash. Delphina leapt aside at the last moment, Falkon's blade screaming through where she'd been a second ago.

"Amusing," said Vanatos. "But enough. Let's finish them."

I tore my dagger out from the back of my thigh, activated Uncanny Aim once more and targeted Vanatos, throwing my blade as I limped toward Falkon. The black and bronze Beggar spoke another word, and my dagger bounced off a second circle of spinning golden light, its edges glowing with runes and arcane marks.

"No!" Delphina's outrage was palpable. "They are mine!"

"They're embarrassing you, my love," said Vanatos.

The orc warrior strode toward Falkon, her expression grim, stone falchions held out to her sides. She prowled like a panther, in no hurry, eyes locked on her prey. The battlemage shot his cuffs, extending his hands which elongated into massive claws that began to burn a deep and fiery crimson. The black and bronze Beggar continued to speak and cast spells, summoning burning circles of different configurations and colors around his friends.

Shit, shit, shit.

I reached Falkon and turned, panting for breath. Delphina extended her hand toward Michaela, cried out a spell, and our undead ally crumpled to the ground just as one of her necrotic bolts slammed into another spinning circle shield above Vanatos.

My mind spun as I tried to think up a plan, a stratagem, something that could get us out of this situation. Blood running down the back of my leg, mundane dagger in hand, and down to one mana, I couldn't think of a single tactic.

Drops of what looked like lava fell from the battlemage's claws. The orc warrior ran the blade of one stone falchion down the length of the other. They moved slowly, closing in with the inexorability of death.

6

"**E**SCAPE," SAID FALKON.

I wanted to be heroic. I wanted to say I'd never abandon my friends; that I'd fight by their side right till the bitter end. But I knew that if worst came to worst, Falkon would respawn and Michaela could admit to working for Guthorios and surrender. My body on its pod in Miami would flatline and that'd be the end of Justin's chances.

"I'll come back for you," I said through gritted teeth.

"Don't take too long," said Falkon, and he flashed me a smile before roaring his defiance once more and charging forth, blade held high.

What a glorious bastard.

I leapt back, intent on diving into the shadows within the keep door, but the battlemage raised one searing fist and, with a cry, he filled the air with burning strands of crimson lightning. They simply flooded out of his fist and arced across the sky, smashing down to shimmer and coruscate like vertical rivers of lava, filling the air with the stench of sulfur and humming with power.

I nearly delved right into one which had fallen slantwise across the keep door, and only managed to save myself from immolation by contorting and falling to the ground. The heat coming off the oblique river of flame was tremendous, and sweat immediately popped out across my brow. Stunned by the power on display, I shot a look at Falkon who ran around one such beam to swing at the orc.

She anticipated the blow with nauseating ease, not even bothering to block or parry, and sidestepped at precisely the right moment so that Falkon staggered past her, overbalanced. Casually, she swung her stone falchion up and around, slamming it into the back of Falkon's armor. The force of the blow blasted him down to his knees, and blood burst from his mouth.

Fury suffused me, and for a second I almost darted back to help him, the elf's laughter melding with the battlemage's sniggering, but I reined myself in. Instead, I leapt to my feet, nearly falling as the pain in my wounded thigh swamped me. Then a circle of blue magic formed around me, a tight knot of concentric circles spinning in opposite directions, the runes that overlaid them growing brighter by the moment.

A quick glance showed me the black and bronze Beggar had his hand outstretched in my direction. I my limbs began to seize up, but before they could completely do so I dove under the spitting beam of fire and into the swirling darkness that filled the keep's door.

I burned my last point of mana and activated Double Step. The darkness embraced me, drank me deep, and I emerged a moment later high on the curtain wall, crouched in the corner beside the goblin tower where the shadows were thickest.

For a moment I considered simply remaining still and observing the enemy below. Falkon was struggling to rise, the orc warrior circling him slowly, giving him time to gather his strength. Michaela wasn't too far from me. Perhaps I could run to her side—

"There." Delphina's voice carried up to me. "He's up on the wall."

Vanatos looked in the direction she was pointing and right at me. "Ah. Balthus. Will you be so kind?"

Balthus, the black and bronze Beggar, turned and raised his palm in my direction. Hell, no. I engaged the second part of Double Step and sank back into the shadows once more, this time flinging myself clear out of the castle and to the far shadows beyond the barbican.

I emerged from their velvety depths at a run, and sprinted as best I could down the slope toward Feldgrau. My thoughts were in disarray, and every few strides I glanced back over my shoulder, fully expecting the Beggars to enact some new, impossible power to capture me. Fear compelled me to activate Adrenaline Surge and I fairly flew down the path, flat-out sprinting as if the very hounds of hell were at my heels.

Adrenaline Surge gave out just as I reached the outskirts of the ruined village. I crashed to the ground in the lee of a small collapsed cottage, sobbing for breath and trying to ignore the stabbing pain in my leg and the vicious stitch in my side. My stomach trembled, then heaved, and I spat up a mass of mostly digested wyvern steak and bile. I turned to look back up the path. Nobody and nothing followed.

What just happened? Where had those guys come from? I'd thought Castle Winter was so far removed from the beaten track that casual passersby were unheard of. I sank back against the warped boards of the cottage wall, watching the castle through eyes half-lidded against my splitting headache.

No, not passersby. Vanatos said he'd been hired. By whom? Brianna? No. She'd have come herself if she wanted something from us; as powerful as the Beggars had been, she was even stronger. Someone who knew of Jeramy's secret, then. It had to be. Why else return to an abandoned castle? Why send such a powerful force if not to ferret out that treasure deep in the dungeon?

Which meant I had to find a way to stop them, or beat them to the punch. Cleansing Lotharia depended on my being useful to Guthorios, not to mention keeping Michaela on our team. But how on earth could I fight the Beggars? Delphina alone had almost been a match for the three of us. All of them combined? Terrifying. And that was without Vanatos joining the fray.

I rubbed at my temple as the horrors of Adrenaline Surge lifted, returning me to a state of clarity. I drew a deep breath and sat up straight. First things first.

I summoned my character sheet. We'd killed four of the goblin spiders. Time to power up.

You have gained 120 experience (120 for defeating four xythagas). You have 217 unused XP. Your total XP is 1067.

Congratulations! You are Level 11!

"Yay," I said weakly, wishing the new level meant I'd have access to something on a par with the Beggars of Solomon. I knew it didn't. Level eleven meant I was now almost a third as powerful as the orc warrior lady. I tried hard not to let despair crush me. I closed my eyes and breathed deeply, slowly. The wound in my thigh was throbbing something awful. I thought of Justin. Thought of my mother lying in the hospital bed the hospice program had delivered to our apartment at the very end. Thought of my dad the last time I'd seen him, my mother and I dropping him off at a hotel when she could no longer stand his cheating. Thought of all the pain I'd already survived, *real* pain, *real* tragedy. The Beggars were nothing, I told myself. Just a bunch of jackasses throwing their weight around in a computer game. I could handle this.

I *would* handle this.

I opened my eyes and swiped to the next window.

 Your attributes have increased!

Mana +1

 You have learned new skills! *Stealth: Basic (IV), Survival: Basic (II)*

That was it? Falkon and Lotharia had warned me the bonanza gains from the early levels were going to slack off, but a single point of mana and a little more Stealth was still a bitter reward. Just when I needed maximum gains, I was getting next to nothing!

I swiped the windows away angrily. Fine. If that was how the system worked, I'd roll with it. I still had a bunch of XP to spend.

A new window opened up:

You have lost the following partial domains:

```
The goblin tower [broken -2] (Castle
Winter)
The Iron Throat tower [broken -4] (Castle
Winter)
The bailey [broken -2] (Castle Winter)
The barbican [broken -4] (Castle Winter)
```

I stared at the text with dull resentment. Damn the Beggars of Solomon. Like that, they'd torn the veil of illusions I'd allowed to build before my eyes. Had I thought myself so tough, killing wyverns and xythagas? Well, they'd walked into my castle and bent me over their knee.

I leaned back and closed my eyes. A new truth was evident. Something that had been right before my eyes all along. As a darkblade, I excelled when I could pick the field of battle, lay out a strategy and execute it. Under the right conditions and at full mana I was lethal even to creatures far beyond my paygrade. But surprise me with a tough encounter in broad daylight? I'd get my ass whupped.

I dug my thumbs into my eyes and rubbed them hard. Every one of my victories had depended on the terrain favoring my shadow magic, on me taking the initiative and surprising my enemies. The spider dude in the tower. The ogres and wyvern. Our second encounter with the xythagas. Plenty of darkness, plenty of mana, and the element of surprise on my side.

I sat up straighter. Well, the Beggars had lost their sole opportunity to catch me unawares. Whatever came next would be fought on my terms, on terrain of my choosing, and only when I was ready.

The thought calmed my nerves. The ball was in my court. Time to man up and get to work.

I swiped away the domains window and looked at the next ones.

 There are five talent advancements available to you:

Wall Climber (I), Cat's Fall, Mute Presence, Heads-Up, and Adrenaline Surge (II). All of them cost seventy-five XP except for Cat's Fall, which clocked in at fifty-five.

 There are three spells available to you:

Evenfall, Ebon Tendrils (II), and Grasping Shadows.

I sat back and thought. I had two hundred and seventeen XP to spend, and I had to make them count. Mute Presence was clearly a must. Anything I tried to enact from here on out would have to be exceptionally stealthy, as engaging with more than one Beggar at a time would prove lethal. That would leave me with one hundred and forty-two XP to spend. Grasping Shadows would allow me to constrain more than one opponent at a time, but I doubted it was a sufficiently powerful spell that I'd be able to use it to slow down the Beggars. Ebon Tendrils (II), however, might allow me to tangle up one of them for just long enough that I could get the drop on them.

On the other hand, Wall Climber could prove key to getting in and out of the castle without burning mana on Shadow Step. That would leave me enough to buy Cat's Fall while I was at it, ensuring that my acrobatics high above the bailey wouldn't prove lethal if I ran out of mana.

I tapped Mute Presence and Ebon Tendrils (II),
re-opened my sheet to see what had replaced th
My new talent was:

```
Stunning Backstab

XP Cost: 75
- Allows you to stun an opponent w
successfully struck by Backstab.
```

And my new spell was:

```
Shadow Clone

XP Cost: 75
- Your affinity with the darkness
you to clone your own shadow and s
forth, directing its movements wit
hundred feet for as long as you co
trate.
- Mana Drain: 2
```

Excellent. Both were contenders for my next
Perhaps Stunning Backstab over Wall Climber
while I headed toward the highland meadow.

Rising to my feet, I dusted myself off and jog
perimeter of Feldgrau. There was a good chance
had killed Falkon in that encounter. If so, I was
with him before he wandered off to investigat
ran past a score of the undead, but despite my
ignored me completely. I also kept a wary eye on

up to the castle, but none of the Beggars made any attempt to descend toward Feldgrau.

All too soon, I reached the highland meadow's road. It seemed like just hours ago when Lotharia, Falkon and I had snuck down through here to capture a plague corpse. I stared morosely at the building behind which she and I had hidden. The wind blew around me, whispering mockingly as if it enjoyed my pain. What I wouldn't do to have her calm, analytical presence with me now, her subtle wit and support. She'd been inside the keep now for almost two days. I didn't want to think about it. Didn't want to think about what might be happening to her in there, where creatures like the xythagas dwelled.

I was panting by the time I reached the meadow, my leg on fire, and as I came to a stop, hands on my knees, it was immediately apparent that there was nobody there. The wind blew down from the cold peaks and set the meadow grasses and flowers to rustling, but nobody stood before the ruined welcome longhouse. Nobody was making their way up along the far path that followed the bluffs toward the high castle gate.

They hadn't killed Falkon.

Disappointment welled up within me, and I sank into a crouch. Only then did it hit me how much I'd been hoping for my friend's presence. Someone with whom to plan, to flesh out a strategy. Instead, I was going to have to go it alone. Just me against the Beggars.

I stayed crouched for a good while. It wasn't that I was frozen, exactly, just that the intensity of my emotions made me stay still, like a small animal huddling while a storm blew overhead. If this had been any normal game I'd have powered on without a thought, but Death March mode changed all that.

Of course, I could simply turn and head out into the wilderness. I wasn't helpless any longer. A month of determined hiking should get me to some sort of civilized land, and then I'd be able to start over. New friends, new opportunities.

Hell, no.

I wanted to save my friends. I wanted to take back Castle Winter. I wanted to bring a little justice to the Beggars who'd waltzed into our domain without so much as a by your leave. But most importantly? I wanted to rescue Lotharia. But how? How could I get revenge without being killed out of hand?

With a wince, I rose to my feet. My only remaining resource was Guthorios. Much as I hated the idea of turning to him for help, I had no choice. Who knew what he'd demand in return? With a heavy heart, I retraced my steps back down to Feldgrau. The sun was dipping toward the horizon by the time I entered the village, and this time I felt nothing but stony determination as I made my way along the Moon's Way toward the far tower.

The dead stilled and watched me as I passed them. Skeletal champions and plague corpses, floating wraiths and cowled figures with burning eyes. If anything, the sheer number of them gave me hope; all I had to do was convince Guthorios to flush out Castle Winter with this horde of undead. As powerful as the Beggars were, they couldn't stand up to literally hundreds upon hundreds of foes. Could they?

I reached the old town square and skirted the charnel pit. Even as I hurried along its edge, a fresh zombie tore itself free of the mud and earth that composed its side and climbed toward me. I shuddered and locked my eyes on the tower doors. They stood closed this time, and I limped up the broad steps to shove them open.

I stepped into the darkness, averting my eyes from the first-floor chamber as I turned to hurry up the steps. Nothing barred my way. No servants, no seneschals. The tower might have been deserted for all I knew. I rounded the final turn and stepped out into the throne room.

Guthorios sat as before. I half expected to interrupt him in the midst of some magical rite or conference with advisors, but instead he seemed to be waiting for me, hands on his knees, eyes burning as he stared through the chill air. I was hit by his terrible presence, the weight of his regard, a sense of power that like a massive hand pressing down on my shoulder. I was desperate, however, and willing to risk his displeasure.

"Dread Lord, excuse my interruption."

He did not respond.

"A group calling themselves the Beggars of Solomon have entered Castle Winter. They've captured Falkon and Michaela and stolen the domain from me. I barely escaped. They spoke of being hired to do a job there."

Still nothing.

Was he asleep? Farseeing? I hesitated, then pressed on. "I've come to ask for your help in rescuing Michaela and Castle Winter. We'd already begun making progress into the keep when they arrived…"

Silence. I took a deep breath and stepped closer. Even with Astute Observer I couldn't tell if he was present in his body. No signs of life, obviously. His eyes were open, however, but unfocused. Perhaps—

"You are skilled at losing your allies." Guthorios' words caused me to startle and step back. "Not an admirable trait."

"Yeah, I'm not fond of it either." It was hard to bite down on what I really wanted to say. "But I'm only level eleven. I don't have a lot of weight to throw around just yet."

"I observed the approach of the Beggars of Solomon. They display greater potential at divining the archmagus' secrets. I am pleased at their arrival."

"Pleased? But they're not working for you. How do you know they won't steal away your treasure?"

Guthorios moved at last, lifting one bony shoulder. "They do work for me."

"They what? Why didn't you tell us they were coming?" My outrage caused me to sputter. "We almost died up there!"

"I am under no obligation to reveal the full extent of my plans to you. Their unexpected arrival is a welcome boon. I had not anticipated their arrival for at least another month. For I will employ any and all tools to accomplish my goals. If you cannot defeat them, then it is clear they are the better tool. I am certain the Beggars shall serve me well."

I ground my teeth as I stared at the floor. My knuckles ached from how tightly I was clenching my fists. How could I convince him to help me? This was it. My last chance. But there was no sane argument I could make in favor of removing the Beggars so that I could resume my work. Their team had over one hundred and thirty levels between them. Mine had barely fifty. Loyalty? No. Sacrifice myself for my friends? I didn't trust Guthorios enough to even examine that option with much seriousness.

"I understand." I had to work hard to speak with an even tone. "I'd still like to attempt to fulfill our bargain. Would you be willing to lend me aid so that I may do so? Insurance in case the Beggars fail?"

Guthorios actually smiled, the stiff muscles of his face ticking as his lips pulled into something akin to a grimace. "Aid that would make your assistance comparable to the Beggars of Solomon? I am not so generous. Should they fail, I shall expend greater wealth in hiring an even more elite team. So, no, Chris Meadows. I shall conserve my resources for where they are best spent. You may still, however, attempt to fulfill your end of the bargain. My completing my part shall depend on whether you ultimately prove more useful than the Beggars."

It was hard to breathe. My throat cramped and my stomach twisted. I simply nodded and turned away. I stumbled down the steps and out into the early evening, where I stood, hands on my hips, staring up at the sky. What to do? I didn't want to stay in Feldgrau, but where could I go? I couldn't approach the castle till I'd recovered my mana.

The Green Liver goblins. Kreekit, Dribbler, and Barfo. They were all I had left. I opened my character sheet and navigated toward my allies. Yep. They were still listed there. But how to find them? They must have fled along with the Big Burpies at the approach of the Beggars. But to where? Somewhere close to the castle. They'd be loath to give up all that meat. That meant somewhere along the high bluffs and cliffs above the highland meadow, no doubt.

I sighed. They were my freaking allies. How did Euphoria not have some sort of paging or location system? Then again, maybe it did. I'd waived all those benefits away when I'd signed up for Death March.

With nothing else for it, I set out. I limped back along the Moon's Way, gratefully leaving the charnel pit behind. This was the first time I felt like I'd lost my momentum in Euphoria. Up until this point, each challenge had been followed by a hard-won victory, new allies, greater abilities. Now, I was adrift. Grasping at straws. Ignoring the rational part of my mind that was trying to tell me I didn't have a chance against a group of high-level PCs.

The path crested and reached the highland meadow once more, and I caught my breath at the sight of a figure standing before the ruined waystation. Falkon? No. A stranger. Another Beggar?

I stood completely still, ready to turn and sprint back down to Feldgrau.

She was standing with her hands on her hips, her bright coppery red hair done up in a high ponytail and blowing in the wind. There was something indescribably young about her despite her voluptuous figure, something fresh, as if she were new to this world, gazing upon it for the very first time. She turned and stared straight at me, and I realized with a start that she was stunningly beautiful.

We studied each other across the grassy meadow, and then she raised one hand, waved, and gave me a bright smile of pure joy.

7

I HESITATED, THEN WAVED back. Her smile widened, and despite it all, despite my pain and despair and loss, I couldn't help but smile back. Her smile was just that infectious. As I approached I couldn't help but wonder: *just how high is her charisma? She's winning me over just with a wave.*

She waited for me to approach, hands returning to her generous hips over which she wore low-slung and form-fitting leggings. Her knee-high boots had folded tops and redundant buckled straps down their length, while a leaf-shaped dagger was shoved in her broad and double-tongued belt with a large, ornate iron buckle.

Everything about her was carefully put together. Her midriff was bare, revealing her athletic figure, and her full breasts were cupped by a black half-corset strapped to a broad leather collar about her slender neck. Bare shoulders, bare upper arms, and then full ivory sleeves from the elbows down to her brown leather gloves.

But it was her face that caught my attention and held it. She had the kind of beauty you only see on glossy magazine covers.

The kind even the real models themselves don't display in person. I'd describe her as elfin if I hadn't just run into Delphina, but she had something of the fey about her, something elusive and ethereal that was undercut by her confident smile and forthright gaze. It was just as easy to picture her meditating in a glade, cherry blossoms falling about her, as it was to imagine her knocking back shots at a bar.

"Hi," she said, and flashed me a slightly more nervous version of her smile. "This isn't quite the reception I was expecting. Are you with Cruel Winter?"

"I am." I was normally pretty comfortable around attractive women, but all that bare skin and cleavage was making it hard to act casual. *Charisma seventeen? Eighteen?* "I'm afraid you're a little late to the party, though. Cruel Winter's about done and gone."

"Done and gone?"

"Yeah. Destroyed. You've walked into quite a situation here." Despite her arresting looks, I felt nothing more than weariness at the prospect of crushing her hopes. "A large undead force killed everyone a long time ago. There's pretty much nothing left."

"That's not true," she said, and with a shy smile she stepped forward and took my hand. "You're still here."

I pulled my hand free and stepped away, heart suddenly pounding. "Yeah, true, but I'm no great shakes." She wasn't fazed by my news. "Who are you? Why'd you choose Cruel Winter of all guilds?"

She linked her hands behind her back. "I'm Sylvana Embers. This is my first time playing Euphoria, but my big brother told me Cruel Winter was the place to be." She paused, as if reflecting. "Of course, that was some time ago. Did I make a mistake?"

"I'm afraid you did." A cold wind rushed down the mountain slopes, driving waves across the high grass and causing me to shiver. Sylvana seemed unaffected. "To be honest, you'd be better off ditching this avatar and starting fresh in a more civilized area."

She raised a fine eyebrow. "Ditch this avatar? That's not an option."

"Course it's an option," I said. "I can tell you put a lot of work into it, but I bet you can recreate it in half the time. Seriously. This is a bad scene here. No place for a newbie."

Her eyes flashed as she raised her chin. "I meant, that's literally not an option for me. I'm playing in Death March mode. I don't get to log out until my six months are up."

I just gaped at her. "You're what?"

"Death March mode," she said. "Surely you know of it?"

"I—yes, but—why?"

She hugged herself and looked away, over the cliff to the vast lands beyond. "I have personal reasons for wanting to raise the cash. I need to help somebody. Somebody I love very much. And toward that end I am willing to sacrifice everything. Even my life, if need be."

I didn't know what to say. Was that a tear running down her cheek? "I'm sorry to hear that. Oh, man." I rubbed the back of my head. "Yeah, then you really are stuck here. That sucks."

"Sucks?" She snapped her head around to stare at me. "Does my presence here inconvenience you?"

"Inconvenience—what? No! Just that this is a really dangerous place. There's a bunch of high-level PCs calling themselves the Beggars of Solomon up in the castle right now, and they've captured my allies. Feldgrau – the town below – is full of the undead. This whole area is filled with high-level mobs and monsters. I've barely managed to survive this long, and that's been mostly due to luck and a lot of experience gaming."

"I'm not a complete fool," she said. "I didn't come entirely unprepared. I contacted a friend who arranged to drop off some gear for me. It's supposed to be waiting in the waystation." She turned to consider the ruined building. "I was expecting it to be in a locker or some such, but now I'm thinking she probably just hid it under some rocks."

"Gear? That'll help. Do you know what she left you?"

"And suddenly you're thrilled that I'm here." She shot me an arch glance as she turned to walk into the waystation. "How surprising."

It was hard not to stare at how closely her leggings gripped her rear, but I did my level best. Was Euphoria turning me into a cad? Or was her charisma simply walloping me over the head? I fixed my gaze between her shoulder blades and followed her into the gloom. She cast around for a moment, then stepped toward a collapsed section of the wall and squatted beside a large rock. "Here. Can you lift this for me, please?"

"Sure," I said. It was a decently sized rock, and I crouched beside it, found purchase with both hands then strained to tip it over. I could barely lift it, and had to exert myself to the maximum till I was finally able to rock it over to one side, revealing a large hole.

"You're so strong," said Sylvana admiringly.

"Uh, not really. I've only got strength fourteen."

She slapped my arm playfully. "You've got to get better at taking compliments from a girl."

Something about that resonated. I frowned as I watched her reach into the hole. Where had I heard that before, that same tone?

"Here we go," she said, pulling out a black silken bag. It was just large enough to maybe slip a basketball into, and my heart immediately sank. So much for a ton of protective gear to keep her alive.

"What class did you pick?" I asked, moving over to sit on a stone.

"Charlatan," she said, sounding distracted as she waved her hand over a small gem pressed into the bag's clasp. "Awful name, isn't it? So negative, when all it means is that you like to socialize and have fun."

The gem glowed and then fragmented.

"There," she said. "Perfect. Now, let's see what my friend left me." She reached in and pulled out a curved, slender blade that was far too long to have fit inside the bag. It was gorgeous, and glimmered gently as if glimpsed at the bottom of a fast-flowing stream. The grip was just long enough for one hand, and the crossbars and basket hilt curled with incredible artistry, depicting a field of platinum flowers that protected her hand completely.

Sylvana raised it and sighted down its length, and a shimmer of light undulated down its blade before forming a star at the tip and disappearing.

"That's... that's some blade," I said.

"Yup. It's a Frostflower Saber." She sounded smug. A scabbard had appeared at her hip, and with surprising skill she slid the blade into it. She gave me a wink. "Don't leave home without it."

"That's some friend you've got."

"The best. Now, what else?" She drew up a folded bundle of shimmering white cloth, which she unfurled into a rich and sumptuous cape. It was made of some thick, luxurious fur, like mountain goat or polar bear. This she swept around her bare shoulders and tied beneath her chin. It fell perfectly to her heels, and immediately gave her a regal presence, like some kind of Russian princess.

"A Tastivan Cloak," she told me. "Level thirty, with protection against enchantments, curses, hallucinations, cold effects, or mind control spells."

I sat back. "Holy shit."

"Language," she said with an impish grin, and crouched once more beside her bag. "Ah, now this is nice." She pulled forth a long black velvet case, which she opened to reveal four ornate silver rings, each with a jewel embedded in its center.

"Four rings of ethereal armor," she said, setting the case down so she could pluck her gloves free and then slide each ring onto a long, delicate finger. "Each with a host of side benefits. There. Now I don't feel quite so naked."

"You sound like you know your stuff," I said. "I thought this was your first time playing."

"It is." She snapped the velvet case shut and tossed it over her shoulder. "But I'm not just looks. I'm smart enough to have done my research before entering the game in Death March mode. Surely you did the same?"

I hesitated. "I never told you I was in Death March mode."

"What?" She recovered so smoothly I barely noticed. "I meant before you entered the game. Didn't you watch any documentaries, read the FAQs, the player interviews…?"

"Yeah, sure," I said. "But I didn't have a friend who was willing to hook me up with insane gear."

She cocked her head to one side. "You didn't?"

"No. Why would I? I mean, there was this one girl who said she'd hook me up, but that all turned out to be lies. Anyway. Doesn't matter now."

"Hmm," she said. "Sounds like there's more to that story than you're letting on. Either way." She returned to her bag, and in short order drew forth a dozen more objects. "Will you look at that. My friend was far, far too generous. There's no way I could use all of these items." She eyed me speculatively. "Would you be interested in some?"

"Uh, would I be interested in artifact-level gear? Yes." I paused. "But I've got nothing to offer you in exchange."

"Oh, that's fine." She beamed at me, and my knees went weak. If she had that smile in the real world, she'd make a fortune in advertising. "Just a little gratitude and company is all I ask for. After all, it seems like we're both stuck here alone, doesn't it? I'd really appreciate benefiting from your wisdom and guidance."

"Sure," I said. "We're both stuck here, like you said."

She moved to kneel before me, and took my hand in both of hers. Her eyes were large, and her expression was suddenly sincere and vulnerable at the same time. "Thank you, Chris. I don't know what I'd do without you."

I slowly pulled my hand free. "How'd you know my name is Chris?"

She froze, then cracked a smile. "What? You told me when I introduced myself."

Had I? I was pretty sure I hadn't.

Sylvana returned to her bag and drew out an amazing looking sword in a bound leather scabbard. It was completely black, a matt darkness that drank in the light, and slightly curved at the tip. It was unlike any blade I had ever seen before; there was no cross-guard, and the hilt was wrapped in one large, continuous sheet of black leather, a silver bolt at the bottom and top affixing it in place.

Sylvana pulled the scabbard away, revealing the blade. It was sharp down one length, the side that ultimately curved up, and this sharpened slope glimmered black-blue, like the depths of the ocean. The rest was matt black but for a small sapphire imprinted at the blade's base.

"A Void Blade," she said, voice hushed. "Here. You should have it."

Reluctantly, I accepted the blade from her. It was just a little longer than a short sword, and surprisingly light.

"Press your thumb on the sapphire," said Sylvana, leaning forward, hands on her knees. "Then force one point of mana inside it. That will permanently key the blade to your essence, making it so nobody else can use its special properties."

"I'm all out of mana," I said. The blade *felt* lethal, much like sitting inside a Ferrari gave one the sense of its potential speed.

"Well, when you recover some, then." She waved her hand impatiently at my objection. "It's an insanely expensive and lethal weapon, but it only really comes into its own when wielded by a darkblade. Once keyed to your essence, you can activate its void power by simply willing it to shift; at that point, the blade will turn to shadow and bypass all armor, stealing the strength from your foes and granting it to you."

I stared at the black sword, eyebrows going up in amazement. "You serious? That's… that's amazing. How…?" I lowered the blade and stared at her. "Why did your friend leave a Void Blade for you?"

"What?" She frowned at me. "Because it's a killer sword, is why. Look, if you don't want it I'm more than happy to dual wield."

"No, I'm not saying that, it's just…" *Just such a coincidence that you'd have this.* "Thank you, Brianna."

"You're welcome," she snapped, then visibly relented and forced herself to smile at me. "Of course you're welcome. We've —what?" She turned pale. "That's not my name."

"You sure?" I pressed the Void Blade's scabbard to my hip. It shimmered, and leather thongs appeared, binding it to my belt. Holy crap. With a blade like this, I might just have a chance of hurting the Beggars.

Sylvana leapt to her feet, red hair swinging wildly from her ponytail. "I told you, my name's Sylvana."

"Sure. Sylvana." I didn't bother standing. "Who just happened to show up here loaded with high-level gear, some of which seems tailored for me, and somehow already knew my name." I held her gaze. "Gig's up, Brianna. But thank you for the sword all the same."

Her jaw trembled and her hand drifted to the pommel of her Frostflower Saber. "You're making baseless accusations. I strongly urge you to take back your insults."

"Insults?" My own anger spiked. "You're kidding me, right?"

"How dare you! Return my blade!"

"Just like you. Giving gifts and then taking them back." I finally stood. "What was your plan here, anyways? Win back my sympathy by—what? Going on a suicidal six-month mission with me?"

Her eyes flashed, her pale cheeks flushing. "I was willing to risk my life for you! And this is how you thank me?"

"Risk your life?" I grinned at her. "Who asked you to? Not only that, but if you were trying to earn my gratitude, what's with all the lies? 'Sylvana Ember'? Risking Death March to save someone you love? Did you deliberately try to copy my situation, or are you just not creative enough to come up with your own story?"

"It's possible I came here to save your life, you ungrateful bastard!" She advanced on me, finger pointed at my chest like a dagger. "Don't you think it's possible I was worried about you? How weak and unprepared you were? Don't you think it's possible I set this all up to help you, to do my part in helping your brother?"

My anger grew flat and dangerous. "Don't bring my brother into this."

"And why not? Only you get to play at being the hero? Only you get to be all noble and self-sacrificing, and everyone else is either a bitch or your inferior?" She got right in my face, strands of copper-red hair falling across her eyes. "Admit it. You just can't stand the idea of someone saving your ass. Of *me* saving you, because you insist on playing the victim, the noble martyr, screwed up by life, your family 'cursed', this whole pathetic drama you've created to make yourself feel important—"

I raised my hand to grab her by the throat. All my anger, all my frustration, all my despair came howling up and focused on her.

"Go on," she whispered, smiling up at me. "Go on, you pathetic little fuck. Grab me and squeeze. Are you man enough to at least do that?"

Then it all came back to me. The tormented, crazy, abusive, out-of-control relationship I'd had with this woman. The way she could get under my skin in seconds flat and turn me into a monster. How she loved to see me enraged; how it turned her on. The hate sex we'd have after our terrible fights, so furious and punishing that I'd be unable to talk, to move, to do anything but lie there loathing myself for ages after.

Even in this gorgeous avatar I recognized that twisted gleam in her eye. This was what she wanted. To reel me back in. Have me shouting and infuriated with her. Involved once more.

"No," I said, pulling my hand back and stepping away. "No. To all of this. I won't let you suck me back into that madness."

She reached up and touched her neck where my fingerprints were only now fading away. "Poor Chris. Such a disappointment. Can't even act like a man."

I pulled the Void Blade from my hip and let it drop. "Don't follow me," I said, backing away from her as if she were a swaying cobra. "Don't search me out. You hear me?"

She froze, eyes narrowing, but I didn't give her a chance to respond. I backed out the waystation door and then turned to take off at a limping run. I half expected her derisive laughter to follow me into the dusk, but nothing came. The grass whispered against my thighs as I charged toward the forest line where eons ago a pair of ogres had emerged and nearly ended my life.

A moment later I was under their dark boughs, racing beneath the canopy, leaving the highland meadow and Brianna's madness behind me.

8

I CLIMBED AS THE sun set far below me, spilling its last aureate rays across the rolling hills and lowlands that stretched out toward that conflagration of fire. The thick woods rose up the mountain slopes, their canopy blocking the last of the evening light so that I clambered in gloom, pushing myself harder and harder, seeking to escape the memory of what Brianna had just drawn out of me. Occasionally I stopped, reeling, and turned upon some outcropping or ledge that had a view over the forest and the distant sunset. Feldgrau far below and to my left. Castle Winter below me now as well. The highland meadow down and to the right, a shadowed plain.

But I couldn't stop. I wasn't even searching for the goblins. I was simply moving. What vigor had been gifted to me by my rage quickly burned out and became mechanical. The wound in the back of my thigh opened and hot blood seeped down the back of my leg. I gritted my teeth and pressed on. The slope became steeper, the forest thin, and soon I was amongst large boulders, their surface gritty and ice cold. The final fingernail rim of the sun dipped beneath the horizon and shadow descended upon the mountain.

Sweat stung my eyes. My spider silk shirt clung to my back. My fingers burned from grasping at countless rocks and roots. My wounded leg was heavy, barely responsive to my needs. Still I fought for height, but each time I stopped to peer upward, the distant peak mocked me. It would take me days upon days to even reach the snowline.

Finally, I collapsed into a small gulley of grass, falling hard onto my side. I lay still, panting for breath, and saw again my hand moving to close around Brianna's pale throat. Felt the righteous rage, the urge to silence her, to still her tongue. Shame poured through me. I'd never struck her. Never slapped her as sometimes she'd demanded. But god damn, I'd wanted to. I'd fled her countless times, shaking with impotent rage, vowing to never speak to her again.

And somehow, every time, she inserted herself back into my life. Even here, in the depths of Euphoria, she'd found a way to return to me. To be valuable. Needed. Because I knew come dawn I'd not be able to turn her away. I had nothing left. No friends, no allies, no costly gear.

No.

I'd not work with her.

I'd sooner bite off my own tongue.

Shivering, I crawled out of the gulley. The rock face before me was cut by a diagonal cleft, dark like a scar cut into the abyss itself. I waited, trembling from the cold and exhaustion, and listened. Waited for Astute Observer to point out any dangers. Tracks. Spoor. Signs that the cave was occupied.

Nothing.

With a groan I crawled across the rough, rocky ground to the cave entrance. It widened inside, but even so I'd not be able to call it more than a large crack. I tried to rise into a crouch, but my leg spasmed and I gave up with a grunt. On all fours, like a wretched wild beast, I entered the cave. I pushed in about a dozen yards and the crack at last opened into a bowl of a chamber.

The cold was starting to slip into me like daggers of ice. I activated Darkvision. Someone had used the small cavern before me; a pile of twigs with larger logs around them had been piled behind a shoulder of rock that would block it from view outside, while a small bedroll was set close by. A tattered notebook was laid on a natural shelf, with two small pairs of boots set neatly just below.

I whispered a prayer of thanks to the last occupant and approached the stack of wood. I'd no idea how I could light the fire, until suddenly I did: what looked like some random stones to one side were clearly a crude set of flint and steel. Unsure as to how I'd suddenly recognized them, I just as quickly realized how to use them and took up the rock and rod of metal. Heck yeah, Survival (Basic II).

It took me five minutes to strike enough sparks into the moss in the heart of the pile for it to catch, and then another five minutes of gently blowing to cause the cottony smoke to flicker into fire. Jubilant, I was reminded of Tom Hanks in *Castaway*, and while I didn't want to leap around the cave bellowing my excitement I still felt the same level of primal pride.

The flames licked up the smaller twigs, and intuition told me to give them a little time before placing the larger logs. I did so, my hands guided by some unexpected wisdom, and after ten minutes

I had a cheerful fire crackling and sending dancing hues of gold, umber and orange across the rough cavern walls and ceiling.

I turned off Darkvision. The walls were decorated with simple paintings; they depicted a goblin in a series of dramatic encounters. In one area, he tumbled into a great crack. In another, he rode what might have been a pony through a flaming landscape. Here, he sat smoking a pipe and smiling beatifically. There, he fought a rearing bear with nothing more than a dagger and a roguish smile.

I couldn't help but be cheered by this goblin's exploits. The last painting showed him being chased by a plump goblin woman. I wondered if she'd caught him. If she'd dragged him down from this mountain and forced him to settle down.

My grin faded, replaced by a weary melancholia. Where was Lotharia now? What I wouldn't give to have her here by my side. Helping me plan our next step, mocking me gently with her wry wit, the fire dancing in her eyes.

I sighed and sat on the goblin's neat pallet and took down his book. It was unsurprisingly filled with what must have been goblin writing. Nothing I could make out. There were a number of amusing drawings scattered throughout, however, including what looked like a series of self-studies, portraits of the goblin making a variety of ridiculous expressions. I chuckled once more, set the book aside, then gazed into the fire.

I should be bandaging up my wound. I should be lying down to sleep, focusing on recovering my mana points. At the very least I should have been coming up with a new plan. But all I could do was replay scenes from my past. A life that I'd managed to forget in the immediacy of Euphoria, but which had finally caught up with me. I saw my mother in her hospital bed, moaning and tossing and turning, lost to me beyond a wall of drugs and cancer. I saw Eva's eyes widening when I'd told her about my brother's situation, told her how I'd not blame her if I had too much baggage to become friends with, and how she'd set her jaw and reached out to squeeze my hand. I thought for the first time in ages of Sarah, the girl I'd been kind of seeing up in Seattle, all punk attitude and toughness on the outside, but like everyone else looking for a connection, for understanding. Where would we be if I hadn't picked up and left for Miami?

I thought of Brianna. The first time I'd seen her, standing at the bar looking so bored she might die. How she'd given me the once-over when I'd stepped up beside her to order a drink and then challenged me to tell her something funny. I'd told her the joke about the general and his armies and she'd laughed, surprised.

We'd talked gaming, she'd talked about herself, and after perhaps four or five drinks we'd left for another bar. I kissed her at the third bar, but she'd pulled away with a knowing, pleased smile and insisted on my calling a cab for her. I didn't know it, not then, but that was to prove her M.O. – dole out intimacy at exactly the right pace, reeling me in then pushing me away, all to drive me ever more crazy with desire for her.

And it had worked. Kind of. Though she hadn't needed to play me so hard. I was hurting so bad I'd have put up with almost anything.

I stared at my hands, turning them over in the firelight. Almost anything.

"Chris?"

I startled, went to stand, but my leg spasmed and I bit back a cry.

"Chris? Don't get mad, all right? I just brought you a healing potion. I'll leave it here for you by the cave entrance."

"How'd you find me?" I growled.

"Well, it wasn't too hard, luckily. I don't even have Survival: Basic (I) yet." I couldn't make her out. The firelight was ruining my night vision. Of course, I could have switched on Darkvision, but I preferred to keep her in shadow. "You're bleeding, you know. You left a pretty obvious trail. I'm surprised nothing else followed you up here, actually."

I closed my eyes. Should have thought of that. A trail of blood leading right to me in a high-danger zone. The last thing I needed was a dire bear or something coming in for a snack.

"You got a second exit, right?" She sounded cautious, afraid of offending me. "You're not just bottled up in there?"

"I—no." I stared at the heart of the fire. "Not that I've found."

"Oh." There was an awkward pause. "I know you don't want anything from me, but I'm going to leave this healing potion here, all right? And—and I'm leaving the Void Blade and the rest of the gear I brought you. Ignore it if you want. But I'm not going to use it, so why let it go to waste? Right?"

I continued staring at the fire. "Fine."

The silence drew out. I thought she might have left, but then the shadows by the cavern entrance shifted. "Chris, I'm sorry."

That got my attention. In all the months I'd been with her, Brianna had never, ever apologized. For anything. Instead of assuaging my anger, her apology made me wary.

"For what?"

She laughed, exasperated. "For… for everything. I mean, where do I start?"

"Where *do* you start?"

"You're not going to make this easy for me, are you?" It didn't sound like a real question. "Well, I'm sorry for tricking you. For trying to find a way to get close to you again. I'll admit, it was a little manipulative."

Sylvana's voice was lighter and completely different from Brianna's huskier tone. In a way, it made it dangerously easier to forgive her. Like I was forgiving Sylvana for Brianna's sins.

I almost didn't want to know. To ask. To open up this conversation. But morbid curiosity compelled me. "What was your plan, when this all started? Why trick me into joining Cruel Winter?"

"You sure you want to know?" Dark amusement in her voice. "I don't think you'd understand my point of view on it."

"Try me."

"Well." I could hear her settle down in the entrance. "I wanted you to appreciate what you'd thrown away. I guess I wanted you to admit you'd been wrong about me. That you did need me. That you were lucky to have me in your life."

The fire cracked and spat forth a stream of sparks. I let it be my answer.

"So I came up with this invitation to Euphoria."

"There never was a raffle, was there?"

"No, not so much. But that's a minor detail. All that mattered was getting you into the game. I knew you'd leap at the chance. Chris Meadows, the all-star Golden Dawn champ turning down a chance to play Euphoria? Not in this lifetime."

I jutted out my jaw and hunched my shoulders. "So. Lies."

"White lies. What mattered was getting you into the game and finding a way to get you to spend time with me. I was going to show you the best Euphoria had to offer. The Glimmerstone Caves. Fly over the EverVortex. Go swimming through the Emerald Dream. All kinds of amazing adventures. We'd fight, level up, *game* together. And you'd see that we really do have a connection. One that was all warped and twisted in the real world, but which here, together, going on quests and having the wildest adventures possible, was true. Because that's what I realized, Chris. The love we had was too big for the boring world. It choked us when kept at the mundane level of bars and parties and sleepovers and bingeing on movies. It needed an epic setting to flourish."

Her voice had picked up in urgency. God damn her charisma. She was causing my heart to beat faster just through her intensity. I *knew* that was Albertus messing with my brain, allowing her character sheet to trigger my hypothalamus or whatever, releasing endorphins and oxytocin, but that didn't mitigate the effect it was having on me.

"But then it went all wrong," she said, her excitement abating. "You weren't on the highland meadow when I arrived to pick you up. And it took me far too long to find you. I hadn't expected you to be quite so enterprising without me."

"Enterprising? You know the first thing I ran into upon arriving here? Two ogres. I was lucky enough to accidentally trigger my Shadow Step ability, because otherwise they'd have crushed my head right there and then. Killing me, Brianna. You hear me? Your plan – your trick – nearly led to my death."

"Like I was supposed to know you were crazy enough to pick Death March mode?" Her outrage was just as sharp as mine. "Who the hell does that? Why didn't you tell me? Why didn't you let me know what you were up to?"

Her words stung, and partially because she was right. Still, I didn't want to concede any ground to her. Bitter experience had taught me to hold my own. "Like you and your friends were so forthcoming when I arrived. What was his name, Arvid? The guy who kept cracking up every time I asked what class I should play, or anything of practical benefit? Brianna, you made it *real* clear that you didn't want to talk shop. You couldn't get me into Euphoria fast enough."

"Fine. I might have been a little pushy, but Death March? I'd have made time to convince you not to commit suicide."

"I had no choice," I said, turning back to glower at the fire. "You wouldn't understand, even if you think you do."

"Sure I understand. Now. Your little brother. Justin. You want to save him." She paused. "I'd no idea things had gotten so tough for you guys."

"No, you wouldn't have. You were too busy enacting your master plan to reveal our true love."

I could sense her stiffen.

"I... I deserve that. You're right. Let's fold that into my general apology."

Again she surprised me. I'd been ready for her cutting rebuttal, but her quiet words disarmed me. Almost. "And why Cruel Winter?"

"Does it matter?" She sounded tired. "You going to grill me over every detail?"

"Yes."

"Fine." She blew out her cheeks. "Cruel Winter's a dead guild. It's as isolated as it gets, in case you hadn't noticed. So it was insurance. A means to ensure you'd join my group and hang out with me."

I smiled bitterly. "Insurance? You mean blackmail. A way to force me to be dependent on you. With no guild to turn to, no way to respawn anywhere but the middle of nowhere."

"Eh, don't be dramatic. You'd agreed to join my party, hadn't you? This changed nothing. Not as long as you planned to remain true to your word."

"Changes nothing?" I opened my mouth to spew out vitriol and then snapped it shut. She just wouldn't get it.

"Hey, I'm apologizing, right? Like, unconditionally? I'm sorry for my setup. I'm also sorry for this whole 'Sylvana Ember' thing. Though... I could have sworn you'd like this avatar."

"Your avatar's fine," I said, voice flat. "I'm just tired of being lied to."

"Yeah, I can tell. And I know you won't believe me, but I did this for you. Because I knew you wouldn't accept my help otherwise. That you'd doubt me and suspect me at every turn if I showed up as Brianna. But as Sylvana? I thought there might be a chance I could do you some good. Earn your trust."

I sank my forehead into my palm. "By lying even more?"

"Well, not when you put it that way." There it was; her impatience with me. "No. I was finding a way to deliver high quality items and back-up to you while you were out here."

"Sure," I said. "And why Death March mode? I mean, are you really in Death March?"

"Yeah," she said, and suddenly sounded despondent. "I had the stupid idea that it would be more romantic. That you'd be more inclined to take me in. That it would unite us. Seems stupid now. I'd take it back if I could."

I laughed weakly. "Brianna, you're incredible. You went with suicide mode because you thought it'd be more romantic? Seriously? *Seriously?*"

"Now you're just being offensive," she said. "I'm leaving the healing potion here, along with the promised gear. I'll wait for you in the waystation. Don't be late or you'll miss breakfast."

"Don't be late? Who said I was going to join you? An apology doesn't absolve you from all you've done." I waited, suddenly furious. "Brianna?"

No response.

"Damn it!" She'd always had a thing about getting in the last word. Used to piss me off no end. Still did. I listened carefully, but after a minute decided she'd really left. With a hiss, I rocked over onto my side and edged my way to the cavern entrance. The moon had yet to rise, and the last of the sunset was turning the clouds to lavender, so I could barely make out the pile she'd left by the cavern entrance.

I turned on Darkvision and surveyed the immediate environs. It would be just like her to hide so as to watch me accept her lar-gesse. But for all I studied the bushes and rocks, I couldn't make her out anywhere.

Frowning, I turned to the pile. A cut-glass bottle was set atop a folded robe. The Void Blade lay beside it, along with three rings, a coiled belt, and an amulet.

If those items were nearly as powerful as I suspected, I'd just hit the jackpot.

I took up the bottle, uncorked it, and then hesitated. Could it be some kind of charm or love potion? I wouldn't put it past Brianna. But fatigue and pain won out over my caution and I tipped the bottle back, chugging the potion quickly. Warmth spread through my body immediately, alleviating my fatigue and aches, healing scrapes and cuts I'd not even realized I'd had till they were gone, and finally smoothing over the agony of my wound, leaving my leg limber and hale.

By the time the last tingles were gone, I felt better than any other time since arriving in Euphoria. I smacked my lips in an excess of energy, grinned, and stoppered the bottle. "Thanks," I told the absent Brianna.

That done, I gathered the items and retreated into my cave, setting them before me in a pile so I could examine them carefully.

I held the robe out before me. It was hard to tell its exact color in the firelight, but it seemed to be a marbled gray, and thick like wool. Only partially warmed by the fire, I pulled the cloak over my shoulders and fastened the clasp under my chin.

Nothing happened.

I popped open my character sheet and checked my stats. Nothing had changed there, either. So either Brianna had just brought me a nice warm cloak, or there was some kind of keyword involved. Quick way to check: I activated Detect Magic and the cloak immediately glowed brightly. Keyword-activated, then.

Next I picked up the rings. Each was distinct from the others. The first was a simple band of glossy black metal. I slipped it onto my pointer finger and a subtle shiver ran through my body. I'd left my character sheet open, so saw the change immediately: my mana total had just jumped to *thirty-six*.

For a second, I just stared. Then I let out a whoop and punched my fist into the air. This ring carried twenty mana points in it! I grinned at one of the depictions of the goblin that I'd started thinking of as Barry. This ring alone opened up a host of new possibilities in combat. I could now drop Night Shrouds and summon Ebon Tendrils with much greater flexibility. Double Step everywhere and not worry about running dry only ten seconds into combat. Amazing.

The next ring was of carved ivory and was composed of a series of small shields being blown around the ring's circumference by gusts of wind. I slipped it on and the air faintly shimmered surround me, so quick and subtle I almost missed it. A ring of armor? I'd confirm with Brianna tomorrow.

The third ring was made from amber with a symbol like a stylized bull affixed to the front. Mystified, I examined it carefully, but found no clue as to its nature; putting it on made no changes to my character sheet, so I shrugged and moved on.

The amulet was simple in design, being a blue gemstone cut in the shape of a hexagon with the cord running through a hole in its center. When I looked through it at the fire I thought I could see faint wisps of smoke curling through the gem. Again, its nature was opaque, so I slipped the cord over my neck and let it sit over my spider silk shirt.

The final item was the belt. I uncoiled it, marveling at its slippery texture, like a band of liquid black ink. There was no buckle nor holes for a belt tongue, so I rose to my knees, removed my own plain leather belt and slipped the black one through the loops of my pants. When I touched the ends together, they melded and cinched to the perfect degree of tightness.

A number flickered on my character sheet.

"Holy crap," I said out loud.

My dex had just jumped to twenty-three.

I remained frozen in place, staring at the new number. My stat had just leapt up four whole levels at exactly the time I'd been warned such gains were doomed to slow down. I reached down and snagged a pebble from the ground, then caused it to dance over my knuckles. I'd never been able to do that. I snatched up a couple more stones and began to juggle, another feat I'd never been able to perform in real life. The three pebbles interwove in the firelight, and somehow my hands knew just how to pluck each one from the air and toss it back up.

It was easy.

Out of curiosity, I reached down and picked up a fourth pebble without breaking the flow and added it to the mix. The pattern changed but remained easy. My hand darted down to the ground once more, quick as a viper, and a fifth pebble was thrown into the pattern. I laughed, marveling at my own ability, then snatched three more pebbles and threw them up into the air.

And like that I was juggling eight pebbles without breaking a sweat, my hands dancing beneath them all, keeping the rocks in motion. I separated the pebbles into two groups, four to a hand, and kept those cycling through the air, no longer crossing them over, then tossed one over from my right, making it five in my left. They tumbled around and around, my left hand catching them and flicking them back up almost quicker than I could follow. I added a sixth. Now I couldn't follow the movements of my own hand. The muscles in my shoulder burned, and my fingers were growing stiffer by the second, but with a determined grin I added the seventh pebble and the whole chain collapsed to the ground.

I laughed and sat back down on the pallet, amazed. Everything had changed. Brianna's gifts had shifted me into an entirely different threat level, and that was without knowing what the cloak, amulet, and ring could do. I'd a Void Blade that could bypass armor and steal my foe's strength, a belt that had boosted my dex to ungodly levels, a ring of armor and another of mana. Add in the cloak, ring, and amulet, and perhaps the situation was no longer quite as dire as I'd thought.

The firelight was dying down. The healing potion had erased my injuries but done little to soothe the emotional exhaustion of the day. I lay down on Barry's pallet, head propped on one hand, and watched the branches collapse into the fire's core, slowly turning to glowing coals.

Brianna had changed the equation. Did that mean I forgave her? I didn't know. Did I trust her? Hell, no. Was I glad she was here? I thought of her exquisite form, her liquid eyes, her coppery red hair. Those full lips, her curvaceous body. I didn't exactly mind having such a beautiful woman by my side. I scowled and thought of Lotharia with a pang of guilt. Was that the effect of her charisma on me? In Euphoria it was impossible to tell.

With a groan, I lay back and covered my face with my elbow.

Life had just become incredibly more complicated.

9

BRIANNA HADN'T BEEN kidding. I could smell the fried eggs and sausage the moment I stepped out of the forest, a faint and indescribably delicious scent that immediately flooded my mouth with spit. Stomach yowling as if I had a furious alley cat trapped in there, I hurried across the meadow, all thoughts of dignified reserve lost before the visions of eggs over easy and greasy links. I came to an abrupt stop, though, at the sight of the dead monsters.

There were three of them. Apparently, I'd not been the only one captivated by the smell of a succulent breakfast. They were all of the same species; some kind of wolf mutant the size of a cow, their frames massively powerful and vaguely humanoid, their fur charcoal colored and thick. Each of them had been ensnared by garlands of vines that had wreathed them cruelly, their lengths covered in morning glory-like flowers, binding them to the ground then apparently shattering their bones. Some of the vines had cut so deep as to nearly slice off their limbs.

I resumed walking. The three monsters lay completely still. The earth was torn and gashed by their claws. They'd fought for their lives, but been unable to break free. I frowned at the longhouse. Brianna might only be level one, but she was clearly packing some firepower.

"Hello?" I ducked in the doorway. Brianna had tossed a white tablecloth over the flattest of the stones, and on this she'd laid out plates, silverware, glasses and a cutting board. An open picnic basket sat to one side, its interior teeming with further table-ware and wrapped bundles. Brianna straightened from where she'd been bent over a cast iron pan and blew a lock of her hair from her face.

"Morning! Hungry?"

"Yeah, like you wouldn't believe." I sat on one of the two rocks beside the table. "Where'd all this come from? You pack break-fast along with Void Blades?"

She laughed, clearly in a good mood. She'd changed out of yes-terday's skimpier outfit into something more practical, a complex combination of crimson-dyed leather and black scale mail that looked at once supple and tough. "Hardly. Did you honestly think I'd slum it just because I was going back to level one?" She took up my plate and slid three sausages that were cooked near to bursting onto it, along with three perfectly fried eggs. "That's a Handsome Gourmand's Everypack," she said, gesturing at the picnic basket with her spatula. "One of my favorite item drops ever. It's like a pantry, washing machine, and Crate and Barrel all in one."

She served her own plate, tossed the frying pan into the basket, then sat and pulled out a carafe filled with orange juice from the basket's depths. "If I were forced to marry and have carnal relations with an object made of wicker, this would be it. OJ?"

"I—sure, yeah." I watched as she filled my glass, then her own, then dropped the carafe back into the basket. It disappeared as neatly as the pan had. "Any coffee?"

"Sure. How do you want it?"

I laughed, amazed. "What, it's got an espresso machine in there too?"

"Now you're seeing why I insisted on bringing it along. Here." She pulled out a steaming mug. "Double shot latte, touch of cream, brown sugar. That still how you like it?"

"Yeah," I said, a little uneasy. She'd remembered. "Thanks."

She flashed me a smile, draped a napkin over her crossed legs, then leaned forward to spear a sausage with her fork, causing grease to burst free of the casing. "Now this is just how I pictured it," she said. "A civilized breakfast on the edge of civilization. Perfect sunlight, a romantic ruin, and delightful company." She picked up her OJ and held out the glass. "Cheers."

"Cheers," I said, clinking my glass with hers. My unease hadn't gone away, but the pull of the sausages was strong, so I set my qualms aside and dug in.

We didn't talk for perhaps five minutes. Brianna appeared to take just as much pleasure from watching me devour my food as from her own. When I finally lowered my silverware and sat back she smiled at me once more, flute of orange juice held up in one hand, elbow resting on an arm tucked across her stomach.

"Thanks," I said. "That was unexpectedly delicious."

"As long as we don't lose the Everypack, we'll always dine in equal style. Now. I see you're wearing the items I brought you. What do you think?"

"Think?" I held out my hand to stare at the rings, then dropped it in my lap. I couldn't help but match her grin. "I'm blown away, and I don't know what half of them do."

"Then let me elucidate. You're wearing a Stone Cloak. As long as it's charged with mana you can command it to petrify, repulsing most physical and even some magical attacks. The command word is 'petrify', obviously enough, but you can change it to whatever you want."

"Awesome," I said. "And I charge it by just willing a point of mana into its fabric?"

"Sure. But it can take up to ten mana and will hold them until used. Just think about how many points you want to expend at a time and it'll offer more or less protection, depending."

"Which normally would make me laugh, but with this mana ring? Twenty mana? Fully charged? That's crazy!"

"Yeah," she said, giving me a feline smile of contentment. "Not a bad little ring. Again, it'll hold your charge until you use it, then you'll have to fill it up whenever you've got extra mana to spare. Given how much trouble we're going to be getting into, I imagine you won't have a lot of downtime with which to fuel it, so, you know. Be smart."

"Not my first rodeo," I said. "And this ring? Armor?"

"Yep. Mostly against physical attacks, though, so don't expect it to stop blasts of fire or whatever. But blades, arrows, clubs – most of them will find their damage greatly reduced if not blocked altogether, dependent of course on the power of your attacker."

"Great. And this bull ring?"

"Ring of the Bull, you mean." She lowered her empty flute into the basket. When she pulled it back out it was filled with more orange juice. "Mimosa," she said. "Want one?"

"No, thanks."

She gave an indolent shrug. "Suit yourself. Anyways, that'll unleash a blast of force in a cone before you, out to a distance of fifteen feet. Enough to knock down doors and send opponents flying. It doesn't take mana, but has an annoyingly long cooldown period. You'll probably only get to use it once a fight."

"Cool. How do I activate it?"

"I think the current power word is 'Blammo'." The corner of her lips tugged up in amusement. "You can change it by thinking the power word then choosing a new one. It'll detect your intention."

"I don't know, I might keep the current version." I ran a finger over the stylized bull's head. "Has a certain charm to it."

She gave me her sinuous one-shouldered shrug again. "Your call."

"And this amulet?"

"Periapt, actually. Quick healing. Not like a troll's regeneration, or anything, but it should halve the amount of time it takes for you to recover from wounds. It's true power, however, comes into play if you ever take enough damage to die, upon which it'll shatter and heal you back up to full."

"Nice," I said, studying the blue gem.

"Nice? You have no idea how much that cost. You can only get one if you complete a level thirty quest that takes almost two weeks. Nice doesn't even begin to cover it."

"Really nice, then. Thank you. And this belt is awesome, too. Plus four dex?"

"Yeah, I thought you'd enjoy the Belt of Shadow Form. But that's just its secondary power. Its true worth lies in its ability to turn you into a living shadow. The effect only lasts for about ten seconds, but you're basically immaterial and impossible to hurt during that time. I mean, there are ways to get around it if your opponent is powerful enough, but it's still pretty broken. All you need do is charge it with mana, and when you need it simply evoke its effect with your thoughts."

"Damn." I shrugged. "I mean, I'm running out of words here. Thanks. Again."

"No problem. Hopefully all this will help you to forgive me in the long run."

"If there is a long run. Even with this crazy gear, we're still in trouble. Have you ever heard of the Beggars of Solomon?"

Brianna made a face. "Yeah. They were one of the up-and-coming cohorts behind my own team. Versatile, powerful, and led by an indiscriminate asshole who calls himself Vanatos."

"That sounds about right," I said. "They've accepted a job offer from an NPC Dread Lord, and showed up yesterday to both claim the castle and explore the dungeons beneath it."

"Like I said, indiscriminate. They'll take on any job, no matter how depraved. What are they looking for?"

So I told her. Everything Guthorios had told us, about Jeramy, about the weirdness in having Albertus take such a direct hand in these events. When I was done I sat back, coffee in hand.

"Huh." She ran a finger around the rim of her mimosa flute. "I've never heard of a quest like it. Sounds like this Jeramy messed enough with the Euphoria system that he attracted Albertus' spam hammer."

"I think it's more than that," I said. "I mean, from what Guthorios told us, Albertus took Jeramy out. Who was able to cast a ward that could keep the AI himself out of his own dungeons?"

Brianna waved a hand. "You're assuming Guthorios told you the truth here. That all sounds really far-fetched. My guess is that Albertus put together this quest to see how we'd react to a slightly weirder setup. Something that sounds like it's getting out of control but really isn't, you know? A test."

"Yeah, maybe." I sipped my coffee. It was so weird to be having this discussion over the remnants of brunch. "But a lot of stuff doesn't add up."

"I'm sure it will in time. Look, when you step back, it's all just a really elaborate story to get you to explore a new and spooky dungeon beneath a castle. I've done that a hundred times, and it's actually pretty refreshing to get a new take on the most common quest in the world. Archmagi, Dread Lords, Albertus Magnus himself – pretty cool setup. What we should really be talking about is how to take out the Beggars."

"Say you're right. How *do* we take them out? They're all in the upper twenties. I'm level eleven. You're, what, level one?"

"Two," she said with a smirk. "Those grimwolvens outside gave me a nice XP bump before breakfast. I'd forgotten how quickly you level up at the start."

"My point still stands. We're going to have to be extra careful and lucky to take down the Beggars."

"True." She tapped her lips. "And Vanatos is no fool."

"What is he?" It was something that had been bothering me ever since the fight. "He never actually did anything."

"Summoner," said Brianna. "And his daemon is pretty damn powerful. You know about summoners? Daemons?"

"No," I said, trying for patience. "You were supposed to give me all those tutorials, remember?"

"Yes, yes, water under the bridge. A summoner doesn't actually fight or wield power directly, but rather summons a daemon to do his fighting for him. The more powerful and talented the summoner, the more lethal his daemon. Vanatos' daemon looks like a really freaky angel. I saw it once in a city-wide quest. It flies, heals wounds ridiculously fast, and throws these weird sunbolts by aligning lenses that are stitched into the ends of all these white scarves it wears. I was actually pretty impressed at the time. It'll line up the lenses, refracting sunlight or torchlight or whatever, and then blast a ray of concentrated energy that can cut through stone. Pretty vicious."

"Great," I said. "Sounds lovely. But it needs light to work?"

"Moonlight, candlelight, yeah, any kind of illumination. The stronger the light, the deadlier its blasts."

"Well, that makes me extra happy to be a darkblade," I said, feeling a little more cheerful. "Nothing a Night Shroud can't take care of."

"Don't be too cocky," she said. "It's pretty smart. Next is Balthus, his second-in-command. Big guy, ornamental mask? He's rocking a classic inquisitor build, specializing in buffs and debuffs. He can drop ongoing effects on both his friends and enemies, with stuff like healing, armor, or even freezing an enemy in place. Inquisitors are usually overlooked in combat, as they're not often dealing out the hurt, but they can easily tip the tide of battle in their team's favor if not taken out early. Ignore them too long and you'll find yourself cursed and slowed down, your armor stripped away while your enemies have been buffed up like crazy."

"Yeah, he was doing just that in our fight," I said. "Though it wasn't much of a fight. We got our asses handed to us. What about Delphina?"

"I love Delphina," said Brianna with a smile. "She's my kind of crazy." Which didn't make me feel any better about having brunch with Brianna. "She plays a witch, and used to be part of the Swamp Queens until they were destroyed in the Immolation.

Witches specialize in twisting shit up. Hallucinations, your ability to stay awake, understand language, filling you with terror. Like Balthus, she's not a front-line fighter, but she can take people out pretty effectively by neutralizing them from the sidelines."

"We were able to hold her off," I said, not sure if I should feel proud of that accomplishment. "Falkon, Michaela and me. We had her running till the others stepped in."

Brianna shrugged. "Like I said, she's not built for the front lines. In a real fight she'd fade into the background and mess you up from a distance."

"Thanks," I said.

"What? Now, if you'd told me you'd gone toe-to-toe with Lagash I'd be impressed. She's probably the most powerful one of the group. And she doesn't fit in with their style, either, which is weird. I think Vanatos has something on her and is forcing her to serve him. Either way, she's a straight fighter. She's famous for taking down the Quartz Man solo, and people say she held the Dismal Gate while everyone else fled, but I don't believe that. She's good, but she's not that good."

"So, what, we just avoid her in a fight?"

"Yeah, if you can. She's built like an ox and as strong as… I don't know, an elephant? Her player's really taken the orc warrior thing to heart and gone all out with her physical stats. I've heard some guys find her weirdly hot, but I don't get it at all. I think she looks more like an animal than anything else."

I realized Brianna was watching me carefully. Waiting to see if I agreed? I moved on. "Last one's the guy with the fire hands."

"Yeah, Makarios. He's a real bastard. He's done some really nasty shit to other PCs, got a reputation for torture and abuse. I've heard he likes to capture new players and break them. If he wasn't protected by being a member of the Beggars I'm sure he'd have been taken out by now. But he's a battlemage specializing in fire and lava. His claws can tear through metal, and he's apparently got some pretty frightening area of effect spells."

"I saw one. He filled the air with stationary bolts of fire. Like a web."

Brianna nodded. "Sounds right. So the way they fight is Makarios, Lagash, and Vanatos' daemon wade into the front lines while Balthus and Delphina provide support from the rear. They've got a bigger rep than they should for their level, and I think it's cause of Vanatos' leadership. They hit well above their paygrade. My team could have taken them down, but it would have been a nasty fight."

"All right. So they're in the castle. How do we defeat them?"

"Well… hear me out here." She toyed with her flute, waggling it slowly back and forth between her fingers. "Why exactly do we have to fight the Beggars? We're both in Death March mode. And while we're now equipped with some respectable gear, we're nowhere close to being able to take on the Beggars. No, wait. What I'm saying is, why not strike out by ourselves? A month's adventures will see us arriving at New Haven on the Amargo River. We can catch a boat from there and sail all the way down to the sea."

"Because," I said, speaking slowly and clearly, "I won't abandon my friends."

"Friends? I don't mean to be rude, but how long have you known these people? A week? Are you telling me you'll risk literal death for them?"

"They're good people," I said. "I won't abandon them."

"Are they in Death March mode?"

I wanted to lie. "No."

"So worst-case scenario, they respawn in the highland meadow and strike off on their own, or quit their avatars and start fresh somewhere else. Hardly an end-of-days scenario." Her gentle disapproval was a palpable force. "So remind me again why you're willing to risk everything on a suicide mission to help people you don't really know and who don't really need your help?"

I set my coffee down and stared at my hands. Brianna had always been exceedingly talented at warping my every argument and stance into something faintly ridiculous. It was like her superpower. But she didn't know about Lotharia. "Because they trusted me. They fought for me. They're my friends. And while they're not putting as much in play as I am, I don't want to be the kind of person who walks away from my friends when they need me."

"Chris." Brianna's tone was frank, her gaze direct. "Euphoria is just a game."

Again, I struggled to refute her position. She was right. Euphoria *was* just a game. But I in turn was the sum of my actions. And Euphoria felt real enough that I couldn't allow myself to act like a sociopath. Emotionally, I was on the hook. I gave Brianna a wry smile. "What can I say? Albertus Magnus has done a good job. I'm taking this stuff seriously. I'm taking responsibility for my actions. My friend Falkon postulated that Albertus was watching the players to learn about humanity, and was paying extra special attention to Death Marchers. So if you can't accept my own morality as reason to stay, then think of this: how we act in Euphoria will influence the world's greatest power in how it understands and treats humanity. And I won't give up on my responsibility to myself and everyone else by acting like a selfish ass."

Brianna shook her head slowly in pitying astonishment, then tossed back the rest of her mimosa and dropped the glass in the basket. "You always were such an idealistic fool, Chris. I have to admit, it's part of your charm. That naive intensity. But I know you well enough to know you won't be convinced to do otherwise, so that's that. I won't abandon you, and you won't abandon these 'friends' of yours. So we'd best get to planning."

"Yes," I said, swallowing my annoyance. Her radiant smile made it all the easier. "Let's."

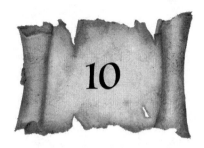

10

THE HARDEST PART was waiting till dusk. No way was I going to tangle with the Beggars of Solomon in the light of day. Nor did I particularly want to spend time hanging out with Brianna in the longhouse, no matter how good the treats from the Everypack were or how luscious her lips. Instead, I spent my time working on my meditation techniques, exploring the various abilities of my gear, and cautiously exploring the environs around the castle. I'd not spent much time outside its walls, so I carefully made my way around it, discovering numerous cave systems, a small and incredibly beautiful hidden waterfall and various lairs I chose to back away from.

The sun was dipping toward the horizon when I ran into the Green Liver goblins. The three of them were hunched miserably on a rocky ledge that overlooked the castle. I spotted them through the scree that separated them from the narrow defile I was descending, and called out so as not to surprise them.

"Hey! Kreekit!" The three goblins leapt to their feet as I backed through the underbrush and out onto the ledge beside them. "There you guys are. You all right?"

Kreekit wrinkled her face into an expression of righteous disgust. "No. No, no, no. Lookit! Shaman Lickit knows no shame!"

A trickle of goblins were passing through the barbican and into the main gate. I wasn't high enough to peer into the bailey floor, but it was clear from the line that extended into the woods close by that the whole tribe was on the move. "Lickit made a deal with the Beggars?"

Dribbler sat with his legs over the edge and threw a pebble into the void. "Lickit make deal with anybody. He make deal as quick as he could."

Kreekit nodded. "Traitor! We all run, but he force us Green Liver to go in different direction. Not hide with him. Now I see why. He want take our place. Claim all meat. Get fatter."

"Huh. I guess I'm not surprised. It's not like the Beggars would really care." I crouched beside Dribbler and rubbed at my chin, peering into the castle. "Though, if they're allied against us, it'll make taking back the castle all the more difficult."

Dribbler looked up at me, eyes wide. "You going to take back castle? How?"

"I'm not sure yet. But Falkon and Michaela are counting on me. I'm not going to leave them out to dry."

Barfo frowned. "You want keep them wet?"

"No," said Kreekit, thwapping him on the arm. "He means he take them home to dry. He good friend. Take friends out of spider tower and bring them home."

Dribbler scratched his cheek. "How he know they wet?"

"Yeah," said Barfo, turning to me. "Why you think they wet?"

"Uh, just a guess. Not really important. But you said they're in the spider tower?"

"Yes," said Kreekit solemnly. "I conduct very sacred, very important ritual earlier. Send spirit down to castle to take look-see. Very impressive ritual. Dangerous. But Kreekit also getting fatter." She patted her little paunch. "Kreekit more dangerous!"

"You can do that? Send your spirit places?"

She nodded. "I go down to see what Lickit up to. He eating all our meat, and bring in two boar trolls to help guard."

"Boar trolls are scary," Barfo told me.

"Hairy, too," said Dribbler. "Hey! Hairy rhyme with scary!"

Kreekit thwapped Dribbler. "As I say. Lickit bring two scary hairy boar trolls to guard. At first, me think he guard meat! But no. He put both trolls outside spider tower. Why? That what I ask myself. So spirit Kreekit poke face through door and see Falkon and dead girl tied up in tower."

"Thank you," I said. "That's really great information. And the Beggars? Were they around?"

"No Beggars," said Kreekit. "Me think they go into keep."

"So Lickit's on guard duty, and he brought in two boar trolls. How's a goblin like him control boar trolls?"

Kreekit shrugged. "Lickit good shaman. Fatty-fat. And now he have lots of meat to give them. He use spirit magic and ogre beef to make boar trolls do what he say."

"Hairy scary boar trolls hard to kill," said Dribbler. "They no stay dead."

Barfo half closed his eyes. "My big dream to cook boar troll steak. Because it heal as fast as you eat it. Endless feast of rich red meat! So tasty and chewy, best goblin treat!"

"Oooh," said Dribbler. "That be yum."

"Mm-hmm," agreed Kreekit, and they all subsided into a meditative state.

"Well, I'm going to try and get my friends out tonight," I said. "Then we'll come up with a plan to capture the castle. If you guys want, head up to Barry's cave. I'll come back there with my friends and we can all plan."

"Barry's cave?" asked Dribbler. "What that?"

"Oh. Right. It's a goblin cave I found high in the mountains. About over that way. Can you follow my tracks back to it?"

"I don't know Barry," said Barfo, looking in confusion at Dribbler and Kreekit.

"Me neither," said Dribbler.

"Of course I know Barry," said Kreekit. "Me know all goblins."

I raised an eyebrow. "You know Barry?"

"Yes." She crossed her arms defiantly. "We best friends."

"Oh," I said, and decided not to push it. "Well, I'll meet you guys at his cave when we get back, then."

"Yes," said Kreekit. "That sound like good plan as long as you no die."

"Here," said Barfo, unslinging a small jar. "Take Barfo's special soup."

"Thanks," I said, pulling the cord over my head so that the jar was slung against my side. "Your soup's the best. Wish me luck."

"Luck!" they all cried out in unison.

I slipped back through the underbrush and made my way down to a cross-wise ridge that led me to the plateau on which the castle was erected. I moved furtively, keeping an eye on the battlements for lookouts, but other than the irregular goblin shadow marching along it I saw no cause for alarm.

They had to be expecting my return. The question was: did they care? Were they complacent in their own superior strength? Did they even care enough about Falkon and Michaela to put up an efficient guard? Or had they thrown the duty to the Big Burpies and called it a day?

I hunkered down and waited. The sun sank ever closer to the horizon, and just before it set altogether Brianna arrived, moving with impressive skill through the underbrush, rapier drawn and held down by her side.

I could tell she was in a foul mood. Her mouth was a thin line and her gaze was more glare as she stood before me. "When you told me to meet you here at sunset I didn't think that meant you'd avoid me all day."

"I've been scouting," I said, trying not to sound defensive. "Gathering information. I've learned which tower my friends are being held in and more about the forces I'll be facing in there."

"You'll be facing?" Her eyes narrowed. "We'll be facing, you mean."

"Brianna, you're still just level two. Trust me, I remember all too well how vulnerable that makes you. I can't risk taking you into the castle."

"My equipment—"

"Brianna. This is what my character class is designed for. I'll be in and out of there before anybody knows what's happened. Shared Darkness will allow me to bring Falkon and Michaela out of the castle, but how does it make sense for me to transport you inside just to bring you right back out? All the while risking you being attacked by some level thirty fighter?"

"I'm not an idiot newb," she said, voice acidic enough to etch metal. "I came here to help—"

"And you have. More than you could know. You have my sincere thanks. Now please. Wait here for us. All right?"

"Fine," she said. "But if you die, it'll be on your head for refusing my help."

"Yes," I said, not even knowing how to make sense of that. "Fine. But I won't. I'll see you soon." And before she could respond, I crept along the last of the ridge along the cliff face that dropped to the rear of the castle. When I was finally forced to stop, the ridge smoothing into the cliff face, I was still some thirty yards away from the castle itself and perched high above the ravine.

Any regular attacking force would have been stymied, perhaps able to fire arrows at the parapets but otherwise left in the open and susceptible to counter-fire. I sank back into the shadows, activated Darkvision, and Double Stepped.

The glory of the writhing darkness as it claimed me was oh so sweet. I fell into its embrace and emerged below the curtain wall. A quick glance showed my former perch high above and on the far side of the ravine. I grinned, exultant, and hurried along the base of the wall, pulling the hood of my stone cloak over my head as I went.

There were three towers along the wall: Jeramy's on the far side, the goblin tower close to the main gate, and the spider tower not far from where I ran. I restrained myself from casting anxious glances up at the battlements for fear a flash of my pale face would be noticed; instead, I focused on the dirt before me, bent double as I ran, till at last I was just outside the wall where the spider tower rose up.

I sank into a crouch and paused. Let my pounding heart grow still. I had thirty-five mana points, more than I'd ever dreamed of. My friends were supposedly just on the far side of this wall.

All I had to do was Shadow Step through, grab one, use Shared Darkness and pull them outside. Rinse, repeat, and then we would all flee for the mountains before anybody was any the wiser.

I restrained the urge to do so and instead drew my Void Blade. I couldn't afford to make any mistakes. What if there was a Beggar in there with them? First, I'd gather intel. I completed my Double Step to the wall top, right into the familiar corner by the tower door. The shadows boiled, then I was high above, crouched in the recess where the parapet met the tower. There was nobody close by, for which I gave thanks – I really didn't want to kill any of the goblins. I listened intently, half closing my eyes. The raucous voices of a the Big Burpies arose from down below in the bailey. An occasional deep snort. Nothing else.

Moving slowly, using as much stealth as I could summon, I drifted to the edge of the wall, passing before the closed tower door, and peered down into the bailey. Three large bonfires had been built, and around these the goblins danced, while Shaman Lickit sat on an impromptu throne over which the flensed wyvern skull had been hung by an excessively complex web of leather straps. Directly below me I could make out two massive hirsute forms, hunched over and lanky. The boar trolls. I scanned the castle for any sign of the Beggars.

Nothing.

I forced myself to watch for a couple more minutes. The Beggars would have chosen the goblin tower as their base of operations, given the inaccessibility of Jeramy's tower and their placing their prisoners in this one. So I studied it carefully, and for a moment deliberated sneaking over to peer into the uppermost chamber.

No. No sense in tempting fate.

I withdrew slowly, careful to make no abrupt movements, and crept up to the spider tower door. It felt like ages since Falkon, Lotharia and I had paused here before mounting our assault against the spider dude within. I could still hear Lotharia's words as she described the large rune Jeramy had supposedly carved on the tower wall, imbuing the stones with the strength of iron.

The urge to sit down and cradle my head arose within me, but I brushed it aside and gritted my teeth. First I'd save Falkon and Michaela. Then we'd drive the Beggars out and depose Shaman Lickit. *Then* we'd enter the keep and rescue Lotharia. It was a daunting task list, but it all began with the next step.

I opened the door a fraction and peered into the darkness below. The tower was still hollowed out, turning it into a tall empty throat, with the webbing that had once choked it pulled away to reveal the bare walls. Far down below I could make out Falkon and Michaela, tightly bound by thick coils of rope, both of them sitting awkwardly against the tower walls and conversing in low tones.

Hesitant, I cast Detect Magic on the tower's interior, and immediately the ropes that bound my friends glowed, along with a series of runes chalked in a band along the inside of the walls. That checked me. I'd not noticed them with my Darkvision. I tried to study their glow, divine something as to their purpose, but I knew next to nothing about magic.

What to do? A trap? Most likely.

"Falkon!" My hiss caused both of them to snap their heads up to stare at me. "Hey! This a trap?"

"Chris! Yes!" Falkon immediately ducked his head and glanced at the door. When he spoke again, it was in a much quieter whisper. "We don't know what it does, though."

Michaela shifted her weight, turning a little to be able to get a better look at me. "It's some kind of summoning spell, but that's all I've been able to figure out."

I bit my lower lip. What to do, what to do? This setup wasn't going to change. There was no advantage to waiting for another day. Could I outrace a summoning spell?

"I'm going to Shadow Step down and grab Michaela," I whispered. "I'll bring her out, then come back for you, Falkon. All right?"

They exchanged a glance. Clearly it wasn't 'all right', but it was better than being held in captivity.

"Chris, try this instead," whispered Michaela. "Appear next to the wall and immediately try to rub one of the runes out. If you tamper with the spell it might not work."

"What's it written with?"

"Chalk, I think."

Chalk. I could brush it with my arm, but that might take precious seconds. Better would be a bucket of water to throw against the wall. Even better would be a bucket of water to pour down the wall and wash the runes away without even activating them. "Hold on!"

I ducked back out of the door and crept to the edge of the wall, peering down to take in the bailey once more. A bucket of water. Where amongst all that madness…? There. Nope, that was a bucket of what looked like wine, and it was right out in the open by the fire. Goblins were dunking their heads in it and scooping out bowls. Where else?

Despite my Astute Observer, I couldn't make out anything immediately handy. No perfectly placed rain barrel or the like just standing off in the corner by itself. My frustration mounted. The longer I waited, the higher my chances of being discovered.

Then inspiration struck me. I crept across the length of the wall to the goblin tower, paused to take stock and then continued on to Jeramy's tower. Nobody had noticed me. The huge rocks the wyvern had dislodged and blocked the tower entrance with lay in small chunks everywhere, turned to sandstone by Lotharia's Imbue spell and then pulverized by the pommel of my sword. We'd rolled the barrels of pitch out of this top chamber, leaving it mostly empty, and into this room I snuck.

There was no obvious means down into the body of the arch-magus' tower, but on a hunch I stopped before where the hidden steps had disgorged Lotharia and me the last time we'd visited, and whispered the passcode: "A whale of a time."

The ground shimmered, undulating like Texas blacktop in the height of summer, and then the steps to the room below appeared.

My elation was only tempered by the knowledge of what I was about to face. I hurried down, then averted my gaze from the beautiful youth who was rising from an ornate chaise longue in the center of the summoning circle.

"Ah, I see—"

"Nope, not gonna chat, just passing through, no demon talky, no demon talky," I said loudly and raced on down the steps to the room below.

This was Jeramy's bedchamber, complete with a full-sized portrait of him shirtless flexing inside a volcano. I slowed. Last time I'd been here he'd been flexing before a waterfall, his foot atop a grizzly's head… huh. I hurried down to the ground floor, which was a combination library/study/lounge. My abrupt arrival caused the ambulatory flock of neon pink flamingoes to run away from me in agitation before collecting themselves on the far side of the room and turning scathing glares in my direction. The stunningly complex orrery revolved overhead, floating without support, and everywhere bookcases with their glass fronts gleamed in the light of a few carefully placed candles.

"Worthington?" I searched for Jeramy's robotic manservant. "You here?"

"How may I be of assistance, Master Meadows?" said Worthington as he stepped into visibility. Bronze-skinned and with the sleek, retro-futuristic lines of an art deco design, he was a mixture of C-3PO and the robot from *Metropolis*.

"Hi." I took a moment to compose myself. "A large bucket of hot water, if you please. And if you could mix a strong detergent into it, I'd be much obliged."

"I must warn you that consuming such a beverage will have deleterious effects on your health."

"Yes, I know. But these are grim times, Worthington." I realized I was feeling a little manic. "Bucket, please?"

"It is there, upon the bar," he said, pointing to one side where the wet bar now sported a large champagne bucket, a mound of bubbles just visible over its gilt brim.

"Not to be greedy, but could I perhaps have two?"

A second bucket appeared beside the first.

"You're the best." I hesitated. "Worthington, since last we spoke I've heard that it was the god of undeath himself who struck down your master. Does that sound right?"

"Master Jeramy is currently meditating on the fourth floor," said Worthington.

"Right, right. The hidden dimensional room. That's a long meditation."

"Mater Jeramy is a man of exceptional talents."

"Yeah. Do you know anything about the ward he placed upon the castle grounds?"

"A powerful spell. He cast it under great duress, and its passing left me nauseous for weeks."

"I'll bet. You sure you can't get a message to Master Jeramy for me?"

Worthington simply shook his head.

"All right. Well, thanks for the champagne buckets."

"Of course, sir. Will there be anything else?"

"No – actually, sure. Can I have a double shot of espresso?"

"But of course." He turned, and then turned back with an espresso cup and saucer in hand. "Master Jeramy preferred the arabica bean, with a little extra crema on top. Sugar?"

"No, thanks." I took up the cup, relishing its warm, smooth sides, inhaled the heady scent of rich espresso, then knocked it back in one scalding gulp. "Ah! That's good. Thank you." I handed him the cup, then jogged over to the buckets and hefted them both. They weren't as heavy as I'd expected, but then I recalled that I was now rocking strength fourteen. I wasn't 1970s Arnold just yet, but I was a sight stronger than I was in real life.

"Take it easy, Worthington!" I hurried back up the steps, through the bedroom and up into the third chamber. A crowd of naked men within the summoning circle immediately began to shriek and claw at the invisible walls. Each of them was me, wounded and caked in filth, all of them with their manhoods torn off and teeth ripped from their bloody, gummy mouths. They howled and begged, and I stumbled, nearly spilling both champagne buckets. Just as quickly the crowd disappeared, replaced by the laughing golden-haired youth lying on his chaise once more.

"Sorry," he said. "Just fucking with you."

Wide-eyed, I chose not to respond. Staring fixedly at the top of the stairs, I ran back into the uppermost chamber, the illusion kicking in as I exited so that the steps were gone when I turned back around. Heart pounding, I put that nightmarish image firmly away and moved to the door. A couple of goblins were stumbling along the parapet toward me, arguing over a wineskin. I Double Stepped past them to the goblin tower, then completed my passage through the shadows by emerging beside the spider tower door.

I listened carefully once again before making a move, giving my Astute Observer skill a chance to pick up on any danger, then pulled the door open once more and peered at my friends below. "I'm back! Hold on. Going to try something."

Then, carefully – oh so carefully – I poured the contents of one of the buckets down the inside of the wall. A film of bubbles and water sluiced down the great stone blocks, followed immediately by the contents of the second bucket. I watched, holding my breath, as the soapy water raced and coursed down the three floors, separating into three main arms that grew thinner and thinner before washing over the runes directly below me.

"It work?" I whispered. "That rub them out?"

"I think so?" Michaela was leaning forward, squinting at the walls. "Chalk's all messed up."

"All right. We'll deal with your bindings once we're outside. Ready?"

They both nodded, and I took a deep breath. This was it. Just to be on the safe side, I activated Mute Presence, then Double Stepped into the base of the tower.

And it all went wrong.

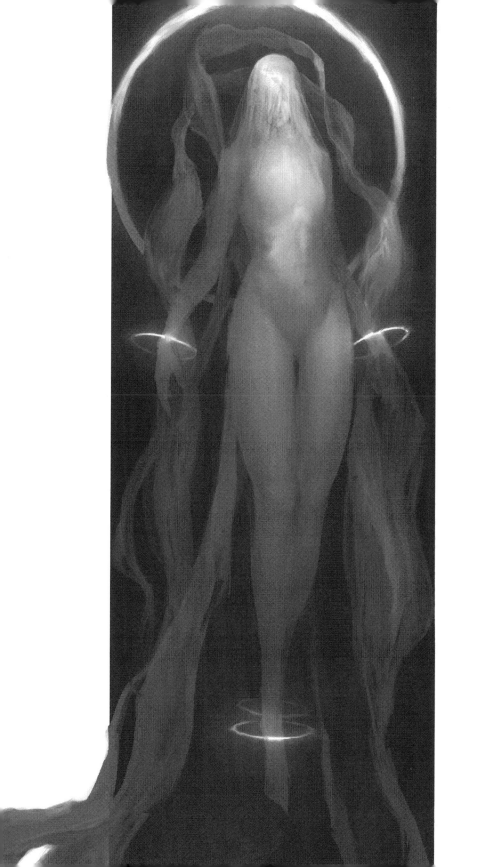

11

WHEN I APPEARED on the tower floor, the runes along the wall flared into blinding white as if each had been cut through the stone to reveal the surface of the sun just beyond.

"Go," shouted Falkon, struggling with his bonds. "Go now!"

I grabbed hold of Michaela and pulled her into the darkness with me, casting Shared Darkness just as a form began to coalesce in the air above our heads. The blinding light was muffled then erased by the shadows, and we emerged a second later on the grassy bank just outside the castle wall.

"It didn't work," gasped Michaela. "I recognized it. A binding spell. We foiled it."

"Then what was that? The thing appearing in the air?"

"I don't know." She shook her head, eyes wide. "Another spell? I don't know."

"I'm going back for Falkon. Hang tight."

"Chris—"

I Double Stepped back into the shadows and emerged a moment later within the tower. The brilliant light had faded away, but with Darkvision I could easily make out the floating entity that had appeared in my wake.

Tall, elegant, ethereal, otherworldly – its skin was pure white and its body was wreathed in broad bands of white cloth that emanated from between its shoulder blades, each one terminating in a hollow disc of the purest gold. More discs floated about its ankles and wrists, while a massive corona of gold – like gilt spiderweb – hovered behind its head, which was an abstract deconstruction of a skull, seamed with gold and without eyes. It was at once angelic and terrifying, a symbol of purity and power, and it oriented on me the moment I stepped out of the shadows.

"Chris, run!" Falkon's scream tore through the air as two of the white scarves slipped into place, golden discs overlapping, their interiors immediately lighting up with a terrible light that shot at me with the sound of a massive choir in rapturous song.

I instinctively completed my Double Step, throwing myself back into the shadows just as the golden beam sliced through where I'd been. Not having picked a destination, I was spat back out above the angel, emerging on the ledge where eons ago Falkon had been trapped by the spider dude's web attack.

"Blammo!" I yelled, pointing my bull ring at the angel, and a torrent of force poured forth from my fist, the air undulating as a hurricane roar filled the tower's interior. The angel whirled around, all of its scarves curling before it to form a shield, its arms crossed in an 'X' before its head. The force of my attack drove it back almost to the wall, but even as it was being blasted it looped three rings over each other and I heard a heavenly host cry out in song.

I dove off the ledge, activating Expert Leaper as I did so, the world incandescing above me as the angel's laser nearly took off my head. My dive turned into a tumble, and mid-fall I summoned my Ebon Tendrils, causing them to writhe up out of the ground around the angel and ensnare it by the legs.

I landed in a crouch, one palm flat on the ground, then charged, drawing the Void Blade and holding it out to the side. The angel surged up against my Tendrils and shattered them both, rising high overhead with gobbets of shadow falling from its ankles and shins.

I jumped, Expert Leaper still in effect, and activated Bleeding Attack as I careened up to collide with the angel. Its broad scarves whipped into place, forming a shield and overlapping the rings just as I brought my Void Blade swinging through them. I willed for the sword to shift it turned into the stuff of shadow, passing through the scarves and into the angel's body.

Two of its golden rings overlapped at the same time, and golden light burst forth – but I'd already Double Stepped away, disappearing just in time to step out high within the tower. Stolen strength surged into me as I crouched on the lip of stone that protruded from the doorway I'd peered down from but minutes ago. The angel reeled, scarves parting to reveal a deep gash from its hip to its shoulder.

The gash closed over and it looked up at me with unerring confidence.

Shit.

Then the angel simply disappeared.

I blinked, straightened, and completed my Double Step down to Falkon's side. "C'mon," I said, reaching for his shoulder. "Time to—"

"Behind you!"

I dove straight at the tower wall, Double Stepping away and appearing on the ledge halfway up the tower. The angel had returned, and this time it had brought someone with it. A leather coat that was black at the hood and gradated to crimson at the hem, both clawed hands glowing with searing, volcanic heat.

Makarios the battlemage.

I flicked on my character sheet then dismissed it. Twenty out of thirty-six mana left. I was still in this fight. I activated Uncanny Aim and Pin Down as I hurled a dagger at Makarios, then completed my Double Step to the ground below.

I emerged from the shadows just as a golden laser flashed up at where I'd been. Makarios' arm was swinging still, having just batted my dagger away. I ran forward, summoning Night Shroud as I went.

The entirety of the tower's base suddenly filled with darkness, causing Makarios' massive claws to dim and the angel to immediately fly straight up and out into the normal gloom.

I grinned, activating Adrenaline Surge to put as much kick behind my attack as I could muster, but just before I could close with Makarios he stomped on the stone floor as if seeking to shatter it.

A shockwave of power exploded out from his foot, picking me up off the ground and hurling me back. I tried to Double Step but couldn't gather my wits before colliding with the wall. I bounced off stone, the wind driven completely out of me, and fell to all fours, heaving for air.

The stomp had also shredded my Night Shroud such that wisps of it were shrinking into tattered rags. Makarios gave a sharp bark of laughter and began marching in my direction, his huge claws dripping gobbets of lava.

A premonition hit me and I looked up just in time to see the angel overlap three of its golden rings. A blinding flash of light filled the air and only my Adrenaline Surged system allowed me to throw myself aside in a roll. 'Throw' might be too grand a word. More like topple. The golden beam caught me in the shoulder, spinning me around as it delivered a scalding burn to my flesh. I caught a brief flare of blue over the invisible forcefield my armor ring provided me as I fell; enough to tell that it had saved me from having my arm surgically sliced away.

There was no time to catch my breath. Strength and stolen power still flooding through my system, I came up to my feet just as Makarios charged me, swiping with both massive claws at my torso. I reflexively parried with the Void Blade, but in my panic willed it into shadow form; it passed straight through Makarios' hand, causing him to shriek in pain even as he slammed his other blades into my ribs.

Pain. I spun away and collapsed again. I hated to think what might have happened without my armor ring. Without my spider silk shirt. Without my stone cloak. Even so, every breath that I now managed to hitch caused stabbing pain in my side; it felt like two or three ribs had broken, and I could feel hot blood running down to pool along the hem of my pants.

"Get out!" I barely registered Falkon's scream. My eyes were locked on Makarios, who was staring at his hand, claws flopping as he shook it in fury.

"What did you do?" He glared at his fist, but it refused his commands. "What did you do?!"

I climbed to my feet once more. Above me, the angel was deliberately overlapping three, four, five rings. Makarios stared at me, eyes wide with a lunatic fury. He pointed the palm of his functional hand at me, which immediately began to burn with actual flames, giving off a wicked plume of sooty smoke even as his claw tips burned white.

Uh-oh.

I grabbed my cloak and hauled it before me, croaking "Petrify," just before Makarios unleashed a livid bolt of screaming flame and the angel blasted me from above with six rings to the sound of a cathedral filled with fervent choristers.

The cloak crackled and hardened and then I was lifted off the ground and thrown back as if I'd been hit by a freight train. I hit the tower door and blasted through it, shattering the timbers and flying out into the bailey in a coruscating explosion of crimson and gold. I tumbled, bounced, rolled, and fetched up against the back of Lickit's throne. My cloak was a shattered quilt of rock, fragments of which were glowing like coals plucked from the fire.

I tried to stand and failed. I coughed, and blood spattered across the floor. Something was terribly wrong with my hips. Three versions of Makarios stepped out through the broken doorway, and a moment later three angels floated out after him.

Warmth spread through my body from the periapt of health around my neck, and my wounds began to itch as they healed. Amazing as it was, the rapid healing was too slow.

"What you doing here?" Shaman Lickit had climbed onto his throne and was peering down at me over its top.

I ignored him and patted my side. Please don't let it be broken. There. Barfo's super soup. I fell down to my shoulder so as to liberate both hands and unscrewed the lid.

"You messed up big time, boy." I couldn't see Makarios' eyes. They were hidden under his cowl, but his grin was wide enough to appear serpentine. "I'm going to enjoy paying you back for this. Oh, yes. You're going to be begging for death by the time I'm done."

"I believe you," I gasped, then chugged the soup, wolfing it down in desperate gulps. I don't think I've ever pounded a beer faster. There was no time for quips. The angel floated up and overhead. Makarios had nearly reached me when I finished the soup and tossed it aside.

"For level ten, you got some bite," said the battlemage, "but ya gotta be out of juice. That's what you get for—"

I dropped another Night Shroud and immediately followed it up with Ebon Tendrils, directing them to snarl around Makarios' legs, gripping them tight. I dove forward, feeling the soup already taking effect, smoothing away the pain, allowing my continuing Adrenaline Surge to help me through the worst of it.

Makarios wasn't done. He raised his fist and a web of flaming filaments filled the Shroud. Wherever the brands burned, the shadow shrank away. I staggered to a halt before I could cut myself in half, and then a bolt of golden light surged down through the Shroud, slamming into me and causing the world to turn white.

I must have passed out briefly, because the next thing I knew I was lying on the ground. The armor ring had seared the skin around my finger, and the periapt was frantically pulsing waves of heat into my body. I could feel the last of Barfo's soup invigorating me from within, and the hood of my stone cloak was in tatters around my badly burned face.

Makarios tore his burning claws through the last of the Tendrils and stepped free with obvious annoyance, turning to kick at the shadowy stumps before they disappeared. High above, the angel placed its two largest rings above each other, resulting in a broad beam of light that covered our immediate area like a cone, banishing all darkness.

It was hard to think. I tried to Shadow Step, but the angel's light prevented me from doing so. A column of shadow fell over me as Makarios stepped next to my head.

"I was going to save you for Delphina, but you're too fucking annoying. End of the road, kid."

He extended his palm, which began to glow white hot. He was going to do that fire bolt thing again. Just then, Adrenaline Surge gave out on me, and the pain I was feeling doubled and then redoubled again as nausea caused me to turn onto my side and spew what was left of Barfo's soup onto the battlemage's boots.

"You serious?" Makarios danced back in disgust. "You don't stop! These are my favorite fuckin' boots!" He pointed his palm at me again and unleashed his bolt of flame.

At the last second, I thought of my belt. Just before Makarios' flame incinerated me, I activated the belt's shadow power, and his flame passed right through me to splatter against the bailey floor.

Cool relief flooded my system as the agony of my body and Adrenaline Surge faded away, leaving me sharp and focused. Brianna had warned me I had ten or so seconds. There was no time to waste.

On instinct, I tried to Shadow Step. Despite the angel's light, despite the fading glow of Makarios' fire blast, I slipped away as easily as if I'd been hidden in the darkest recess of the blackest shadow.

I appeared thirty yards above the bailey floor, right behind the angel. I summoned Night Shroud, then summoned it again. The angel's reactions were superb; it immediately dropped its arms to its sides as it sought to fly straight up once more, but I caught it with Ebon Tendrils, summoning them from within the layered Shroud. Twice. Four tentacles emerged from the darkness to wrap around the angel, clasping it tight.

With great reluctance, I dropped my shadow form, and was immediately hit with an overpowering wave of pain. I was already swinging my arms, however, the Void Blade grasped in both hands, and brought its edge straight through the angel's neck.

It spasmed, shaking violently within its constraints, and then simply disappeared. I fell, nearly delirious with pain, and managed to Double Step away just before punching out the bottom of the Night Shroud.

I appeared within the spider tower and collapsed beside Falkon. He started to speak, to protest, but I reached out, still shuddering with nausea, and grabbed his boot. I cast Shared Darkness and we both appeared a moment later outside the walls.

Michaela startled at our appearance. My XP chime sounded. She'd risen to her knees and sweat dripped from her brow. She'd clearly been trying to do something, escape from her bonds, perhaps, but to no avail.

"Chris, what the fuck?" Falkon sounded stunned. "How—?"

"No time," I growled. It took all my remaining strength to push myself up to my hands and knees, then slide the tip of the Void Blade under the ropes that bound his hands. With a grunt, I shoved it down and it sliced through the bonds as if they were putty.

"Those are anti-magic ropes," said Michaela. "You can't—"

I cut hers, too. "Falkon. Help me to the ravine's edge."

"How are you still breathing?" He slid an army gingerly under my own and levered me to my feet. He was watching the skies, however. "This is—I mean, Vanatos' daemon—"

"Don't worry about it," I rasped. "Edge."

Michaela got under my other arm and together we hurried to where I'd Shadow Stepped in all of – what, fifteen minutes ago? Once we reached it, I sighted up at the far ledge. "Michaela first."

I didn't give them time to respond. I burned three more mana on Shared Darkness and we both appeared high above, balanced precariously on the tapering end of the ridge.

"Head that way," I rasped. "Be right back."

I Double Stepped back down to Falkon, drew his blade so I could avail myself of its mana, then folded my Double Step into a Shared Darkness. Together we appeared high on the ridge. I summoned my character sheet.

In less than three minutes or whatever I'd burned through thirty or more points.

"I don't see the daemon," said Michaela. "What happened in there? I heard a bunch of screams and explosions—"

"Daemon's gone," I said. And then, miraculously, like the cool waters of benediction flowing over me, the side effects of Adrenaline Surge faded away. I grunted as I managed to stand a little straighter, but a blanket of pain still enveloped me. The periapt was pouring its healing into me, but even so the burns across my scalp and shoulders was blisteringly insane. "We've got to go. Brianna's waiting for us. Up ahead."

"Gone?" Falkon blinked and then slipped under my arm again to help me along the ridge. "What the hell do you mean, 'gone'? It's a nearly level thirty greater daemon. Did it just lose interest or something?"

"Yeah," I said. "Something like that. I cut its throat." Despite the pain, I couldn't resist a wolfish grin. "It seemed to lose interest after that."

"You… holy crap." Falkon glanced down at what I was holding. "Is that a fucking Void Blade?!"

I sheathed it somewhat self-consciously.

"We'll talk when we're safe," said Michaela, voice authoritative. "For now, let's get the hell out of here. And who's Brianna?"

"Trouble," said Falkon. "You'll find out soon enough."

We hurried along the ridge until it finally leveled out and opened up to a broad ledge. Brianna had been pacing, and at the sight of us ran forward, concern writ large on her features.

"Whoa," said Falkon, throwing up an arm as if to block a blow. "Go easy on the charisma there. Holy crap, I'm not even interested in girls and you've got me curious."

"Falkon," said Brianna, in a tone I recognized as her trying to be civil, even engaging. "Michaela. I'm thrilled that Chris brought you out of the castle alive." She gave me a sidelong look that made me feel unexpectedly pleased. "Not that I had any doubt."

Michaela was studying Brianna with something akin to cold curiosity. "You're the source of these high-level items? You don't seem too powerful yourself."

Brianna made a little moue of distaste. "My other avatar is level thirty-six. I simply dropped a bunch of gear here before creating this one."

"My other car is a TARDIS," said Falkon.

Michaela wasn't thrown off. "And why would you do that?"

"Listen," I said, hobbling forward. "Brianna's basically come to help. I know her from real life. Without her equipment, you guys would still be back in the castle and I'd be stuck out here alone."

"I'm not attacking her," said Michaela. "I'm simply confused. A Void Blade is an incredibly potent weapon. I've only seen two the whole time I've been in Euphoria, and never wielded by anyone under level forty."

"I've got some powerful friends," Brianna said. "And I knew Chris was in Death March mode. I had to do something."

"Especially since you were the one to dick him over so bad in the first place," said Falkon. "What? Should I not have said that?"

"Let's get out of sight," I said. "Barry's cave's not too far away. I'd appreciate the chance to sit down." In fact, I was already feeling better. Ever since I'd left the castle, the periapt had been pumping me full of high-potency healing. At this rate, I'd be feeling fine within an hour or so.

"Sure," said Michaela. "Who's Barry?"

"Barry's the best," I said, walking past them all and toward the far end of the ledge. "An inspiration to us all. C'mon."

We climbed up the mountain's flank, and only my Survival skill allowed me to navigate the dark woods back to the cave. When we were close, I instructed everyone to collect branches, then led them toward the entrance.

"Chris!" The voice came from the undergrowth. "No move! Wait!"

I startled and then held my hand out to reassure the others. "Allies."

Dribbler emerged from the bushes. "Look! Trip wire. Careful. Attached to bucket of Barfo's Face Melta Pudding up in tree. Here, follow me."

We carefully stepped over the filament.

"Good, good. Now watch here, foot spike trap with fire wasps. Nasty. Don't step!"

The area before the cave entrance was surprisingly dense with traps. Dribbler helped us pass a dozen of them, all within ten yards of the cave. It was as if they'd set up a blender.

"There," said Dribbler, turning at last and beaming at us. "Welcome to Barry's cave!"

Barfo's head popped up from over the entrance where he'd been hiding. "Where Barry? I want to meet him."

"I don't know," I said. "Cave was empty when I found it."

Barfo grinned. "Kreekit read from his diary. Very funny! He sleep with elf!"

"Yes," agreed Dribbler. "Very sexy. We all become very aroused."

"Uh." I didn't know quite what to say. "Yeah. Barry's an enterprising goblin."

"C'mon," said Falkon. "You're about to fall down. Let's get you inside."

We ducked our heads, leaving the two goblins outside on watch, and headed around the cave's turn to where Kreekit was seated by the fire, reading from Barry's diary.

"This very special cave," she said. "Very important goblin live here."

"Yeah," I said, sitting down heavily beside the flames. The cave was much cozier with five of us inside; we huddled around the flickering fire, shoulders and hips pressed against each other. I groaned as I elbowed my way out of my cloak, and then gave the others a few minutes to admire Barry's artwork on the walls.

"Barry does indeed appear to be the man," said Falkon. "Looks like he's got a hydra in a headlock over here. All seven heads."

"At the very least Barry seems to think highly of himself," said Michaela, a hint of a smile at the corner of her lips.

Kreekit, I saw, was nodding judiciously, as if taking personal pride in Barry's accomplishments.

"Dinner?" Brianna opened the Everypack and pulled out stemless glasses of red wine. "This is one of my favorite vintages. Blackberry, currants, with a hint of leather and oak. From a winery on the slopes of Etrubius."

Falkon took his glass and held it up against the firelight. "Isn't Etrubius a volcano on the Sword Coast?"

"They are very nervous vintners," said Brianna with a pleased smile.

I took a sip. I'm not much of a wine connoisseur, but this was delicious. "Adventuring is going to get a whole ton of a lot more civilized with Brianna around."

"As it should be," said Brianna, handing Michaela her glass. "And I thought perhaps chicken wings with a chili lime seasoning?" She twisted around to pull out a large platter of wings piled in a steaming pyramid.

"Oh, god, yes," said Falkon. "The Beggars didn't think us fit to feed. And I am so tired of wyvern steak."

For a few minutes we simply chowed down, grinning at each other as we devoured wing after drumstick, the sauce rich with garlic and ginger overtones, washing everything down with large sips of the wine.

Brianna dumped everything in the Everypack when we were done, and we all leaned back against the smooth walls, bunching cloaks and packs for cushioning.

"So," said Falkon. "Strategy. Tactics. Stuff. We want to talk about it?"

"If I may," said Brianna, wiping her fingers with a wet wipe which she then tossed into the Everypack. "I've some experience in Euphoria, as it seems we all do. And my experience tells me we've been exceedingly fortunate against the Beggars thus far. The equipment I gave Chris allowed us to surprise them, but we won't have that advantage again."

"No, Brianna," I said. "We're not abandoning Lotharia."

"And I literally can't leave," said Michaela. "I'm tied to Guthorios, and have some measure of free will only as long as I am following his orders."

"I'm with Chris," said Falkon. "Though you're testing my loyalties with this wining and dining thing you've got going."

"Chris?" Brianna turned to me, eyes wide, expression plaintive. "Step back and just think for a moment. We're both in Death March mode—"

"Hold on," said Falkon. His eyes were blazing green. "That's a lie."

"What?" Brianna whipped around to glare at him. "Of course I am—"

"Nope. Sorry, hon. I'm in Euphoria's IT department and smuggled in a little analysis tool. You're level two, loaded with some epic gear, and playing in Tough Cookie mode. You're not in Death March mode at all."

I GAVE A BARK of laughter. I shouldn't have been surprised. But apparently Brianna could not only still fool me, she could also still hurt me. "Tough Cookie mode?"

"One level tougher than Cake Walk," said Falkon.

"Chris." She held her hands up as if I were a wild animal. "I can explain."

"You can always explain," I said. "You've had an explanation for everything you ever did. What I can't explain is why I ever listened."

"I wanted you to feel a sense of solidarity, to not feel alone—"

"Brianna, stop. I don't care." I shoved my emotions aside. I wouldn't let Euphoria play me with her stats. Wouldn't let the turmoil I was feeling mess with me anymore. "If you want to help us, great. You've already done me a huge favor with this gear. Let's leave it at that. No more explanations, no more lies, no more anything. All right?"

Her eyes filled with tears and she tucked her chin to her chest, a strand of coppery-red hair falling before her face. "I'm sorry," she said, voice shaking. "I'm so sorry." Then she stood and rushed out of the cave.

And despite it all, I took a step after her. I clenched my fists and stared into the fire instead.

"I see what you meant about her being trouble," said Michaela dryly. "Let me guess. An ex-girlfriend?"

"Yeah," I said. "Wasn't a very healthy relationship."

"No kidding," said Falkon, tossing a log on the fire. "I mean, I haven't been in a lot of relationships, but even I know you don't create solidarity through blatant lies."

"One might even argue that achieves precisely the opposite effect," said Michaela.

"Yeah." My voice was soft. I blinked several times as my sight grew unfocused. I wanted nothing so much as to sit down. "She doesn't see it that way. Never did." There was so much I could share with them. Anecdotes. Explanations. But I didn't want to go there. I didn't want to open all those doors and pull out those painful memories, let them sap me of my vitality and will to keep going. So instead I took a deep breath and forced myself to sit up straight.

"Regardless, she gave me some insane loot. Check this out." I laid the Void Blade across my knees. "I cut through Makarios' left fist with this thing. I think his actual hand is within his claws, like they're some kind of gauntlet, because while I didn't cut his hand off, he wasn't able to use it after."

"He's going to be *pissed*," said Falkon in a sing-song voice.

"And then I cut Vanatos' daemon's head off," I said. "It disappeared completely. Do you guys think it's permanently dead?"

"Oh, man," said Falkon. "Vanatos is going to be piiiih-isssssed."

"Not permanently dead," said Michaela, voice slow, thoughtful. "More akin to banished. It hurts Vanatos, but he can regenerate his daemon in time."

"Then we can't allow him to have that time," I said. "That thing was ridiculous."

"No," said Falkon. "What's ridiculous is you taking it out. At what. Level eleven?" His eyes blazed green. "Nope. Level thirteen. *That's* ridiculous. You keep this up you're going to be level fifty by next week."

"It's not ridiculous," said Michaela. "He keeps placing himself in horrendously dangerous situations that he should have no chance at winning. There's no quicker way to earn XP."

"Or die," I said. "But the blade's not the only thing Brianna gave me." I showed them the rest of the gear. "I'm like a walking arsenal. And having mana thirty-six was crucial. I'd have died a hundred times over without it."

"Dang," said Falkon. "Quadruple dang. You sure you need all that gear? Because if it's too heavy, I'd be happy to—"

Michaela smacked his arm without even looking at him. "This undoubtedly gives us an edge, but is it enough? How do we take down the Beggars without being killed?"

"Did you learn anything from them while you were their prisoners?" I asked.

Falkon made a face. "Not really. They're on a pretty simple mission for Guthorios himself, turns out. The double-dealing bastard. Clear the keep, go into the dungeons, and find out what the treasure at the heart of it all is."

"Yeah, I know," I said. "I spoke with Guthorios after I ran from the castle."

"Oh?" They both sat up.

"Didn't go well. Guthorios isn't interested in helping as long as the Beggars are trying to accomplish his goals. May the best tool win, or whatever."

Michaela rubbed her chin. "Perhaps we can simply let the Beggars do all our fighting for us."

"No," I said. "For one, that might mean their killing Lotharia."

"If they do," said Falkon, "then she'll just respawn in the meadow. We can grab her there and take her to Guthorios to be cleansed."

"He won't cleanse her if we're not doing our part of the job," said Michaela.

"Oh," said Falkon. "Well, so much for that then."

"Also, our only chance of defeating the Beggars is to ambush them right after a big fight," I said. "When their reserves are at their lowest. Just like they did to us."

"Not a bad idea, though tricky to pull off." Falkon frowned at the fire. "That'd involve knowing when they went into the keep, and then sneaking in and hanging back without their noticing till the right moment."

"I've acquired a new talent called Mute Presence," I said. "The daemon spotted me, but the other Beggars might have trouble. Even if they do, I can get out of there fast without them being able to stop me."

"But if they do spot you, we'll lose the element of surprise," said Michaela.

"That might not matter. They still have to clear the keep. Knowing we're around won't stop them from doing that. Even if they're waiting for us, they'll still be resource depleted after a big fight."

"All right," said Falkon. "Sounds like a plan. How do we know when they enter the keep, though? We can't hang around the castle."

"Maybe we can." I smiled. "Where's the one place they can't get into?"

Falkon hesitated. "Jeramy's tower?"

"To which I know the pass phrase. We go in, you guys hang out in the lounge, have some drinks, and I'll keep an eye out. When they enter the keep, we'll sneak in after them."

"Feasible," said Michaela. "You can get us in through your Shared Darkness spell. Though that will burn up a lot of your mana."

"I've got lots to spare," I said. "Or will, once I recharge my mana stones. Actually, how do I do that? That's twenty-five points I need to generate."

Michaela laughed. "It'll take you three full rests, or meditating all day, sleeping, then meditating the next day. You can only generate your natural number of mana points per regen period."

"Or you can give us your stones when we rest tonight, we'll regenerate them for you, and then you can top them off tomorrow," said Falkon. "I'm already back to full due to spending all day meditating."

"Sounds like a plan," I said, and tossed Falkon my mana marble and Michaela my larger stone. "Thank you. We can move in tomorrow at dusk. Michaela, why don't you take Barry's pallet? I'll rest right here by the fire."

"And Brianna?" asked Falkon.

"She can figure herself out," I said. "She's probably waiting for me to chase after her to have an argument. Let her wait."

Falkon grunted his approval and settled down more comfortably. Michaela rose and gave me a shallow bow.

"Thank you, Chris. For coming to our rescue. I appreciate the risks you took. It was noble of you."

I gave her a pained smile. "We're a team, yeah? That's what teammates do for each other. No problem."

Michaela hesitated as if to say something more, then frowned and lay down on the bed of straw, lying with her back to us and facing the wall.

"You doing OK?" asked Falkon, his eyes reflecting the glow from across the fire.

I didn't answer at once. Was I? It had felt so good to fight both Makarios and the angel. To find it within me to marshal my powers and wits, go toe-to-toe and come out ahead. Yet that combat did little to mask my anxiety. Lotharia was now several days missing. The Beggars could easily crush us if we weren't careful. Worse, Brianna had injected a sense of unease and frustration into my life that I'd hoped to never experience again. Especially not here in Euphoria.

"I'll be fine," I said at last.

"About what Michaela said. You coming to save us. I've seen some incredible things here in Euphoria, but all of it felt like a game. Fake. Easily risked. But you coming back to Castle Winter for us – that was some real heroism. Nobody has ever literally risked their life for me. I don't think I even know anybody in the real world who would."

Falkon was staring into the flames, his expression haunted. He paused long enough that I thought he was waiting for a response, but I had nothing to say. Nothing that wouldn't cheapen what he was expressing.

"So thank you, Chris. For real. You're a legit fucking hero." Then his somber expression broke into a smile. "Or craziest idiot I've ever met."

"Maybe both," I said. "But you're welcome."

"I said I was meditating all day, but that's not true." He shifted around, army crawling around the fire to get closer to me, dropping his voice into a whisper as he did so. "I logged out for a while there."

"Understandable," I said. "Why spend all that time just sitting on your ass?"

"No, I wanted to do some snooping around. I called a friend of mine who's on the Brussels Senior Dev team. Hadn't talked to the guy since the big Vegas convention earlier this year, but I told him right off I was cheating on my in-game time so he got to the point." Falkon inched closer again, resting on one elbow. "I asked him to look up Jeramy's player. He promised to do so, but ran into some kind of unusual red tape. I didn't want to wait too long, so I told him I'd check back in soon. I'll have to wait a little longer before seeing what's he's learned."

"What was unusual about the red tape?"

"Swen's got clearance for that kind of information. It's why I called him. It violates a whole bunch of privacy laws for him to share it with me, but after Vegas… meh. He owes me. So for him to run into red tape would be like a head librarian finding a book they weren't allowed to read."

"Some libraries have rare books," I said. "Not allowed for general circulation."

"Exactly," said Falkon. "Whoever Jeramy's player was, he's the equivalent of a rare book. Anyway, Swen said he was going to look into it. Each of our days is about half an hour for him, so I'll check back in tomorrow evening just before we hit the Beggars. Maybe he'll be able to shed some light on this whole mystery."

"Thanks, Falkon." I tried to think through the complexities of the situation but my mind was dulled by exhaustion and pain. "Guess you're getting curious about this situation, too."

"Yeah," he said. "It's weird as all get out. I mean, everyone I work with both loves and is a bit freaked out by Euphoria. There are entire sections of the code that we can't parse. Like, Albertus has created his own code that's something between binary and what we've being using. Everyone I know has tried to crack it. I was part of a club that was trying to hand code a transcriptor for it, but we didn't get anywhere."

"I don't know anything about coding," I said, "but that sounds pretty freaky."

"You've no idea. I mean, just last week I heard about this new theory out of MIT that Albertus' code works more along the lines of genetics, with RNA coding, decoding, regulating and expressing a genetic code. All we've seen so far is the equivalent of messenger RNA and the proteins it works with. We don't even know where this base genetic code might be. And that's if their theory is even correct."

I tried to wrap my head around that, but didn't feel bad when I failed. My inability to understand it apparently was in line with even the best coders and hackers out there.

"Anyways," said Falkon. "The reason I bring all this up is because nobody really knows what Albertus is up to. We know what he's telling us, and he's really, really convincing, but when faced with that alien code? Who knows? He's creating autonomous server warehouses all over the world on which to store it, built by machines he designed himself. Nobody allowed inside. I'm telling you, it's pretty freaky stuff. So when I hear about him personally snuffing out a player who has the ability to create unique wards he can't bypass? You bet your ass I get curious."

"Well, in light of all that, isn't this grounds to just log out and go tell everybody what you've stumbled onto here?"

"Yeah, I won't lie. I've given some serious thought to that. But that'd mean abandoning you in here." He rolled his head and looked up at me. "The amount of time it would take me to connect and convince the right people would mean you being in here by yourself for months and months without my help. And… yeah. I'm not going to ditch you like that."

I won't lie, my throat tightened up a little. "Thanks, man. I really appreciate it."

"Hell yeah, dude. You just literally risked your life for me." He picked up a stick and poked the fire. "Plus you're kinda cute. Be a real shame to cut out on you now."

I gave him a shove and he laughed, spilling out onto the floor. "Thanks," I said. "Just as I was about to get all sentimental."

"Couldn't risk that, now, could I?" Falkon rolled back onto his side and propped his head up on his palm. "Though if you get cold, don't hesitate to come over and ask for a cuddle, all right?"

"Sure," I said. "Thanks. Duly noted. And on that note, I'm going to get some sleep. Big day tomorrow."

"Big day indeed. Night, Chris."

"Night, Falkon."

He made his way back over to his side of the fire and after peeling off his armor lay down, head propped on his arm. I did the same, and lay for a while staring into the dancing fire.

A shadow at the back of the cave shifted and I realized Kreekit had been there the whole time. She leaned forward now, Barry's diary in hand.

"Be careful, Chris."

"No worries on that front," I said, fighting off a yawn.

"No." Her tone caught my attention. "You gather attention from spirit world. Big spirit watching you. You walk fine line. Your friend, his talk, it angers the spirit. Do not make it angry."

That made my blood run cold. "Albertus?"

"Kreekit not know any Albertus. But I know the big spirit. It move through all of Euphoria. It hear all, see all, is all. Do not anger it, Chris. Do not speak with Falkon about such things again. Very dangerous. Very, very dangerous. Now. You want me read you bedtime story?"

I gulped and then gave her a shaky smile. "No, thanks. Maybe some other night."

Kreekit nodded and moved back into the shadows. I tried to puzzle out Falkon's revelations, to understand what it might mean to upset Albertus through our investigations, but eventually gave that up. Instead I lay there thinking of Lotharia in the darkness of the keep, surprised at the intensity of the ache that throbbed within me, a yearning to hold her in my arms as I drifted off to sleep. And at the very last, just before I fell asleep, I thought of my little brother Justin.

BRIANNA HAD BREAKFAST ready when we woke up. She must have snuck in and snagged the Everypack while we slept, because she'd laid out a feast when we emerged into the early morning sunlight. Kreekit sat at the head of the table, looking solemn and dignified, while Dribbler and Barfo stood to attention with white towels draped over their arms, both of them eyeing the food and drooling down their chins.

I caught a glimpse of croissants, a big bowl of scrambled eggs, fresh-cut fruit, tiered trays of small cakes, waffles drenched in syrup, carafes of coffee and orange juice, but I didn't stop. Instead, I took hold of Brianna's hand and dragged her away from the cave entrance, ignoring her protests till we were safely out of sight.

"What?" She snatched her hand back and rubbed. "Croissants in the morning piss you off now?"

"Stop."

"Stop what? You never want to eat again?"

"No. Brianna. Stop. This campaign to win me over. It's not going to work."

She froze. "Not going to work."

"No. I'm not saying we can't be friends. That we can't work together. But you have to quit this… this attempt to win me back."

"I just made breakfast."

"I know you, Brianna. You didn't 'just make breakfast'. You've never 'just made breakfast' in your life. If anything, you've always expected everyone else to make you breakfast, which makes this whole charade all the less convincing. Everything you do has an ulterior motive. Inviting me into Euphoria. Giving me this gear. Saying you're also in Death March mode. Making breakfast. It's your M.O., and it normally works, but not anymore."

I realized I'd raised my voice, so I forced myself to calm down. "Like I said, you're welcome to help us, especially now I know you won't actually die doing so. But if you're going to be part of our team, then enough with this charm offensive. No more lying. No more putting on this sweet and sugary act. Be yourself."

"Be myself." She gave a bitter laugh. "You don't even know who that is."

"See? After all we've been through, that's frankly pretty terrifying. Do *you* know who you are? I mean, really? Who are you when you're not putting on an act, manipulating people, trying to get an advantage or score a point?"

"You must really hate me if you think of me that way," she said, voice bleak. "Why the hell did you ever even date me if you have such a low opinion of me?"

I pinched the bridge of my nose. "I didn't know how awful you were at first. Took me months. Now I know better."

Her eyes filled with tears and she took a step back.

The impulse to apologize was overwhelming. It was so easy to think of her as a new Brianna, a red-headed, stunning woman I'd just met and was being incredibly cruel to. I could feel Euphoria's influence pounding at my walls, seeking to undermine my conviction, to forgive this Sylvana Embers and make amends. The apology was right there on the tip of my tongue.

Instead, I closed my eyes. "Your charisma is killing me, Brianna. Any way you can switch it off?"

"No," she said, voice sharp. "Maybe that's not my charisma. Maybe that's what's left of your basic human decency."

"Nope," I said, opening my eyes again. "That's your charisma. And don't pretend to cry. I know it's an act."

"How dare—"

"Nope. No fake outrage either. C'mon, Brianna. Drop it."

She glared at me, pale skin mottling with fury, and then she wiped the tears away on her voluminous cream sleeves. "Fine. You want to be an asshole? I can play that game."

"Yup," I said. "I know you can. But that's not what I want. I want you on my team, like, the real Brianna. Whoever she is. Not as an enemy. Not as an ex. Just as a friend. Can you do that? Can you be that? Just my friend?"

She gave another bitter laugh and turned away, striding to the edge of the small forested glade in which we stood. For a moment she stood still, then she drew her Frostflower Saber and cut at the air with a scream.

I tensed as a blizzard-like wind flew from her blade, cutting in a great diagonal slash across the trees. The trunks splintered from the cold even as icy blue and white flowers wreathed the trees, and a moment later half of them collapsed in an explosion of splinters and frozen shards.

Falkon and Michaela ran out, weapons drawn.

"We unda attack?" asked Falkon through a mouth full of food, bastard sword in hand. "Wha happun?"

"No," I said. "Brianna's letting off some steam, is all."

My friends stared wide-eyed at the shattered line of trees. "Letting off steam?" asked Michaela. "Remind me to stay out of her way."

Brianna turned, eyes glittering, Frostflower Saber held out to her side. It glimmered in the morning sunlight.

"We'll be back there by the cheesecake," said Falkon, pointing a thumb over his shoulder. "Cool? Cool."

They both backed away, leaving me with Brianna. I crossed my arms over my chest and raised an eyebrow. "Done?"

"You are such a miserable bastard," she hissed, taking a step toward me. "Arrogant, rude, conceited, unappreciative—"

"Yeah," I said. "I get the gist."

"No. You don't." She leveled the tip of her saber in the direction of my throat. "What drives me insane about you is that you're a nobody. You're a fucking *public-school teacher*, for fuck's sake, and that's not even your career. You don't have a career. You don't have friends. You don't have money. You don't have a future. All you used to do was play Golden Dawn, and then your brother got arrested and you stopped even doing that. And by the way, boo fucking hoo about your brother and your mother. Shit happens to everybody. So your mother got sick and died and now your brother's in jail. You think that makes you special? No. It makes you just like millions of other people, and there's a name for people who are like millions of other people: nobodies."

"Uh-huh. There you are. Nice to see you again, Brianna."

The tip of her sword wavered. If she chose to blast me with it, I was probably a dead man. But I was done dancing to her tune. So I walked forward till the blade was touching my neck.

"But you know what? If I'm such a nobody, why are you all torn up about me? Why are you here making breakfast and acting like an idiot, hmm? Doesn't add up, does it? You know what I think?"

"I don't care what you think."

"I think your life is so shitty that I'm actually the nicest guy you ever met. I mean, yeah, boo hoo about my family life, but what about yours?"

"Shut up."

"Big rich dad who's world famous for doing something with nanobots and leukemia, but he never had time for you, did he? Still doesn't. You think I forgot how he handled that breakdown of yours? How much did he give you? Two thousand dollars in cash right there on the spot? That was pretty sweet of him."

The tip of her blade danced even more. "Shut the fuck up."

"You always talk up your life, your money, your connections, all that fancy stuff, but you're not out there playing with Arvid and the rest of your gang, are you? No. You're here, playing a level two avatar so as to hang out with me. Why is that?"

She didn't answer.

"So how about this. You quit trying to insult me and manipulate me and seduce me or whatever it is you're doing. Stop trying to control me or own me or break me. Just quit it. And instead, just help me. Work with me. Who knows? Maybe we'll become friends. Maybe you'll make some new friends. Maybe you'll have some honest-to-god fun. But if you don't want to? If you think you can't stop? Then just leave. I'll give you back all this gear and you can drop this Sylvana avatar and go back to playing with your old crew."

Tears filled her eyes and she angrily dashed them away. "Fuck you, Chris." She sheathed her blade and strode away into the forest and was gone.

I let out a huge breath and my shoulders sagged. Had I been in real danger? Maybe. Probably not. Hard to tell. I rubbed at my face and made my way back to where brunch was laid out. Falkon and Michaela looked up at me with concern.

"Cheesy eggy thing?" asked Kreekit, holding out a platter.

"Thanks," I said.

"We could hear a bit from here," said Michaela. "Apologies if that was a private conversation."

"No, it's fine." I took a bite of the cheesy eggy thing.

"I've got only one request." Falkon poured me a mug of coffee. "Whatever it takes, you've got to convince her to leave the Everypack. After living like this, I can't go back. Please, Chris. Don't make me."

I couldn't help myself. I laughed, rubbed at my eyes, then picked up the mug. "Fine. I'll do whatever it takes."

"Seriously, though," said Michaela. "What's the upshot?"

"I don't know. She ran off. Which is classic Brianna. She'll stew for a bit and then make up her mind. Guess we'll find out sooner or later whether she's leaving."

"She must really like you," said Michaela with studied caution, pouring herself a mimosa.

"You know, I used to think that. I used to think all our crazy fighting was because our feelings for each other were so intense. But that's not it." I stared down at my hands. "I think she's just a fundamentally lost person. Like, she doesn't know how to interact with people in a normal way. She comes from this world where everybody's trying to take advantage of each other. Everybody has an angle, an ulterior motive. And me not being like that drove her crazy."

"I agree on the crazy bit," said Falkon.

Michaela, however, was nodding. "I think I understand. In the real world, I work in drug research and development. It's not an environment that's very friendly toward women. As a result, I see a lot of women grow hard, try to act like men. Not all of them, but enough that I think it's a definite trend. We mold ourselves to excel in our given environment. But when we're removed from that environment, it can be quite challenging to revert to or act in what might once have been a normal manner."

"I guess," I said. "I don't think she even really loves me or anything. She just doesn't have the vocabulary to be friends. And then when I broke up with her, she went nuts."

Falkon blew out his cheeks. "Well, that sounds like exactly the kind of person I want to have on my team."

I gave a sad smile. "She's a great gamer. It's what we originally bonded over. She's really, really good. If we can just find a way to get past all this stuff—"

"Get past all her character-defining neuroses," said Michaela blandly.

"Right. If we can, then I think she'd be an amazing asset."

We sat in silence, munching on our incredible breakfast, then Falkon startled and dug something out of his pouch. "Here's your mana marble, by the way. Fully charged."

"Mmph," said Michaela, hunching over as she bit into a large piece of waffle and tried to dig out my ring. "Here'sh yoursh. Haf recharge."

"Half? Perfect. Thank you both." I slipped the ring back on, dropped the marble in my pouch, then smacked myself in the forehead. "I haven't even spent my new XP. You know things are getting crazy when you forget that."

"Have at it," said Falkon. "I'll be right here eating… what's this? Blackberry tarts? With whipped cream topping? Oh, yes. Yes indeed."

I grinned and opened my character sheet. Time to level up.

13

YOU HAVE GAINED **145** experience (80 for defeating the daemon Eletherios, 65 for rescuing Falkon and Michaela from the Beggars of Solomon). You have 212 unused XP. You total XP is 1212.

Congratulations! You are Level 12!

Congratulations! You are Level 13!

I took a bite from my croissant sandwich and flicked the windows away. Despite everyone's predictions, I was still leveling up like a madman. All it took was to continuously solo impossibly lethal threats. Surely that wouldn't backfire at some point, right?

Your attributes have increased!

Mana +2
Constitution +1

You have learned new skills! *Stealth: Basic (V), Survival: Basic (III), Athletics: Basic (V), Backstab (V)*

Huh. I'd really impressed Euphoria with my attacks on Makarios and Eletherios, as I guessed the angel was called. All my running around the mountain and finding Barry's cave and lighting fires had paid off with my Survival, too. Pretty neat. 'Course, the plus two to mana didn't hurt, either. If I kept this up, I'd be hitting mana forty soon. Insane.

I swiped the window away.

 There are five talent advancements available to you:

Wall Climber (I), Cat's Fall, Stunning Backstab, Heads-Up, and *Adrenaline Surge (II).*

All of them cost seventy-five XP except for Cat's Fall, which clocked in at fifty-five.

 There are three spells available to you:

Evenfall, Shadow Clone, and *Grasping Shadows.*

I didn't rush. They key to picking one's talents and spells depended almost entirely on one's ability to guess what challenges lay immediately ahead. I'd be tracking the Beggars through the keep, seeking to evade their notice and then ambush them when the time was right. Furthermore, we couldn't stand to take them all at once; constraining as many of them as possible so as to gang up on a single member was the optimal strategy. Toward that end, Grasping Shadows and Stunning Backstab were obvious picks. Combine them with Ebon Tendrils, Night Shroud, and Pin Down, and I had a veritable arsenal of choices with which to confuse and imprison my foes.

I tapped Grasping Shadows and Stunning Backstab; both options lit up in gold, moving to appear on my character sheet. They cost me one hundred and seventy-five XP, leaving me with thirty-seven. I could live with that.

I took a moment to gaze over my sheet. I'd been leveling so fast I was running the danger of gaining too many powers too quickly. That was one of the problems of inheriting an already leveled avatar in Golden Dawn, for example; you had a wealth of abilities and powers at your fingertips, but no familiarity born of usage with them. Which meant in the heat of battle, you could forget a key power – to everybody's detriment.

Add in all my new gear, and I was nearly overwhelmed with options. Experimenting, I pressed my finger on Sabotage Defenses, and tried dragging it down the list. It worked. I sat up and quickly sorted my talents into four groups: attacks, including things like Bleeding Attack and Pin Down; movement abilities like Shadow Step, Expert Leaper and Ledge Runner; observation abilities like Darkvision and Astute Observer; and finally my random abilities like Minor Magic and Mute Presence.

Much better. At a glance, I could now navigate my long list of talents with ease. I didn't yet need to do the same for my spells; I only had five of them, and they were all interlinked through the play of shadows. Instead, I went through my list of gear, tapping each one to see its status. My Ring of the Bull and Belt of Shadow

Form were charged once more. Stone Cloak was empty, however, and my mana ring needed to be topped up.

"Hey, Michaela, how's your mana looking?"

She blinked, coming back from some reverie, and lowered her mug. "I'm at full. Why?"

"Here." I took my mana marble and extended it to her. Michaela would no doubt burn though mana quicker than Falkon. "There's no need for me to be running around with nearly twice your mana. You've got some awesome spells. You'll get some good use out of this."

Her eyebrows went up as she looked from the glimmering marble to me. "Are you sure?"

"Yeah. Go on, take it."

She did so, holding it up with two pale, slightly rotted fingers, then closed her fist about it and smiled. "Why, thank you, Chris. This is a princely gift."

"No prob. And I was hoping you could recharge my Stone Cloak at some point today? It can take up to ten mana points, and I'm going to be focusing on my ring."

"Of course." She took the cloak when I handed it over and folded it neatly on her lap. "I've always wanted a Stone Cloak. Much more common than a Void Blade, but still far out of my reach. I've heard it said they're made from the hides of stone goats. It's a quest just to get up to the heights where they live."

"They must be tough to kill," I said. "But I'm grateful for their hides all the same. That cloak saved my life last night." I polished off the last of my coffee and stood. "I'm going to find a quiet corner to meditate. Maybe inside Barry's cave. You guys all set?"

They both nodded, and Falkon reached out to pat the Everypack. "We're just about to start edging into elevensies," he said. "I'm going to stay here so I don't miss it."

I laughed, gave a wave, and walked away.

THE BATTLEMENTS OF Castle Winter were much busier that night, with patrols of goblins marching to and fro with foot-stamping self-importance. It had taken delicate timing to transport Falkon and Michaela into Jeramy's tower; Brianna never returned, and when dusk had fallen we'd given up waiting for her. Now I sat crouched within the wyvern's nest atop the tower, huddled within the dense interweavings of thick branches, peering down at the bailey far below.

A large bonfire had been lit in the center of the courtyard, around which the Big Burpie goblins were feasting on what remained of the ogres. It was pretty impressive; they must have eaten without stopping ever since they'd arrived, for the carcasses were nearly picked clean and now they were intent on smashing the bones open with stone hammers to get at the marrow. Many of the goblins lay in what looked like feverish dreams, clutching their swollen stomachs and shuddering as they turned their heads from side to side. The others cast envious glances at these fallen comrades and ate all the quicker.

Lickit sat atop his throne, looking like he'd gained a hundred pounds. A team of goblins labored to feed him, forcing raw meat down his gullet as the shaman gurgled and weakly flailed his swollen limbs. Every once in a while, he'd choke and spew the meat back up, only for the goblins to assiduously capture the mess in their hands and force it back down.

It was pretty fucking disgusting.

There was no sign of the Beggars, however. Lights shone through the cracks of the goblin tower door, and from the fearful glances the goblins shot at it as they walked by I guessed the Beggars had yet to make their next assault on the keep.

I shifted my weight so as not to grow stiff. The wyvern's nest was a fascinating place. Vast swaths of wyvern skin had been sloughed off here, the scales as hard as iron and looking like prime armor-making material. Animal and goblin bones were interwoven with the branches, and at the base of the nest sat a large egg which I'd discovered to be ice cold to the touch. That had filled me with a stab of remorse; I'd no idea the wyvern was a mother-to-be. I tried telling myself that it was a good thing another such monster hadn't been loosed upon the world, but I couldn't help but feel like crap every time I caught sight of that egg out of the corner of my eye.

It was getting bitterly cold, and as wonderful as my stone cloak was it did little to keep me warm. Nor could I risk catching the attention of the goblins walking the walls by moving around. Instead, I was forced to stay still, shifting my weight and stretching my legs every few minutes as I kept watch. After the first hour had passed I found a vantage point from which I could meditate and still keep watch below; I sank into a mindful trance during which everything around me took on the faint golden sheen of its inherent magic, and time lost its meaning.

The stars slowly wheeled overhead. The moon rose up, crescent shaped and looking exactly like our own. I watched it, thoughts drifting, as it wheeled higher into the sky then swung back down. My mana points slowly ticked back up. I knew I was cold, but the cold didn't touch me in my meditative state. The main bonfire below died down; more and more of the Big Burpie goblins fell into a state of feverish torpor. Shaman Lickit was finally left alone by his minders, looking half dead as his breath snarfled around a half-swallowed piece of steak.

A flock of pale moths the size of condors drifted overhead. Green flames wandered the streets of Feldgrau far below. Will-o-the-wisps? The thoughts came and left just as easily. My mana pool reached full, but still I remained meditating. No sense in feeling the cold.

The eastern sky lightened, turning cobalt then ultramarine blue. The stars over the mountains faded, and as the sky lightened further to pale gray a fine dew appeared on everything, dampening my hair and cloak. A few high cirrus clouds lit up in deep peach and salmon pinks, then their farthest edge became burnished gold as the sun finally broke over the mountain peaks.

The door to the goblin tower opened and a grim-looking Vanatos stepped out, followed in short order by the rest of the Beggars. I blinked, rousing myself from my meditation. Makarios came last, his ruined hand held in a sling across his chest, face as sour as a spoiled grapefruit. They strode across the bailey, picking their path between the fallen goblins, heading toward the keep door.

I gasped as sensation returned to me, and for a moment I felt like an old man; my limbs were locked in place and my muscles spasmed as I forced myself to move, to crawl to the edge of the tower and look down over its ruined battlements at the wall. The goblin patrols were nowhere in evidence. With a grimace, I swung out and dropped to the parapet, knees popping and hips twanging with pain, then hurried into the tower and whispered the passcode.

I dashed down, racing past the demon in its summoning circle who watched me from his chaise with what looked like a romance novel in his hands. Down through the bedroom and into the bottom floor lounge, where Falkon was passed out on a couch and Michaela had fallen asleep at the desk, cheek resting on arms crossed over a large book.

"Wake up, guys," I said. "Show time."

"Show time?" Falkon smacked his lips and sat up, blinking in confusion. "What are we—oh. They finally make a move?"

"Yep. They should already be in the keep." I headed over to where the Everypack sat on a low table. I opened it and reached in for a coffee which I set before Michaela, then another for Falkon. I grabbed a chocolate croissant to accompany my own coffee, then focused on wolfing them both down.

"No sign of Brianna?" asked Michaela, pulling her skull mask out of her satchel.

"Nope." I washed down the last of the croissant with a final gulp and dropped everything back into the Everypack. "Ready?"

Falkon stretched, windmilled his arms, then set to buckling on his pauldrons and greaves. "Gimme a moment and I will be."

I waited by the front door and looked askance at Falkon when he stepped up, Everypack slung over his shoulder.

"What?" he asked, pretending to be genuinely surprised. "We might need crepes while we're in there."

I snorted. "Fair enough. Ready?"

Michaela slid her mask on and nodded. "Ready."

I cracked open the tower door and peered out into the courtyard. Hundreds of Big Burpies lay everywhere, as if in the wake of a disastrous battle. They shivered with minor twitches as if fighting off wicked nightmares. "What the hell...?"

Falkon crowded in close behind me. "No idea."

The Beggars had made it across the bailey without a problem, so I took a breath and slipped outside into the dawn shadows. I led my companions along a weaving path between the goblins. Up close, they didn't even look like goblins anymore; their bones seemed to be straining against their muscles, stretching them out, while their features were becoming more boxy, their jaws reinforced, teeth more jagged. Some kind of metamorphosis?

I didn't waste any time gawking, however, and headed straight toward the keep door. Its interior still swirled with shadow, and when we reached it I held up a hand, then listened carefully. Nothing but the faint susurrus of a whispery wind. We'd already agreed upon the plan, so I drew my Void Blade, activated Darkvision and Mute Presence and stepped inside.

The shadows resolved themselves into the short hallway that led to the great kitchen. I immediately dropped into a crouch, pulse pounding in my ears, and pressed against the rough stone wall. Silence. Was that sound coming from the stairwell? I bit my lower lip and strained to hear more, but the thick stone walls were terrible for acoustics.

After a moment, I pushed my arm back through the veil of shadow and beckoned for my friends to follow, then moved forward as silently as I could to the kitchen entrance. The furniture here was shattered and overturned by violence, and not all of it wrought by us during our last raid. One wall was blackened and melted to a smooth surface like glass; a slowly spinning circle of crimson runes filled the fireplace, assuredly Balthus' work. Gobbets and smears of intestines were splattered everywhere, along with hewn-off limbs and the scorched remnants of xythagas.

"Looks like the Beggars cleaned up good," said Falkon.

"Hold here," I whispered. "Let me scout ahead." I crept through the kitchen, nerves on edge, but the silence was heavy and thick like an oppressive blanket. I moved to one of the doorways and peered into a large pantry with a trapdoor in its center; it too was scorched to sooty ruin. Another doorway led to what might have been a barracks. A terrible fight had taken place here, as evinced by the damage done to the walls and shattered furniture. Whatever the Beggars had fought was now gone.

I crept back to the others. "I think they've cleared the ground floor. I heard noises from upstairs. Let's take a look."

"That's where the grand hall is," said Falkon, voice grim. "Stairs open directly onto it. You've got a library, chapel, privy, two guest bedrooms and meeting room directly off it. Stairs'll continue up to the third floor."

I nodded and made my way up. I trod on each one as if it could be trapped, and remembered how, as a kid, I'd believed that ninjas walked by placing the ball of their feet down first, then twisting the heel off to one side. I'd never asked why, but had crept around like that all summer in sixth grade.

I resisted the urge to do so now, and instead reached the bend and peered around it. I could hear voices. Not the quiet murmur of companions debating their next move, but loud statements of two different parties addressing each other. Curious, I climbed higher till I could peer over the topmost step, and gaped.

The grand hall was utterly unlike the dismal, brutal first floor. Gone were the rough stone walls and gloomy lighting. The vast chamber into which I peered was cavernous, brilliantly lit with buttery yellow light from countless cut-glass lanterns, and decorated sumptuously with golden drapes, vividly colored tapestries, hanging bronze and silver shields, and other items of equal splendor. The ceiling was vaulted and painted bronze, and large crystals hung in the air, spinning slowly and glimmering so that everything was covered by wondrous sparkles.

The Beggars stood in a group before a bald child whose lower body was encased in a ball of mud and who floated above some kind of slowly exploding golden throne that cycled endlessly through a variety of geometric shapes. A dozen sourceless flames revolved around the child, who was listening to Vanatos address him.

"…in opposition to you. However, you seem inflexible on this point. Know that this road will lead only to your perdition."

The ball of mud opened itself in a vertical slit, revealing a writhing interior akin to the unhealed flesh beneath a scab, edged with teeth and disgorging a long tongue that flopped about idiotically as it spoke. "Gracious healing and boredom, tempt not the foulness in the air, it squeezes about your head and inserts itself into your head cracks, crushing, crushing your very sense of self. Toys are made for breaking."

The voice was at once lascivious and amused, and clotted up as if spoken by someone with a throat filled with phlegm. The boy's head atop the sphere of mud blinked owlishly but did not otherwise comment.

Vanatos raised his chin, mouth thinning into a slit. Balthus leaned in to whisper in his ear, and I took the opportunity to retreat back down to the entrance hallway.

"So?" asked Falkon. He and Michaela were blessedly normal compared to what I'd just seen.

"The Beggars are in the grand hall talking to some crazy mudball child. It looks like they're trying to reason with it, but it's not working."

"Perfect," said Michaela. "Then we wait here for the outcome."

A shout came from above, quickly followed by what sounded like tearing flesh. We all startled, and then flinched away from the keep's front door as the roiling shadows coalesced into a slab of solid obsidian.

"What the hell?" Falkon stepped up to it, hesitated, then rapped his gauntlet on the black surface. "Solid rock."

More shouts, and then the very walls and floor of the keep shook as if from a palpable blow. I activated Detect Magic. The door radiated powerfully with necrotic light. "Looks like we're locked in with the Beggars," I said. "I might be able to get us out with Shadow Step, though."

"Save your mana for now," said Falkon. "Let's see how the fight's going."

At that moment Lotharia's face emerged through the wall beside us, pushing through as if the massive stones were but water, ripples flowing eerily away in every direction. Her black hair was slicked back as if by an excessive amount of gel, and the silver band she always wore across her brow was missing. Her face was pale, as if bloodless, and her eyes were jet black. "Too late," she whispered.

"Lotharia?" I stepped forward, unsure of myself, wondering for a second if I could reach into the rock and pull her free. "That you? Too late for what?"

"The hole in the wainscoting has been blocked, the crack in the basement filled, the gaps under the eaves choked with rotting flesh." Without an iris and pupil it was impossible to tell whom she was looking at, but the slick surface of her eyes gleamed as if her eyeballs were turning from side to side. "The door is locked and the windows barred. There is no way out till all are dead."

"Hoo, boy," said Falkon. "That doesn't sound good."

"Lotharia — is this you? Are you in the wall?" I avoided the others' glances but I had to ask.

"This is me as your shadow is you, a fragment, a figment of a broken collective. No, this is not me. That me is dead."

"Agreed," said Michaela. "Not good at all."

The keep shook again, and a scream echoed down the stairwell, followed by a thunderous crash like a building toppling over.

"Lotharia, where are you? How can we get to you?"

"All roads lead to me. I am the center of the web. The shortest distance between two points is to fold the paper and punch a hole, but here that means tearing me in half. I'm sorry, Chris. Come to me and die."

I ran my hand through my hair. "You're the center of all this? What are you saying?"

"This keep is but a shell that contains broken multitudes. A labyrinth filled with madness. My arrival drove Xylagothoth to join with me. We are both greater than the sum of our parts. We hunger. Come to me, Chris. Free me by allowing me to consume you."

And with that, her face withdrew into the wall.

"Freaky deaky," said Falkon. "How about we say 'no' to that invite and come back tomorrow?"

The keep shook again and dust sifted down upon us. The sounds of fighting were even louder; the clash of weapons, the hoarse bellow of curses and commands.

"I don't think we can," said Michaela. "She made that quite clear."

I gripped my Void Blade tightly. "No way out until we're all dead or we defeat this Xylagothoth. It was listed as the owner of the keep."

"Can we let the Beggars do the heavy lifting?" asked Falkon.

Lagash the orc warrior was thrown into view. She crashed into the elbow of the stairwell above us, bounced off the wall and dropped to all fours. The three of us stared, stunned into silence, while she growled, shook her head, rose unsteadily to her feet then charged back up.

"Uh," said Falkon. "Maybe this one's too heavy for them."

"Come on," I said. "I don't think we can sit this one out. We're going to need allies. Hurry!" Void Blade in hand, I charged up the steps.

14

I RAN UP TO the bend in the stairwell and peered into the
grand hall. It was now brilliantly lit up, ropes of golden flame
rising from the top of each cut-glass lantern to arc under the roof
into a swirling mass of incandescent fire. The crystals reflected
and refracted this light in revolving motes that danced over every
surface, and when one passed over my hand it seared my skin.

I hissed and drew my hand back, but instead of retreating, this
only convinced me to climb higher up the steps. Spindly crab legs
had emerged from the bald child's muddy sphere to stab down
at the floor, elevating it to a height of around three yards, while
a ferocious array of serrated pincers and claws had punched out
of its side. Its vertical maw was disgorging struggling shapes contained within amniotic sacks, and the boy's head was screaming
incoherently in something akin to pain or panic.

The Beggars were besieged by a small army of half-crusta-
cean children, each complete with a scorpion stinger and still
dripping with birthing fluids. These children were nauseating to

gaze upon, all of them screaming like the original head, and all of them moved with lightning-fast staccato speed, leaping like facehuggers right at the Beggars.

Vanatos had summoned his angel, who was raking the ranks of the scorpion children with blasts of golden light while Balthus struggled to replace the wards around his companions that kept getting torn asunder. Lagash was the only one directly assaulting the mud fiend, dodging and striking at it from amongst its huge legs, while Delphina and Makarios fought to throw blasts of magic at it that had little effect.

In short, it was a shitshow I had no business in entering, but if the Beggars lost this fight we were all doomed. The sheer amount of lighting banished all the shadows, severely limiting me. Damn, but the light-quenching spell Evensong would've been useful right now!

No time for regrets. Gritting my teeth, I raced forward, running around the bulk of the massed scorpion children to circle around toward the mud fiend. One of them caught sight of me and veered in my direction, skittering at me with terrifying speed and then leaping for my head. I almost triggered Adrenaline Surge, but held off; its cooldown would kill me in here.

My every instinct was to dodge, but instead I gripped the Void Blade with both hands and slashed at the scorpion fiend just before it hit me, cutting it in two so that each half flew past me in a welter of milky blood. I kept running and activated Expert Leaper, taking off just moments before two more sprinted at my legs. Midair I activated Ledge Runner, and purposefully abused the power by trying to train it on one of the beams of fiery light that ran from a lantern to the central sphere of fire.

My boots pulled up toward the beam, and for three delirious seconds I ran upside down over the horde below, and then
the talent lost traction and I fell. My ridiculous dexterity kicked
in, however, and I turned my fall into a tumble so that I hit the
ground rolling and came up before the mud demon.

Lagash roared as she parried a huge claw, knocking it aside
with a sweep of a stone falchion. Then she leapt at the monster,
slamming both falchions down upon its muddy side with such
force the fiend actually staggered back, its multitude of crab
legs scrabbling for purchase. A huge claw closed around the orc
warrior, its serrated edges punching into her gut. Her blood burst
forth, and where it landed on the demon it burned it like acid;
the demon's vertical mouth spat out another amniotic sack and
then screeched in pain. With a flick of its claw it sent Lagash
flying to crash into a far wall.

If I stopped to consider the power of the being I was about to
face I'd lose my nerve. Just one hit would kill me. No time; no
time at all. I summoned Night Shroud upon us both, activated
Uncanny Aim and Distracting Attack as I hurled a knife at the
child's head, then Double Stepped into action.

The shadows claimed me a mere second before something
swiped through where I'd been standing – did it have Darkvision as well? Then I was spat out high above it, falling with a
mad laugh, Void Blade swooping down with Bleeding Attack
added for extra juice.

The child's head snapped up to look at me. Its screaming mouth
spread grotesquely wide as it spat forth its tongue which elongated like a spear, streaking up toward me. Before I could Double
Step away it hit a concave barrier of green light that flickered

into life around me – Michaela's Unholy Ward. I swiped my Void Blade through the tongue, severing it but missing my attack on the head. A claw whipped around as I completed my Double Step, appearing behind the child's head once more and stabbing at it with my blade.

The mud fiend leapt straight up at me even as I fell toward it. One moment it was stationary, the next it was surging right up at the vaulted ceiling and ropes of fire. My blow was thrown off; Michaela's Unholy Ward flared and then shattered, and just before I was crushed against the ceiling I Double Stepped away.

This time, I purposefully emerged on the edge of my Shroud, and took off sprinting through the mass of scorpion children, activating Adrenaline Surge for what would truly be a suicidal move without it. My feet took flight and I blew through their midst, dropping two Night Shrouds as I went. A line of fire opened up on my thigh, something stabbed into my calf, then I was amongst the Beggars. They stared at me, shocked, but I had no time for them – I wheeled around and cast Grasping Shadows on the mass of Night Shrouds and all the scorpion fiends contained within.

The enemy had been momentarily thrown off by the cloying darkness, but just as they were gathering their wits hundreds of small arms reached out of the shadows to clasp them by the arms, tails, and necks. Shrieks of frustration erupted as the scorpion creatures fought and bit and clawed at their constraints.

"Hurry," I gasped, turning to the others. "I've got them locked. Focus on the boss."

Vanatos gave a curt nod and the angel flew higher, interlocking four rings so that a blast of searing golden light flew straight into the mud demon's body, carving entire chunks of its corpus away. The cuts in my legs were ridiculous painful, but my periapt was already flooding my system with healing. Grunting, I moved into the closest Shroud and completed my Double Step into the Shroud that now lay behind the mud fiend. As I emerged, I saw that it was charging away from me toward the Beggars. Falkon was helping Lagash to her feet. Michaela was still in the stairwell, throwing Necrotic Bolts at the demon.

A massive bolt of flame zigzagged its way from Makarios' fist into the fiend's side, sending huge amounts of mud splattering but failing to halt its charge. A revolving circle of runes appeared around the child's head only to be sucked into its mouth.

I had moments left of my Adrenaline Surge. The mud demon charged through the first Shroud covering its children, high enough that it could wade through without being completely submerged, and I took the opportunity to cast Ebon Tendrils. I directed my tentacles to grasp the fiend's crab legs, and it tripped, knocked off balance, and crashed down to one side.

The angel unleashed another series of bolts upon the demon just as Lagash and Falkon charged into its side, blades whirling. Makarios fired off another bolt of fire just as Michaela caused a mass of writhing maggots of virulent green electricity to erupt around the fiend's body.

Adrenaline Surge crashed and nausea wracked me – until a revolving circle of soothing blue runes appeared over my head. It sucked the pain and sickness out of me, neutralizing the cooldown. Never had I been so pleased. I ran forward. The Beggars and my friends were pummeling the mud fiend, reducing its bloated body to torn gobbets of muddy flesh. It tore its legs free of the Tendrils and tried to charge once more, only to have two legs hewn out from under it by Lagash. Falkon let out a roar that lifted my spirits a moment before he fended off a claw that was about to swoop down on the orc, and then I was in the Shroud, racing past the nd, swiping out at its legs with my shadow-formed Void Blade as I went.

I cut through four legs before I emerged out the other side, my blade not severing the legs but passing through their chitinous exterior as easily as a breeze, causing them to buckle beneath the fiend's own weight. It fell again onto its side.

I turned, panting. The angel overlapped all six of its circlets and, with the sound of a full cathedral choir in song, it disintegrated the child's head.

The mud demon sagged onto its side and went still, and the scorpion children deliquesced into milky pools of goo.

After a moment, I dispelled my Shrouds and turned to check on Falkon and then Michaela, assuring myself that they were fine. Falkon gave me a shaky thumbs up, while Michaela visibly forced her shoulders back and lifted her chin.

"Unexpected," said Vanatos, turning toward me. His angel lowered to hover just above and behind him, its scarves and golden rings undulating as if underwater. "To what do we owe this unexpected pleasure?"

"She's losing a lot of blood," said Balthus, voice grim. He was kneeling beside Delphina. A cut had opened her from clavicle to hip.

Vanatos half turned to consider. "Can you save her?"

"We'll see," said Balthus, and wove webbings of runes over her wound, muttering and flicking his fingers as if knitting them into place.

Falkon and Michaela stepped up alongside me. Their presence bolstered my own confidence. "If she needs healing, I can help."

Vanatos raised a perfect eyebrow in polite disbelief. "A dark-blade with the capacity to heal?"

"No, a darkblade with a periapt of healing." I pulled it over my head and extended it to him. "Here. Put this on her."

He hesitated, eyes narrowing. "What's your angle here? What's going on?"

"Take the damn periapt," said Lagash, voice a low snarl. "She's fading. Fast."

Vanatos did so, gloved hand closing delicately about the arti-fact as if expecting a trap, then holding it back out to Balthus without turning to look at him. Nobody spoke as Balthus slipped the necklace over Delphina's head. The effect was immediate; the circling runes brightened and began to spin faster, and Delphina gave a sigh of relief and settled more comfortably on the floor.

"Hey, Vanatos," said Makarios from his crouch. "Why don't you ask the little shit why we don't kill him and keep his gear?"

"Language," said Vanatos. "But it's a good question. You've been a thorn in our side since we got here. Why did you risk yourself for us?"

"I think we're in this one together," I said. "The keep's been locked down. The only way out is through respawning after we've been killed."

"Is that so?" Vanatos raised his hand and made a gesture, and his angel flickered out of existence only to immediately reap-pear. He turned to it in surprise and annoyance. "Teleportation's blocked, at any rate. Perhaps he's telling the truth. Balthus?"

The inquisitor looked up from Delphina. "I'll have to see one of the blocked exits first."

"How long till Delphina's capable of walking?"

Balthus considered her wound. "Another twenty minutes."

"Very well. We won't split up. Time for a short rest. So, *Chris*." He said my name with obvious disdain. "What else can you tell us about what's going on here? How did you come by this information?"

Despite Vanatos' proclamation, nobody moved to sit or relax.

"A friend of ours is trapped in here. An enchantress by the name of Lotharia. She appeared to us below while you were fighting and told us as much. From what I could gather, she's joined with the owner of the keep. Something that goes by the name of 'Xylagothoth'. I'd hoped it was that mud baby thing, but since we're still stuck in here… I guess we're not that lucky."

"Yes," said Vanatos, "I saw its name in the Castle Winter domains list. Any idea what it is?"

"No," I said.

"Whatever it is," said Lagash, the leather wrappings of her stone falchions' hilts creaking as she tightened her grip on them, "we'll kill it."

"We're going to have to work together," I said. "That's why we came up to help. The ogres we killed were level thirty plus, and they were scared of what's in here. Had the place all boarded up. If we're to survive this, we're going to have to forget our rivalry."

"Very well," said Vanatos. "I concede that your aid wasn't negligible in that last fight. I can find use for you. However, if we're to work together, you will do so under my command. There cannot be any room for chaos or confusion on the battlefield. Am I clear?"

"To a point. It'll depend on the command, to be honest."

Vanatos' expression tightened with displeasure. "So you're to be a wildcard. That will hamper our effectiveness."

Falkon laid a hand on my shoulder. "In all honesty, it'll probably work to our benefit. Chris is at his best when he's doing whatever he sees needs doing. Let's just agree to cooperate and go from there."

"Little shit's got some moves, I'll give him that," said Makarios. "Question is, where'd he get all the elite gear from?"

I gave the battlemage a mocking smile. "Ever hear of Santa Claus?"

Makarios snorted in disgust.

"So that is why you're here?" asked Vanatos, and for a moment I thought he was talking about Father Christmas. "To save your friend Lotharia?"

"In part," said Michaela, her voice made hollow by her mask. "I work for Dread Lord Guthorios, and they've agreed to help me in my mission to pierce the ward that prevents NPCs from going below ground and discovering what lies at the heart of the dungeon."

"Guthorios, hmm?" Vanatos crossed his arms over his still-spotless white coat. "Interesting. We're allies, then. We're working for him too. Our goals are the same."

"What've you learned about what's below?" I asked. "Have you found the entrance to the dungeons yet?"

"Yes. A simple trapdoor, but it's been enchanted by this Xylagothoth. We can't open it without removing his ward, and none of us were able to dispel it. Hence our desire to kill him and end his magic."

"So our goals really are aligned," said Falkon. "We all want Zai-Zai dead."

"What do you know about the cause of all this?" I asked. "What did Guthorios tell you about how this situation came about?"

"The Beggars of Solomon have a policy of not asking too many questions," said Vanatos with a hard smile. "It makes it easier for all manner of employers to give us work. Guthorios is paying us handsomely. Toward that end, I don't really care what the quest setup is, or that this castle once belonged to the Cruel Winter guild and the treasure below has some meaning to them. To you, I suppose."

"Must make it easy to just smash and grab," said Falkon.

"Yes," said Vanatos, his smile widening a fraction.

I wasn't ready to let go. "So you know nothing about Archmagus Jeramy?"

"Just that he was the creator of the treasure."

"And you're not curious about this ward he put in place to keep Albertus and the Dread Lords out?"

"Honestly, do you question every quest's setup? Obviously it's just a means of forcing players into this adventure and explaining why the more powerful NPCs haven't grabbed it. Simple."

"All right. I guess you've got it all figured out," I said. "Balthus. How's she looking?"

"Better." He reached out and tweaked his runes, causing several new ones to incandesce into existence. "The synergy between your periapt and my magic is very powerful. She's healing faster than I expected."

"What happens if you guys die?" I asked. "None of you are in Death March mode, right?"

"Of course not," said Makarios. "Think we're stupid?"

"We respawn back in Goldfall," said Vanatos. "Without our equipment. So yes, there are some serious consequences to death for us, too."

Conversation died after that, and we simply stood around watching the doorways that led deeper into the keep while we waited for

Delphina to heal. Falkon stepped in close, gesturing for Michaela to lean in.

"By the way, this room's all wrong. It's far larger than the old grand hall. The way it is now, it should extend right out the back wall of the keep, and the ceiling's high enough to eat into the third floor. No way it's contained within the keep walls."

"Like a bag of holding," said Michaela. "Larger on the inside than without."

"Lotharia hinted at that," I said. "Something about the keep being a shell that contains multitudes. Great. Who knows how big it is now?"

"Another thing," said Falkon. "You notice we didn't get any XP for winning this fight?"

I opened my character sheet. No new windows popped up. "You're right. What's up with that?"

Falkon shrugged uneasily. "My best guess? Maybe the keep's being treated as one extended encounter. It means we won't level up while we're in here."

"Which really blows," said Michaela.

"Great," I said, rubbing the back of my neck. "Just great."

Delphina finally roused herself and rose groggily to her feet. It took her a moment to understand what had happened, and when she finally did she gave me a bleary salute. I decided to let her keep the periapt for a while longer; the gash along her side had scarred over, but was still horribly inflamed and red.

"Very well. Time to test the keep's defenses," said Vanatos, voice overly hearty. "Come." He led us down the stairwell to the front door, and there stepped aside for Balthus to move forward and inspect it. The inquisitor ran his heavy black gloves over the obsidian stone, then muttered a spell and sank a single rune into it.

"Strong," he said, stepping back. "Blocks teleportation, spirit transfer, all kinds of stuff. I'm guessing it's nearly impossible to shatter, too. Looks just like the ward over the dungeon entrance."

Vanatos hissed in displeasure. "In which case there's little point in our expending mana trying to blast our way out. Unfortunate. Xylagothoth is really starting to irk me."

"Let's irk him back," said Makarios. "Let's go irk the fuck out of him."

"Indeed. Delphina, are you ready to proceed?"

The elf curled an errant strand of hair behind one pointed ear. "I still feel a little achy breaky, but yes."

I didn't believe her. She had a perilously delicate look to her, as if she were made of fine china and would break from one solid blow. Her ashen skin was nearly gray, and her sinuous body was drawn and wasted within her armor. My periapt still glowed on her chest, however. I really wanted it back, but it would be needlessly cruel to demand it when she was in such rough shape.

"Then let's return to the second floor and resume our explorations. The way we operate is as follows: Lagash takes point, with Balthus and Makarios just behind. Delphina and I move in the following rank, with Eletherios covering our rear. I suggest Falkon join Lagash, Michaela move with myself and Delphina, and Chris – well, you've already made it clear you'll do as you wish."

"Sounds good to me," I said. "Falkon, remember you're a third of Lagash's level, all right? Don't try to impress her."

Falkon flushed even as Lagash threw a brawny arm around his armored shoulders. "Come, little man. Let's go find danger."

"Little man? First, I'm not even a dude—" I could hear Falkon protesting half-heartedly as the pair of them climbed the steps. I decided to come right after, moving ahead of Balthus and Makarios.

We tromped up the steps back into the grand hall, and then walked down its glittering length to a broad doorway in the back.

"This should have taken us to a private meeting room in the old keep," said Falkon quietly. "Now? No idea."

I did a quick mana check: eighteen points left. I'd have to be much more conservative moving forward. Lagash rolled her broad shoulders, cracked her neck to one side then the other, then placed the pommels of her falchions against the doors and pushed. Muscles coiled across her back and then, with a creaking, laborious groan, the heavy doors gave way.

15

I FOLLOWED LAGASH INTO the next chamber, which proved to be an extended hallway of great height and length. No doubting the impossibility of these internal geometries now. The floor was paved in great pale green flagstones, while the walls were draped with exquisite tapestries. A single archway at the hallway's end led to the next room. Lanterns burned with a pale, ivory radiance between the tapestries, and the air was cool and smelled of damp.

Lagash moved forward carefully, one falchion extended before her, the other raised just above her head. Balthus muttered something behind me, and a disc of spinning crimson runes flew out from under our feet to whisk down the length of the hallway and back.

"No traps," he muttered. "At least, none I can detect."

"Comforting," said Falkon by my side.

Lagash continued to pace forward, and I took the opportunity to glance at the tapestries. I'd grown up on enough fantasy fare to half expect the creatures depicted within to animate and attack, but mercifully they stayed still.

Mercifully, because they were a particularly horrendous bunch; if anything, they looked like fan art created by Lovecraftian aficionados. The tapestries depicted great cyclopean rooms in which strange, tentacled monstrosities lurked. There was something Dali-esque to it all, or maybe more accurately Escher-esque, as geometries and gravity were all broken and strange, such that different creatures stood on different walls, or bled around corners, or transposed themselves through each other. My gorge rose and mouth flooded with sour saliva as I tried to figure out the images, so I tore my eyes away from the tapestries and focused on the hallway once more.

"Look," said Delphina from the back. "Aren't those the xythagas we fought downstairs?"

She was gesturing with a curved dagger at one of the tapestries, where a dozen of the spider goblin creatures hidden in the shadows of a vast room in which a shoggoth-like travesty heaved itself out of the wall.

"And there," said Michaela, her voice a whisper. "The mud child we just fought."

"A regular rogue's gallery," said Vanatos.

"I hope not," I replied. "That'd mean there's a chance we'll be fighting some of these other horrors."

No one responded. Instead, we followed Lagash all the way down to the archway, and out into a T-junction hallway which extended into the gloom in both directions. Lagash grunted and turned right, and since nobody gainsaid her I simply followed behind Falkon.

The silence was unnerving and absorbed the sound of our footsteps. The air had a thick, underwater feel to it, and the lantern light here was tinged a faint green. Lagash stopped at the first doorway. We gathered around her, and when she pressed it open with the hilt of a falchion I tensed, ready for violence – only to see the inside of what seemed to be a broom cupboard.

"Huh," said Falkon. "I guess even Zai-Zai needs to clean up every once in a while."

We moved on to the next door, which opened into a library. Or many libraries. With lay an elegant room with floor-to-ceiling bookcases – minus its ceiling. Instead, another library room had been dropped atop the first, and this higher one turned on its side. Looking up, I saw a bookcase across what would have been the ceiling of the second room, but none of those books were affected by gravity. Furniture appeared to stick to the wall directly above our heads. Its 'ceiling' was also missing, with a third library attached to it, leading out of sight ahead of us.

"We go in?" asked Lagash, turning to Vanatos.

"Let me send Eletherios to take a look," he replied, and the angel slipped by us to float up into the room, spinning in place as it took in the warmly lit environs and then rising to the second floor. I craned my neck to keep it in sight, then watched as it flew forward and disappeared into the third room beyond.

"Can it communicate with you while out of sight?" asked Michaela.

"Alas, no." Vanatos rubbed his thumb into the palm of his other hand. "It must be close for us to communicate."

The seconds crawled by, and then Eletherios retreated into view, flying hastily and with several thick slashes lacerating its body. These healed as it descended toward us, and it turned to regard Vanatos.

"The rooms continue," Vanatos said. "Looks like a warren of them, with branches bifurcating and then splitting again, becoming a small labyrinth. All the rooms alike. Some kind of spider beast lives up there. It threw gusts of wind at Eletherios that cut like an ax."

We all exchanged glances.

"Shall we come back to this one?" asked Falkon. "Find something a little less daunting?"

"I'd vote for that," said Delphina, her voice robbed of its usual mockery.

"Very well," said Vanatos. "We'll come back if we must."

The next door opened onto a small chamber whose walls were lined with mirrors.

"No," said Lagash, closing the door firmly. "Never go into a room full of mirrors."

"Agreed," said Balthus, voice low.

"At this rate we're not going to go into any room," snarled Makarios. "What is this, a sightseeing tour?"

"There's no real rush," said Vanatos. "Let's proceed apace. We can always return."

I turned to continue down the hall, only to see that a door had appeared just a few yards beyond, truncating its seemingly endless length.

"Um," I said. "Did I somehow miss that door before?"

"No," said Lagash. "It's new."

Balthus rubbed at the side of his stylized skull mask. "Which means the keep is changing around us. Not good."

"Shall we knock?" asked Falkon, looking to Lagash. "Want me to?"

"Move back," said Lagash, her tone flat and hard. Nobody argued, all of us shuffling away as she examined the door, sniffed at it, then levered the handle down with the tip of a falchion and pulled it open.

"Watch out!" bellowed Lagash, crossing both falchions before her as a heavily muscled man burst through the door, a hand ax in each hand. His head was completely encased within a horned helm of dull iron, huge wire mesh bulbs extruding on each side like insect eyes. His skin was gray, and he was muscled in the manner of real laborers, compact and massive and without an ounce of fat. His lower half was armored in overlapping black plate, and a huge shaggy fur draped down from his waist so that for a moment I mistook him for a satyr-like monstrosity.

His first ax crashed down on Lagash's crossed blades while the second came sweeping in from the side. Falkon lunged forward to parry it, but a second man came out from behind the first, his helm spiked and insectile, a spear clenched in both hands. He stepped up alongside his companion and thrust his spear's head deep into Falkon's side. Falkon screamed and fell back.

There were more of them behind the first two, a shadowed crowd right within the door. Lagash roared and threw the first back, knocking him onto his heels so that he stumbled into those behind him, and then Michaela shouted and a shield of faint green light flickered into being between us and them.

The helmed warriors immediately began to hammer at the Unholy Ward, which looked like it was about to collapse till Balthus threw out his hand and a spinning vortex of blue runes burst into being and embedded themselves in Michaela's magic.

"Falkon?" I pulled him back. He drew his hand away from his side. It was dark and wet with blood. "Delphina! Give him the periapt!" I shoved him back, past Balthus and Makarios.

"On my count," barked Vanatos, "drop the shield. Makarios, to the front! Thunderstomp, then fall back. Anyone with a ranged attack, let loose as soon as the enemy falls. Everyone else against the walls. Michaela, Balthus, prepare to throw the ward back up if we fail to rout them!"

The helmed warriors were bellowing as they attacked the curving green wall, throwing themselves at it in a barbaric frenzy. Each blow caused white cracks to flow out, only for Balthus' runes to seal them over.

Makarios elbowed his way roughly past me and then more carefully past Lagash, and then turned to nod at Vanatos.

"One!"

Should I summon my Grasping Shadows? No. I needed to conserve my mana.

"Two!"

An ax blow shattered through the ward, emerging in a shower of green sparks.

"Three!"

The ward fell and Makarios stomped his foot, unleashing a thunderous blast of power and energy that he fortunately directed away from us. The helmed warriors before him staggered, most falling to their knees or lurching against the hallway walls. Scores of them were lined up beyond the door, weapons raised, eager to join the fray. They shook and fell about, and then Vanatos screamed:

"Fire!"

A massive bolt of golden light blew past me, accompanied by the deafening sound of a heavenly choir run amok, while

Makarios unleashed his flaming blast and Michaela threw her own Necrotic Bolt. They slammed into the front ranks, causing the helmed warriors to blow apart in a welter of gore, arms severing from shoulders, chests exploding, heads vaporizing despite their helms.

The hallway before us emptied of combatants, but a roar from beyond the door rose and more foes overran their fallen comrades to charge at us from the shadows. Almost I cast Ebon Tendrils, but I checked the impulse.

"Again!"

Once more the blast of fire and gold, the green Necrotic Bolt. Another dozen warriors collapsed, falling apart in sprays of red. Corpses lay just beyond us now at knee height.

More shouts, and a third wave came charging out, axes and spears held high, completely undeterred.

"Again!"

This time, Eletherios kept his attack up, raking the hallway from side to side with his heavenly blast, the choral song rising higher and higher in pitch. It illuminated the corridor beyond, and what I saw chilled me to the bone: his beam cut down scores of warriors. A vast crowd choked the passageway, receding into the far distance, pressing forward to attack.

"Wards up!"

Michaela's green shield flickered into place, reinforced immediately by Balthus' runes.

Lagash leapt through it, straight at the oncoming tide, her powerful thighs working as she muscled through the corpse-choked hall.

"Lagash! Get back here! Now!" Vanatos' bellow was colored by something akin to panic, but the orc warrior ignored him. She grasped the open doors, and with a mighty roar forced them to close. Bodies and limbs slid before them, and her whole body shook as she wrestled against the weight.

Eletherios shot a beam no wider than my wrist over Lagash's shoulder to drop the closest warrior. A moment later and the orc somehow forced the doors closed, then turned and pressed her back to them.

Powerful thuds and thumps sounded from the far side, jostling Lagash where she stood. Falkon ran up to press his shoulder against the door beside her. For a few moments more the thumps sounded, then everything went still.

Nobody moved. We stared, waiting, and then finally Lagash stepped back, turning to regard the doors.

"The doors are thick with magic," said Balthus. "As long as they're closed, it seems the warriors cannot pass."

"Let's keep 'em closed, then," said Makarios. "I'm starting to run low on mana here."

"Agreed," said Vanatos shakily. "Good—good thinking, Lagash."

The orc gave her leader a flat stare, then looked away.

"Looks like a dead end, then," I said. "So either the mirror chamber, the library maze, or we try the other corridor. I vote for the latter. Thoughts?"

"I'm with Lagash," said Falkon. "Avoid mirror rooms."

"I've no desire to climb around a library maze," said Balthus pensively. "Vanatos?"

"Back," he said, then, in a firmer voice, "We need to bring the fight directly to the main enemy, not waste our resources on his pets. Let's try the other fork."

We resumed our formation. Falkon moved to stand before me, but I pulled his arm aside. The wound was still grave. "Why don't you hang back till that patches up?"

He grimaced, glanced at Lagash, then pressed his arm back to his side. "I'm fine."

We moved back past the doors to the fork, then proceeded down it till it passed through an archway into a large feasting hall.

Two long tables ran down its length, each with a full complement of warriors seated down their length. A third table completed the horseshoe shape on a raised dais at the back, and at this table's center sat a massively armored warrior in monstrous full plate. He shouldn't have been able to move under all that iron, and when he did the metal scraped against itself horrendously.

Flames leapt high from a massive firepit in the center of the room, and support beams of intricately carved wood arose behind the tables to hold up the raftered roof. The warriors all had the look of seasoned fighters to them, bearded and broad-shouldered beneath cloaks of wolf fur and with their weapons set by their side.

Vanatos stepped forward, gaze locked on the massive knight seated at the end of the room. "Greetings. Apologies if we interrupt your feast."

The knight rose to his feet, shoving his throne back. He was a beast of a man, seven feet tall and with room inside his armor for three regular-sized people. His helm had the classic 'Y' slit down the front, with more grooves cut alongside his cheeks that gave him the appearance of a skull, while a bear's skin fell from his shoulders, further increasing his size. Bronze runes were inlaid across his armor, and the haft of a spear was propped against the table by his side.

"Well met, interlopers," said the knight, his voice gravelly as if he'd been gargling on flakes of rust after a lifetime spent chain-smoking raw tobacco. "If you wish it, you may be seated at my table and feast upon my food. Swear allegiance unto me, and you shall be gifted with life everlasting."

Vanatos gave an apologetic smile. "Thank you for the hospitality. If possible, however, we would rather be on our way."

We were all crowded within the great door. Lagash had the foresight to ease her way in and step aside so the wall was to her back, but the rest of us were bottled up. Rather than contribute to the problem, I did the opposite of Lagash, stepping out of sight and behind the archway's left side. I caught Michaela's eye and nodded; she then did the same.

"You refuse immortality? Seated here are the finest heroes to have graced the lands of Euphoria. The bravest and most bold. You would turn down the chance to join their ranks?"

"We seek not to feast, but to find our prey. Now, my thanks once more, but we must insist on passing through."

I itched to watch, but caution prevailed. I was the only one here in Death March mode. Whatever happened, I'd know soon enough.

"Very well. It grieves me to hear your refusal, but I shall not contest it. Come. Make your way through my hall."

I could see Vanatos' back from where I stood. He rocked from his heels to the balls of his feet. He was clearly as suspicious as I was. Balthus murmured a spell, and Delphina did the same, whispering to herself as she knitted a cat's cradle of glowing green lines between her fingertips.

"Thank you," said Vanatos at last. "We seek the one that calls himself Xylagothoth. Do you know where we can find him?"

"I am not familiar with the name."

"Do you know what lies beyond your hall?"

"Only lesser experiences."

"Very well," said Vanatos. "Then we shall proceed."

Eletherios ducked its head and floated into the room, rings almost overlapping as if ready to fire at the slightest provocation. Vanatos stepped forward, leaving my line of sight. Footsteps joined his own, and I surmised that Lagash and Falkon had fallen in behind him. Balthus and Makarios moved into the room next.

I took a breath and stepped into the doorway. Over forty warriors sat along the lengths of both tables. The great black knight yet stood at his solitary table, his gauntlet closed around his large spear. Vanatos had stepped to the left, intent on following the wall to the sole other doorway.

The knight hefted his spear at the precise moment Vanatos moved behind one of the support pillars.

"Watch out!" I yelled, my voice overlapping with those of Lagash and Balthus.

Vanatos had the wit to freeze in place, but faster than I'd have ever believed the knight hurled his spear straight through the column. It smashed its way through the wood, sending splinters and shards flying, and then burst through Michaela's ward and buried itself in Vanatos' neck, lifting him off his feet and slamming him into the wall where the spearhead impaled itself in the stone.

Chaos erupted in the feast hall. The forty warriors screamed with bloodlust and leapt to their feet, snatching up their weapons and knocking over their benches. Overhead, Eletherios disappeared.

I dropped a Night Shroud on the table closest to Falkon and Lagash just as Makarios summoned his fire web, filling the hall with filaments of fiery orange and crimson. Lagash and Falkon's charge faltered as their closest foes were enveloped in darkness, but a moment later five warriors burst free of the shadows to attack them.

The urge to blast through my mana was nearly overwhelming, but instead I forced myself to calm down and observe. I was down to sixteen points. I had to make each one count.

The huge knight pulled another spear from the shadows and lifted it to his shoulder, sighting with unerring accuracy at where Lagash fought.

Warriors were running toward where I stood with Balthus, Makarios and Michaela in the doorway, weaving their way through the flaming strands, screaming in fury where they failed to negotiate a path.

Time to act.

I dove into my Shroud and then Double Stepped. A second later I emerged, crouched in the shadows behind the vast form of the knight. He drew the spear back, armor scraping and creaking, and I lashed out with my sword, activating its shadow ability to cut through his knee.

My blade passed through his leg like a breeze and the knight grunted and staggered, dropping his spear as he caught his weight on the broad table, which buckled and nearly broke. He was fearsomely fast, however, and swung a massive gauntleted fist down in a hammer blow toward my head.

No thanks.

I completed my Double Step and emerged back within my Shroud, crouched beneath the feasting table. A crowd of warriors bulged around the doorway. Michaela and the others had retreated to make it a choke point, but none of them were front-line fighters or tanks. A quick glance showed me Lagash was more than holding her own, hewing down her assailants with insanely vicious blows, Falkon darting out from behind her to parry or stab at her opponents as the opportunities presented themselves.

I raised my fist at the twenty or so warriors hacking at Michaela's ward and whispered, "Blammo."

A torrent of wind poured out from my Ring of the Bull and hit the back of the crowd with hurricane force. Warriors were lifted off their feet and thrown into each other, crushing those unfortunate enough to be standing by the wall. In a cacophony of crashing metal and cursing they collapsed to the ground, and then I was out from under the table, Void Blade in hand.

I simply held the blade's dark, shadowy edge down at a diagonal as I raced around the outer edge of the fallen group, allowing its tip to pass through helms, pauldrons and breastplates. Men screamed, jerked, and died. I dodged around a flaming tendril of fire only to come face to face with one of the enemy that hadn't fallen. He roared, spraying spittle, and swung his blade at my head.

I had barely enough wit to phase my blade back into its solid form in time to parry. The force of the blow numbed my arm, and I backpedaled, allowing my ridiculous dexterity to compensate for my Melee: Basic (III).

A slash got through and would have sliced open my shoulder but for a flare of blue from my armor ring; three more blocks and then he drove the point of his sword straight into my gut. My armor ring once again blunted the attack and my spider silk shirt stopped it completely, but the force of the stab knocked the wind out of me, forcing me to stagger back.

Another warrior appeared to my left and brought a warhammer down upon my head with a roar. For a second, I contemplated trying to parry, and then simply pulled the hem of my cloak over me as I fell into a crouch against the wall.

The shock of the hammer blow hit a mere moment after I willed my cloak into stone form, followed by the rasp of a futile slash. Three more blows and then suddenly they multiplied into what felt like dozens – the other warriors had no doubt gained their feet and turned on me.

My cloak was running out of mana. I was about to Shadow Step from out of its enclosing darkness when a roar filled the air, followed by a wave of heat, and then the blows stopped.

I dropped my cloak and blinked at the cindered bodies that lay around me. Makarios gave me the middle finger as he turned to search for another opponent, only to be lifted off his feet as a huge spear caught him in the chest and drove him back through the doorway as if he'd been hit by a truck.

"No!" I screamed, leaping up, but it was too late. I couldn't see him, but there could be no doubt that Makarios was dead.

I activated Ledge Runner and Expert Leaper and jumped up onto the closest table, racing down its length, my feet finding clear spaces between the bowls, platters and flagons with impossible ease. The black knight was drawing another spear from the shadows, propping himself up with his other hand, and he turned to stare at me as I ran toward the far end of his own table.

He drew the spear back. I leapt up nimbly onto his table, pivoted with consummate skill and charged him. I could see writhing sparks of green electricity playing over his body, but they had no effect. With a grunt, he hurled the spear right at my chest, and at the last moment I activated my shadow belt so his weapon passed right through me.

Then I was upon him. I slashed my Void Blade through his head as I ran past, and he jerked back and fell. I was livid, furious at myself for not having done this the first time, for only having cut through one leg instead of both. But there was no time for recriminations. I reached the end of the table and was ready to leap to Lagash's help when a wet, muscular sound came from behind me.

I spun and dropped into a crouch, nearly sliding right off the end of the table before my boots found traction. Corgi-sized black slugs were thrashing up from the fallen knight's body, erupting through the plate armor and slapping at the table with such force they shattered its boards.

I leapt easily down to the ground and stared, mesmerized, as the monstrosity tore itself free of the knight's corpse. It rose up like a construct made of pitch-black slugs that contorted their bodies to form a vaguely humanoid shape, two glowing spots of red lighting up within the slimy crevices of its head.

The room filled with cries of ecstasy and pain, and the remaining warriors – down to twenty or so – contorted and staggered as tentacles and insect legs burst out of their armpits or from under their chins or groins.

"Ssssit at my table," hissed the monstrous aberration, and it extended its arm and unleashed a firehose of slugs in my direction, something right out of *Akira* when Tetsuo loses control of his body. I screamed and vaulted over the tilted table, tumbling out of the way just before a deluge of slugs slammed into the wall behind me.

I rolled over plates and mugs, and then my Ledge Runner feet found purchase and hauled me upright just as a warrior swung his blade at my shins. I turned my momentum into a somersault, spinning over his blade, but Ledge Runner and Expert Leaper gave out right then so that I crashed down hard upon the table, cracking my chin against the wood and spilling out onto the floor.

Sheer survival instinct caused me to roll over and then scoot forward into my Shroud, where I came to a stop, trying to get my bearings. Who had my periapt? Falkon. He fought desperately beside Lagash, both pinned against the wall and facing a semi-circle of blades.

Delphina and Michaela were hidden from view, standing behind Balthus who in turn stood behind a pair of slain warriors that had turned to fight their own comrades. The pair of them filled the doorway, flickering with protective magics as they parried blow after blow.

I looked over my shoulder. The sluggoid knight-thing was massing up toward the ceiling, a column that bent forward over the table, an arm extending toward Lagash. Its form rippled and glistened, bloated with power, and I knew that nobody was going to tackle it but me.

I took a deep breath, steadying my nerves, and forced myself to focus on the boss. Its left shoulder swelled up violently, a swelling which surged down its arm in what was no doubt going to be an explosive slug attack on Lagash.

Double Step. No time to think. Through the shadows, out behind the throne, Void Blade hissing down to cut through the arm at the wrist just before the boss unleashed its attack.

It was like cutting a firehose in half. Slugs exploded in every direction, battering me as if a dozen people were hurling sirloin steaks at my head with everything they had. I crossed my arms and dropped a Night Shroud just before the sluggoid knight directed the deluge into a vicious stream at where I stood, completing my Double Step to appear on its far side a second later.

I activated Stunning Backstab and sank my Void Blade into the knight's back, the blade sliding in to the hilt. It shrieked and arched its back, but the blow had only killed the slugs my blade had passed through. Those were immediately pushed out and replaced by fresh slugs, and then the knight's back exploded out in my direction, lifting me off my feet as if I'd been clotheslined by an avalanche of cooked whole chickens.

I Double Stepped just before I was thrown clear of my Shroud, and appeared at the apex close to its head. This time I activated Bleeding Attack and hacked at its corpus as I dropped, slicing free an entire hunk of its side, the component slugs of which immediately shriveled and died.

Before it could react, I completed the Double Step and appeared high on its other side. This time I layered Sabotage Defenses over my other active buffs, and hacked the Void Blade through its head.

The sluggoid knight exploded in every direction with a roar. I was lifted up and thrown free of the Shroud, tumbling through the air only to feel a cordon of slugs tighten around my waist. I hit a table, bounced, rolled over onto my side. The slugs were a rope that sought to crush me to death; a dozen of them were interlaced around me.

My Void Blade was too long and dangerous to bring to bear, so I summoned my Death Dagger in my left hand and slashed through the crushing belt of slugs. In moments I was free. I pushed myself up to sitting. The boss was reforming itself.

How the hell were we supposed to kill it? An area of effect attack like a fireball? Did it have a core I'd missed?

Half a body flew past me, spraying gore, and Lagash screamed in defiance as she stepped in after it, stone falchions dripping blood, her body slashed and cut. I blinked. She'd somehow killed the ten warriors that had been facing her.

"Help the others," she growled. "I'll finish the boss."

Falkon staggered up, looking awestruck, and all I could do was nod. Lagash leapt atop the table and ran toward the slug column, falchions held out to each side, kicking and powering her way through the platters and bowls.

"She's a freaking force of nature," gasped Falkon. "C'mon!"

I followed him straight into full-on melee combat. We hit the rear of the other group by surprise, and I dropped one warrior with a blow of my Void Blade, Falkon's attack taking another's arm off at the shoulder.

The others turned to face us and Falkon bellowed in their faces, his cry a soul-stirring evocation: "For the king!"

Strength flooded through me and I parried the downward swing of an ax with my Void Blade, stepping in and slamming my Death Dagger into the warrior's neck. He gurgled, a tentacle lashing at my face before he fell away. Two more leapt at me, and I danced away from a spear only to take a hammer blow to my shoulder. My arm went numb and I dropped my Void Blade, which clattered to the floor.

Falkon lunged and slid the tip of his bastard sword into the warrior's neck before it could finish off the job, but my friend took a wicked cut in the side for his efforts. I reversed my grip on my Death Dagger and threw a ball of Light into the spear wielder's eyes before stepping in and hacking at his face.

A third warrior rammed into Falkon, knocking him to one knee and tangling him with my legs. I braced myself on his shoulder and went to parry the next blow only to see a bolt of green flame envelop the third warrior's head and char it down to the skull.

Michaela moved into view. Her hands had turned into fearsome claws of bone; she punched straight through another warrior's chest just as he turned to face her, and then two undead warriors moved in to protect her flanks.

With Delphina's and Balthus' support we made short work of the remaining five warriors, and like that the fight was over. Swaying with exhaustion and pain, I turned to stare at the front of the room.

Lagash was defeating the sluggoid knight through sheer ferocity. Screaming in defiance, she hacked again and again at its reforming column. It exploded outward, but she braced herself and crossed her falchions before her, only to return to the attack. Each blow spattered dozens of the massive slugs. Her strength seemed illimitable.

The column collapsed. The rest of us just stood there, gaping, as the orc warrior continued to hack and chop at what remained about her feet, bellowing in a paroxysm of rage. Finally, she straightened, sweat coursing down her features, and kicked a last slug so that it sailed through the air and squelched against the wall.

"Dead," she grunted, voice hoarse. "And stay dead."

"Holy shit," said Falkon, sinking down onto a bench. "We did it."

16

I PICKED UP THE Void Blade and sheathed it with trembling
hands. It took me three attempts to slide the sword home. My
chest tightened and the urge to laugh was bubbled up within me,
a wild laugh I knew I had to hold back.

"You all right?" Michaela stepped up by my side, hand going
to my shoulder.

"Fine." I took a deep breath, trying to swamp the squirmy sensation of post-combat terror with the sheer volume of air, then
exhaled and forced a smile. "Just… that was close. Really close."

Balthus stood surveying the hall, hands on his hips. "They hurt
us badly by taking out Vanatos and Makarios. Our lethality is
greatly reduced."

"Come on, Balthus!" Delphina's laugh was exactly the crazed
kind that I was trying to keep bottled up. "Vanatos ain't here. We
don't need to talk all fancy and in character. If we're going to die,
we might as well loosen up for once!"

Balthus turned his entire torso toward the elf, and even through the black silk mask that covered his lower face I could see his frown deepen. Before Delphina could react, he muttered a spell and flicked his fingers at her; a revolving circle of golden runes descended over her head, and Delphina let out a shuddering breath. Her shoulders relaxed, and the haunted look left her delicate features.

"I—thanks," she whispered.

"Not a problem," rumbled Balthus. "We are all of us under a lot of stress. For that matter, would anybody else appreciate a dose of courage?"

"I shit courage for breakfast," said Falkon, wincing as he sat and leaned over to examine his bloodied side. "I'd appreciate some healing, though."

The wound was fearsome. It had mangled his armor and looked to have cleaved through several ribs. I immediately moved to his side.

"You still got the periapt?"

He nodded. "It's what's keeping me going right now. Freaking wonderful. But yeah. Some more healing would be appreciated."

Balthus muttered another spell, and a revolving wheel of green runes appeared around Falkon's wound. He immediately let out a sigh of relief.

Lagash stepped up, and the sheer intensity of her presence caused us all to orient on her. Her eyes were narrowed as she searched the floor.

"What is it?" asked Delphina, a sliver of nervousness entering her tone once more.

"Gear," said Lagash. "Vanatos and Makarios should have dropped theirs when they died. They didn't."

As a group, we spun around and examined the floor, but it was immediately obvious that she was right.

"What does that mean?" asked Michaela. "That they didn't truly die?"

"They died," said Balthus. "I saw them take mortal wounds."

Delphina held up a finger. "Unless they were teleported away, and we simply saw illusions of their deaths."

"But why go through such effort?" asked Michaela.

"To demoralize us, perhaps," said Balthus.

My racing heart had slowed. The back and forth of conversation had given me something to focus on, to get past the pain in my shoulder and the realization that I'd very nearly died. "Listen up."

They turned to regard me. Balthus, Delphina, and Lagash. Michaela and Falkon.

"If they're not dead, we stand a chance of rescuing them. For all we know, they could be in the same place Lotharia is. So we focus on healing up and we press on. Let's go round. Report if you're hurt and how much mana you have left. My shoulder's busted and I'm down to a little less than a third of my points. Michaela?"

It was as I'd suspected. Everybody had burned through their resources. Balthus was nearly tapped out, while Lagash was only halfway depleted. Everyone else was roughly at where I was.

"That means we can survive maybe one more big encounter," I said. "We can't escape the keep to rest. Perhaps we can try and meditate here, set up camp."

"I don't like it," said Lagash. "This place won't let us rest. I can feel it."

Balthus grunted. "I agree, though I wouldn't mind being proved wrong."

Falkon stood carefully and swung his arm a couple of times. "I'll be ready to move on soon. Don't rest because of me."

"Look sharp," said Delphina, voice suddenly taut. "Slugs are massing."

Lagash hissed and marched back to the high table where she set about slashing at the mound of slugs that had been coalescing while we'd talked.

"There's our answer right there," said Michaela, "unless we come up with a permanent way of destroying that guy."

"Let's try and find a more defensible spot," I said. "What about retreating to the ground floor of the keep? Resting in the kitchen or pantry?"

"Smart," said Balthus. "That, I approve of."

"Agreed," said Michaela. "If the keep works like any regular dungeon, that should be a safe move."

"If," snorted Delphina. "Big fucking 'if'."

Lagash booted a final slug against the wall, then turned to face us. "Retreat?"

"Retreat," I confirmed. "Falkon?"

"Ready," he said. He held out the periapt. "Here. Heal up."

"Keep it a little longer," I said. "You're still looking peaky."

"Peaky?" he asked, eyebrow raising, then laughed. "Fine. Let's go."

Lagash marched down one of the long tables, stepping over corpses and kicking goblets aside, then dropped down and moved to the archway through which she'd entered. She stopped.

"Passage has changed," she said.

We crowded in behind her and saw a short corridor that ended in a new doorway of black wood banded with gold.

"I'm starting to think this place doesn't want us to have a good time," said Falkon.

"Told you," said Delphina.

I took another deep breath and carefully rotated my injured arm. My shoulder crunched and popped, causing me to wince. Thank Brianna for my armor ring. That and my spider silk shirt were the reason I still had an arm. "So much for that, then. You guys ready?"

Balthus punched one heavy-gloved hand into the palm of the other. "Mostly."

"Come on, then." I walked alongside Lagash to the gold-banded doorway, our steps loud in the tight hallway. The hinges were on the other side, indicating that it swung into the far room. I drew my Void Blade and nodded to Lagash, who pushed the door open with the tip of her falchion and moved inside.

The room beyond was a large, gleaming white hall, with slowly revolving columns whose surfaces were covered with shards of broken mirror. The ceiling was high above us, easily some twenty feet up, and I couldn't see the source of the glittering, harsh light that reflected off the broken mirrors and forced me to slit my eyes.

"Vanatos," called Lagash, and I saw that she was right: he stood at the far end of the room, Eletherios hovering above and behind him. Makarios stood off to one side.

It was hard to make him out in the glare, so I stepped forward, one hand raised to shield my eyes. It wasn't just the light that was making it hard to focus on him, however; my gaze kept being drawn to the slowly spinning columns and my broken reflection.

A feverish flush ran through me, and I shuddered violently. My vision blurred, then stung.

"Back," I shouted, but my voice sounded strange. "Something's wrong. Get back!"

A rushing, roaring sound filled my ears, and I shook my head in an attempt to clear it. I felt different. I was different. I no longer held the Void Blade, but rather a stone falchion in each green-fisted hand.

Shit.

Someone slammed into me and knocked me staggering away just as a thick beam of searing light slashed through where I'd been standing. My body regained its balance with incredible ease, however, and as the roaring in my mind cleared away I was suffused with a physical prowess that was exhilarating.

Holy crap. I was in Lagash' body.

Which meant—

I saw myself – my body, that is, *me* – racing away to dive behind a pillar.

Hot damn, Lagash's player was faster on the uptake than I was.

At the far end of the room Eletherios overlapped its rings once more. The glare didn't faze Lagash's avatar as much as it did mine. Makarios was racing wide, looping around to my left.

All right. A ripple of excitement ran through me. Let's see what a level thirty-one fighter could do.

I punched up Lagash's sheet as I threw myself into a forward roll, aiming to come up behind one of the glittering pillars. My leap covered some six or seven yards alone, and the roll was so soft and smooth I felt as if I were performing it on a mattress. I came up into a crouch as my sheet popped up before me. No time to dig in deep: I just needed to know what I was working with.

My back to the column, the rough edges of which rubbed against my piecemeal plate armor and furs, I studied the sheet before me. Strength twenty-four. Dex twenty-two. Con twenty-six. Hot damn!

The skills list was too long to absorb, but the talents list was slightly shorter. I caught sight of abilities like Behemoth Blow, Eviscerate, Chest Tunnel, and Tornado Cleave.

Just then, the pillar over my head exploded into an avalanche of stone chunks and mirror fragments as a beam of light as thick as my leg cut through it. I dismissed the sheet and bolted away. Makarios was almost level with me, a good twenty yards away and with two columns between us. At the sight of my approach, his eyes widened and he slammed his boot into the ground, cratering it as a wave of force slammed out in every direction.

I leapt, activating Expert Leaper in the hope Lagash had it. She did. I soared up, falchions crossed before me, spinning through the air and over the wave of force to come down in a sprint only ten yards from Makarios.

He backpedaled frantically and then slashed at the air before him with both claws to create a net of fire that snarled into life, the gaps between each fiery thread only a foot wide.

I slid to a halt, stymied. How to cross through and get at him?

"Makarios!" I yelled, my voice that of Lagash yet with cadences that were mine. "What the hell are you doing?"

"New master," he said. "Apologies and all that. Ain't got a choice. You'll understand when you join us. Now. Time to burn!"

He slammed both fists together and fired off a swath of flame that billowed through the net and unfurled around me.

I crossed both falchions before me and dove forward, feeling my shoulders and face blister, but the crossed falchions somehow caused the worst of the fire to part before me. I felt like a space shuttle re-entering the atmosphere, the heat building up, flames on all sides, then I roared and was through, powering right at Makarios, who yelled in fear and turned to run.

I somehow noticed the bolt of searing light a split second before it hit me, and threw myself into a dive just before it burned away my head. I came up right behind Makarios and slashed a falchion through his back, activating Behemoth Blow as I did so.

Makarios parted before my blade in a welter of gore. I staggered to a stop, confused, and then realized I'd cut him in two. The parts fell to the ground then disappeared, but still no gear was left behind.

I whipped around, taking in the hall. Eletherios was firing off blasts of light every few seconds as it drifted forward. Falkon was desperately dodging even as Michaela threw bolts of burning green light at it. Delphina and Balthus were crouched behind pillars.

I had to take out Vanatos. I took off at a run, angling to keep as many pillars between us as I could. A bolt of searing light flashed toward me and I dove once more, this time taking a hit across my leg that seared me as if I'd dipped it in scalding water.

My roll turned into a spill and I hit the ground hard. It didn't faze me. I did a push-up that lifted me high enough to get my feet back under me, and even with my mangled leg I powered on.

I opened my character sheet again, searching the Talents. There had to be something here. Suicide Charge. Demon Speed. Unstoppable Wrath.

I activated each in turn and swelled with bloodcurdling fury even as my legs blurred beneath me. A roar tore itself from my throat, a bellowing scream of defiance, and flame flickered about my feet as I gained even more speed.

Eletherios fired blast after blast at me, but I was able to dodge and weave with such skill that each went wide. Vanatos turned to run, not in panic but simply out of a desire to stay alive, circling around to put Eletherios between us.

A bolt of necrotic green light splashed the ground before me and I leapt over it, seeing Michaela trying to close to one side. She raised her hands and suddenly pain tore through my body as my bones shuddered within their casement of flesh. I staggered and collapsed onto my side, momentum causing me to slide a good six yards.

Growling, I fought to overcome the pain, but my bones were wrenching themselves within me, fighting my own musculature. The agony was excruciating.

Michaela's damned Bone Puppet spell, I realized. She'd somehow been turned. Could the keep control her through her bond to the Dread Lord?

I rose to my feet with jittery awkwardness and was forced to turn toward my remaining allies. She was going to force me to fight for her. I roared and tried to tear myself away, only to feel sinews and tendons sprain and nearly snap as my bones began to march.

Michaela's laughter was abruptly cut off as she was enveloped in green light, disappearing an instant later as my Chris avatar appeared behind her to slice his Void Blade through where she'd stood.

Had the keep saved her?

Immediately, the spell that had ensorcelled my skeleton disappeared. Lagash in my Chris avatar sprinted on, disappearing behind a column.

The pain faded quicker than I'd anticipated, and I scooped up my falchions as I resumed my charge toward Vanatos.

Someone came sprinting toward me and I wheeled to see Falkon as he roared and swung his bastard sword.

I blocked it with a flick of my falchion, my arms seeming to know what to do before I did, and then backed away as he attacked with everything he had, roaring his fury and slamming at me with powerful blows.

"Falkon—what—"

He grimaced and thrust his sword at my chest. I wheeled away, parrying the attack and slamming my elbow into the side of his head without meaning to. He stumbled, caught himself, then riposted with wicked ferocity.

This time I caught the attack between my falchions, crossing them into a large 'X' so that his swing was stopped cold.

"Falkon!" I shouted at him in desperation, but his eyes were wide, his gaze unfocused. Damn it! They'd gotten him as well. He snatched his blade away then came at me, slicing and slashing, low then high, trying to find a chink in my defenses.

This was Lagash, however. He didn't stand a chance. It was surreal to move with such confidence and speed when I'd never fought at this level of intensity before, but I parried Falkon's every blow, noting how he telegraphed each attack, seeing how I could easily slide my blade into him from any number of different directions as he left himself open to a counter-attack.

Yet I couldn't. His familiar face was contorted in effort, but it was *Falkon*. My friend. The thought of striking him down was abhorrent.

He screamed in frustration and then leapt, blade rising high for a downward cleave.

I sidestepped his swing, let him fall into a crouch, then slammed the pommel of my falchion into his temple.

He crumpled as a blast from Eletherios took me full in the side.

Pain. White, annihilating pain. I was lying on the ground, my arm and ribs a river of magma. I groaned and stirred, and my body on instinct activated Pain Resistance: Major (II). Immediately, the agony receded like a low tide, and I managed to sit up.

My right arm was a mangled mess, bone showing here and there, while the flesh and armor from my side had been seared away to reveal ribs. My hip was churned flesh, and blood steamed as it seeped through the cooked flesh.

How was I still alive?

I didn't have time to take in the horror of my condition. Falkon was rising to his feet, blade in hand. He blinked several times, then turned on me.

Gritting my teeth, I searched for my falchions. They lay out of reach.

Falkon lifted his blade with both hands, eyes going wide as he took in my condition, then stepped forward, teeth gritted.

I drew one of the daggers at my hip and activated Uncanny Aim and Chest Tunnel. Just before Falkon swung his blade, I hurled my dagger at him. It hit his breastplate full on and punched through the metal, disappearing into his chest and leaving a gory hole in its wake.

Falkon staggered to a stop, face pale, and his sword slid from his grip to clatter on the floor. A moment later a gout of blood erupted from the wound and he toppled down to crash upon his side.

Horror flashed through me and I convulsed, doing everything I could to reach his side. I had an overwhelming instinct to comfort him, to apologize – all irrational, but I couldn't help it. He lay staring at me, eyes wide, and then they glazed over in death and he disappeared.

With grim determination, I crawled over to where a single item had been left behind. The sole piece of gear that hadn't been his: the periapt.

My clawed hand closed around the necklace and immediately soothing warmth flooded into my body. My chest unlocked a fraction, allowing me to take a deeper breath.

Another moment's crawl took me to the falchions. I looped the periapt over my head and took them up. Only then did I survey the hall.

Eletherios had disappeared, and a moment later I confirmed that Vanatos was also gone. Balthus was striding toward a gravely wounded Delphina, who was limping away from him. I couldn't see myself anywhere, but that wasn't too surprising.

"Balthus!" My yell drew a glance from him, but had no other effect. With a grimace, I used a falchion like a walking stick to climb to my feet. The periapt was synergizing with some talent of Lagash's to heal me even faster than normal; glistening flesh had already crawled out to cover the exposed bones.

Delphina whispered something and black mist flew from her lips in Balthus' direction. He raised a warding arm and the mist faded away before it could envelop him.

I was too far to reach them in time. I drew a second dagger, activated Uncanny Aim and saw that Chest Tunnel wasn't available yet. Instead, I picked Eviscerate and hurled the blade, nearly falling over as I did so.

The dagger flicked through the brilliantly lit room. Two spinning shields of green runes flared into life and were torn apart by the dagger before it ricocheted off a third. Balthus smirked as he loomed over Delphina, but then a sphere of impenetrable darkness appeared around them both and I could make nothing out.

I hobbled forward, growing stronger by the second. The was a muffled gasp, the sound of tearing flesh, a pained grunt, and then the Shroud disappeared. My Chris avatar stood over Balthus' fallen body.

A wave of relief passed through me.

"I was too late," said Lagash in my voice.

"Too late?" I stumbled up and saw Delphina's eyes rolling up as a network of runes ate their way into her stomach. I went to pull free the periapt and then stopped when Lagash shook his head. My head. Whatever.

Delphina's eyes fluttered open. "This game sucks," she whispered, then died.

Her body disappeared, along with its gear.

I turned warily, Lagash moving to stand at my back. We slowly scanned the grand hall, and I saw Delphina appear toward the back. "There."

"She's good with mind magic, fear spells, hallucinations, things like that," said Lagash. "If we come at her from both sides we can overwhelm her."

"Got it," I said. We broke away, both of us running out wide then closing back in.

Delphina was fully healed, and probably had her mana points back. She immediately set to weaving a cat's cradle of glowing red lines, then threw the construct toward where Lagash in my body was curving in toward her. At the last moment she ducked behind a column and disappeared.

I gritted my teeth and put on a burst of speed, activating Suicide Charge, Demon Speed and Unstoppable Wrath once more. I fell upon Delphina just as she unleashed a spell upon me, causing my vision to blur and begin to fold in on itself as if I were staring through a kaleidoscope tube, but it was too late for her. I swung my falchion with grim ferocity, and she died.

A moment later, my vision cleared. Lagash emerged from behind another column, and I stared mutely down at Delphina as she faded away.

Neither of us said anything, and for the first time I was able to make out the slow grind of the revolving pillars.

"We're outclassed here," said Lagash. It was truly weird hearing my own voice. "This keep's meant for much, much higher levels. It's not just the mobs that are too tough. We're failing to understand how the keep works. How to solve it."

"Solve it?" I asked, sinking into a crouch so as to take the weight off my wounded leg. "Yeah. I see what you mean."

Lagash sheathed the Void Blade. "We already know the keep's larger on the inside than without. Which means there's no limit to how many encounters we might have to face. Forcing our way through could be pointless."

I forced myself to think, to draw on the years of gaming experience I'd accumulated, to engage the gamer mindset that had helped me overcome and outwit so many scenarios.

"You're right," I said. "I've been approaching this as if it were a real, set map. I've not been meta-gaming or thinking strategy at all." I snorted. "Just survival, really."

"Right." Lagash crouched before me, eyeing the damage I'd taken. "You could stand to think more about survival, though. I'm partial to that body."

"Yeah, sorry." I winced as I shifted my weight. "Going from my character to yours was like upgrading from a golf cart to a racing car. Your options here are pretty overwhelming."

She tried not to smile too smugly and barely managed. "You've got a decent setup yourself. I'd not appreciated how versatile darkblades are. Even in a room this well-lit you're pretty good at hit and run."

I laughed. "Whereas you seem like you can run through walls with this body. Strength twenty-four? Con twenty-six!?"

"Yeah." Her smile faded. "Any idea how we can swap?"

I surveyed the room with its revolving mirrored pillars. "Nope. Maybe the effect only works while we're in here."

"I hope you're right. I've put a lot of work into Lagash. I want her back."

For a moment, I was tempted to ask about the player. Was she a boy or a girl? What was their real name? But I set that urge aside. "That makes two of us."

"Fair enough," Lagash said. "So. Thoughts on our next move?"

I rose experimentally onto the balls of my feet. The orc body was completely healed. I felt light, lethal, and explosive. "We need to find a way to get in touch with Lotharia. She didn't appear here to fight us, and spoke to me at the start in a way that made me think she was somehow mixed up with the keep. So let's leave the room, see if our bodies swap back, then try to summon her somehow and get more answers."

"Deal," said Lagash. "What's your connection to her? You guys involved?"

"No," I said, but coming from Lagash I didn't feel embarrassed or defensive. It was a clinical question. "Not yet. I guess we were developing feelings for each other, maybe. But nothing had happened."

"There's got to be a reason she was pulled in deeper while Vanatos was just recycled as a mob," she said. "No ideas?"

"She was heavily tainted by a necrotic staff when she ran in," I said. "But then again, Michaela being undead means she was necrotic, too."

"Michaela vanished just before I could kill her," said Lagash. "The only one who did. Perhaps there's a connection there." Lagash drew the Void Blade, then nodded toward the door at the far end of the hall. "Let's see what lies on the other side."

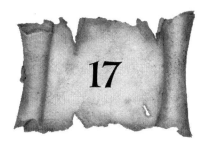

17

I STEPPED THROUGH THE doorway into the hallway beyond. It was bare and lit by infrequent torches that gave way to darkness perhaps twenty yards ahead. No doorways, no decorations.

I activated Darkvision. The hallway beyond the torchlight extended for another few yards before turning into a tunnel of unworked stone; it was as if the builder of the keep had lost hope and abandoned his attempt to civilize a cave system.

Lagash stepped up behind me and we glanced at each other, expectant. Seconds went by, and no reversion took place. After perhaps thirty seconds or so, I sighed. "Looks like the swap's not so easily undone."

Lagash twisted my face into a scowl. "I'm really starting to hate this place."

I turned back to the hallway. "You're starting to sound like Delphina. All right. I've no desire to enter that cave system up ahead. Ready for something different?"

"Let's do it," said Lagash.

I hesitated, unsure how to proceed, then stepped up to the wall and placed my hand flat against the stone. It was cool to the touch, slightly damp, and I felt the fool as I closed my eyes and tried to reach out in some way for Lotharia.

I thought of her face. Recalled the way her lips would curve when she was happily surprised. The single vertical bar that would appear between her brows when she chewed over a problem. Her laughter, her habit of chewing on a strand of hair when upset.

Lotharia wasn't her avatar. She was the player behind the image, and as such I tried to focus my thoughts on her. Tried to summon the warmth she evoked in me. The way her wry comments had drawn my laughter even when I'd been on the brink of despair. Her own secret pain that had darkened her eyes on more than one occasion.

Lotharia, I thought. *Are you out there?*

I tried to sense an answer. From the darkness behind my eyelids, I tried to envision her swimming through the stone toward me. Emerging from whatever prison she was held in. I could feel the powerful pound of my body's pulse. Became aware of the sound of my own breathing.

Focus, I told myself, and pushed past that physicality back out into the darkness, the shadows in which I'd made my home these past few weeks. *Lotharia!*

Nothing. I stepped back and dropped my hand, fighting hard to control my bitter disappointment.

Lagash's gaze was flicking from me to the wall, eyebrow raised. "And?"

"And nothing." My orcish body imparted a rumbling growl to my words. "Not sure what I was trying to do, and it clearly didn't work."

Lagash rubbed at her – my – jawline. "Then perhaps there's an angle we're not considering—"

"Chris?"

Lotharia's voice made me jump. Her face emerged from the stone, pushing through as if rising from a pool of molten lead, eyes wide and sightless, her face as pale as alabaster.

"Lotharia?"

She was staring at Lagash, of course, but turned to me, confused. "Chris?"

"Here," I said, stepping forward. "Lotharia, it's me. We've switched bodies."

"I'm fading," she said, voice quiet, resigned. "The me in Lotharia dwindles. Where are you? I can't wait much longer."

"Ask her—" began Lagash but I waved her short.

"How do we get to you?" I asked.

"I've been watching you," she said, face starting to sink into the wall. "Like mice trapped in a maze with no exit. Watching you through the walls that are your prison. In this place designed to trap another..."

"Lotharia," I said, fighting for calm. "How do we get to you?"

"I can't wait much longer," she whispered, the stone wall closing over her ears, seeping up around her cheeks. "I'm in the darkness, Chris. I'm in the dark."

Then she was gone.

"Damn it!" said Lagash. "This girlfriend of yours is fucking useless at actionable advice."

I stared at where she'd disappeared. Such loneliness. Such sorrow. The thought of her very sense of self dying away while we fumbled around in these fights was excruciating.

"Call her back," said Lagash. "And this time let me do the talking. Simple, direct questions."

"No," I said slowly. "She told us everything she could."

"Which wasn't enough," snapped Lagash. "How did—"

I raised a hand. "Wait a minute. Think on what she said."

"That she's watching us through the walls," said Lagash. "We knew that."

"No, we surmised, we didn't know. Now we do. These corridors and hallways are a maze meant to trap us. So moving forward is a waste of time. That's confirmation. We need to move out of them."

Lagash stood silent. I could feel him fighting for patience, for calm.

"At the end there. She said she's in the darkness. Waiting for us."

"Right?" Lagash's tone was strained but calm once more. "I imagine it's pretty dark inside a stone wall. How does that help us?"

"My avatar," I said. "My ability called Shadow Step. It allows me to move from one place of shadow to another."

"I know," said Lagash. "I used it to—oh."

"Exactly." I couldn't help but grin. "In the past I've not always known where to direct it, have done Hail Mary kind of moves that have popped me out in random places. Maybe we can try that."

"And use Shared Darkness to bring you with me." Lagash ran a hand through her hair – my hair, damn it – and then smiled back. "OK. Sounds like a plan. Any pointers?"

"You can kind of aim where you want to come out," I said. "Activate the power and then will yourself into the wall. With a little luck, it'll lock onto the closest darkness in that direction and take us there."

"Well, all right then. Let's kill these torches so I can save on mana. Your avatar is down to five points. Come on."

We jogged down the length of the hall, pulling torches from their sconces and grinding them against the floor, putting them out till at last we were swallowed by a darkness so absolute I could barely make out my own hand even with Darkvision. Lagash reached out to take hold of my shoulder and I drew both falchions.

She took a deep breath and the the darkness writhed. There was a moment of piercing cold, and suddenly we were through.

We emerged into a bewildering new reality. Gone were the walls, the floor and ceiling: we stood upon a massive branch of glistening silver material the size of a redwood tree that extended before us only to divide into further branches, connecting with others in a manner I could only compare to images I'd seen of neurons in our brains.

This forest of connecting silver strands was illuminated by a soft, pearlescent glow, and hung in the void, growing smaller and fading into the gloom in every direction. There was no wind, but the air was frigid, as if we'd stepped into a walk-in freezer, and my breath puffed out before me.

The sheer immensity of the drop into nothingness caused me to fall into a crouch, and I placed a hand on the silver surface of the branch only to find it sticky and cold. With disgust I pulled my hand free, dozens of strands of goo stretching from my palm to the branch only to attenuate and finally snap.

"What the hell?" whispered Lagash, slowly turning in a circle by my side. "What is this place?"

"I've no clue," I whispered back.

"Look," said Lagash. "You see over there? I can make out a hallway."

She was right. Stretching through the darkness was a shadowy corridor, translucent and barely discernible against the black.

Faint specks of light burned where torches hung, and I followed its trajectory to a large room that I realized was the feasting hall in which we'd fought.

Now I knew what to look for I saw hallways and corridors all around us, floating in the void. They moved slowly, changing their configuration, some fading away altogether while new ones appeared as if birthed by the shadows. Some held mobs within them, groups of warriors or eldritch-looking monsters standing quietly as they awaited visitors. Others were altogether empty.

"Just like she said," whispered Lagash. "A maze. We'd never have broken free."

The scope of the keep's innards was chilling. I tried to trace our path back to the ground floor with its kitchen and entrance, but kept losing the trail. Hallways branched off into new rooms, stairways descended to new levels – we'd never have been able to return.

"What is this place?" I asked, repeating Lagash's own words. "I've never seen a dungeon like it."

"Me neither," she said. "My best guess is it's a dungeon for level forty or fifty players. If I'd known this was what we were getting into I'd never have agreed to come, Vanatos be damned. Hell, I'd not venture in here without an archmagus."

"That's it," I said, standing once more. "That's what this is. A trap for an archmagus." Pieces slid into place, clicked, and I was filled with a sense of certainty. "This must be Albertus' doing. He gutted the keep and replaced it with… this, whatever it is, in an attempt to trap Jeramy. It's all just an extremely potent trap."

Lagash shook her head. "That doesn't make any sense. Why would the Universal Doctor try to trap a player? Dungeons and quests are designed to challenge and reward, not capture and trap."

"We're still trying to figure that out," I said. "All we know is that Albertus turned on Jeramy in its attempt to acquire his 'treasure'. This was part of its plan, but I'm guessing it failed, since Jeramy is supposed to be meditating within his tower."

"I still don't get it," said Lagash. "Albertus controls all of Euphoria. By definition, there can't be a 'treasure' it can't acquire. Or have created."

"Feel free to come up with a better explanation," I said. The cold and silence were getting to me. "For now, we're still no closer to getting free. None of these strands or branches or whatever they are seem to lead anywhere but into the dark."

"It's some kind of web," said Lagash, raising a foot so that sticky strands stuck to the sole. "And if it's a web, there's got to be a spider somewhere."

"Xylagothoth," I said.

"Exactly. We find it, we kill it, we get out."

I couldn't help but laugh. "Fine. As good a plan as any. So. Just start walking?"

"Unless you want to jump." Lagash moved forward, each step accompanied by a sticky squelching sound. "At least this gooey stuff means we're not likely to slide off into oblivion."

Gravity held us to whichever branch we walked along. When we reached a bifurcation and opted for the right branch that rose up steeply before us, our 'down' oriented toward the new branch's center. I quickly lost all sense of direction, but that growing concern ended when we came across our first cocoon.

It was a humanoid shaped hummock layered in sticky silk. We stopped; then, with a sense of inevitability, I moved forward and carefully used the tip of my stone falchion to slice open one end.

"Damn," whispered Lagash, crouching beside the slit and tearing it open to reveal a waxen face beneath. It was that of a young man, noble in bearing and with flaxen hair strewn across his features. He looked dead, purple around his eyes, lips white.

"You know him?" I asked.

"No," said Lagash.

"Maybe a previous victim of the keep, then," I said.

"Maybe." Lagash sighted along the length of the branch on which we were walking. "Look. More up ahead."

We didn't recognize the woman in the second hummock, nor the older man in the third, but the fourth contained Falkon. The sight of my friend's dark features reduced to an ashen pallor shook me hard.

"He should have respawned in the meadow," I said. "He died. What the hell's he doing here?"

"Trapped," said Lagash. "If that's what this place is, then death is no escape."

"For, what, the duration of his session in Euphoria?"

"Maybe."

"Falkon's player works in Euphoria's IT. If he's lost his avatar, he'll be working even now to help us out."

"Yeah, fine," said Lagash. "But remember how slowly time moves here? Help from him could be days or even weeks off."

I studied my friend's profile. Such was the realism of Euphoria, so vital and alive had Falkon seemed, that it really felt as if I were studying a corpse. With a shudder, I drew back. There was nothing more to be said. We stood and resumed our hunt.

The uniformity of the strands was numbing. Only the occasional hummock broke up the monotony of walking along their sticky lengths. I sheathed the stone falchions and strode ahead, at first eager to find some sign of the spider's presence, but eventually slowing into a trudging march. The wonder of shifting my center of gravity as I chose different branches along which to walk soon lost its novelty, and even the translucent hallways that morphed in the air before us soon became little more than a background pattern I tuned out.

What if Xylagothoth chose not to reveal itself? It could defeat us by simply hiding, allowing us to run ourselves ragged in a futile pursuit. Where was Lotharia? I searched the distant branches for some sign of her presence – a shadow, perhaps, a retreating figure – but saw nothing.

Frustration grew within me. Was it the orc's nature that was influencing my mood, or my anger alone? I wanted action. Resolution. I hated this trudging limbo. Ever since I arrived in Euphoria I'd had a plan of attack, a means to progress, whether from level to level or goal to goal. Even when Vanatos had kicked me out of Castle Winter I'd moved from one desultory objective to the next, crossing items off my list till I'd run into Brianna.

Here? There was nothing but an increasingly pointless series of decisions to make as to which path to follow. Did it matter whether I went left or right, up or down if the path itself never changed?

In a way, we'd exchanged the maze of the corridors for this open-air labyrinth of spider strands. Perhaps we needed to delve one layer deeper. Penetrate the mystery just a little further, so as to emerge in the web's center. But no matter how I racked my brain, I couldn't divine a way to do so.

My frustration continued to mount, giving rise to a restless irritability that I recognized. That I'd fled to Seattle to forget. An anger that barely hid the terror. That sensation of helplessness, of being unable to make a change in the unfolding tragedy before one's eyes.

It was all too easy to remember the waiting rooms. The strangely harsh hospital lighting; that distinctive smell of sterility, disinfectants, and ion air filters, like putting your nose inside one of those disposable latex gloves. The voices over the intercoms. The distant beeping.

Sitting in waiting rooms had changed in the end to sitting in my mother's hospital room. I'd always heard of loved ones reading to comatose relatives, staying up all night and patiently reading their favorite books, but I'd never done so. I'd felt too... empty. Horrified. Bereft. Watching my mother on that hospital bed, murmuring in pain and wondering why the doctors couldn't give her more pain medication had filled those hours with a blankness I couldn't overcome.

Instead, I'd been filled with a panicky anger. This frustrated inability to *do* anything. To make a difference. To do anything other than wait. To witness death stealing into the room, knowing that at some point Dr. Avisham would discharge her to go home and into a hospice program.

It had been too much for Justin. He'd come visit for an hour or so then catch a ride back to the apartment. I didn't blame him. He was only – what – fifteen at the time? Too much for a kid. I'd made myself stay. Made myself sleep on those god-awful couch beds, go down to the hospital cafeteria at odd hours along with the other ghosts and forlorn relatives to grab an apple or a cup of coffee.

Something was dying with my mother, something she represented. Something more than just her person. A sense of... I'd wrestled to put it into words. I'd grown up always feeling like my life was charmed. That I was destined for greatness, to be a hero, just like in my favorite books and movies. That my family was special. That sense had taken a serious blow when my father left us. But seeing my mother die?

It was too much. It was a crash course in reality. Knowing I wasn't special. That anything could happen to me. My parents could get divorced. My mother could die of such a rare form of cancer even the latest genome therapy couldn't help.

I sat there in the armchair by my mother's hospital bed. Hunched over an armrest, head propped on my hand, staring at the white sheet that rose and fell with each of her hitched breaths.

Nothing special. No hero. No charmed life. I wasn't going to experience great things. I was not different from all the other millions of people out there going about their lives. Eating at drive-throughs, watching the latest summer blockbusters, hoping on Saturday nights at the bar to touch the magic but instead stumbling home drunk and alone.

I leaned back in the chair, which stretched with a plasticky sound beneath my weight. That was our culture's biggest crime. I watched as the sheet rose and fell. Every story, every movie, every commercial and game told us we were different. Made us feel special. Did everything to make our banal lives bearable. Lied to us to keep us going, to keep us working, to keep us spending our hard-earned cash on entertainment that would only lie to us some more.

And I'd fallen for it. Well, not any longer. I took a deep, shuddering breath. The scales were finally falling from my eyes. I'd never tell myself I was special again. Never imagine myself the hero. Different from everyone else.

The door to our room opened and a nurse entered. They were always sneaking in to check vitals, adjust IV bags, press buttons, and then slipping back out. Making it impossible to rest. To sleep.

"Chris?"

I didn't recognize her. She wore a nurse's uniform, but didn't look like a nurse. Didn't have that air of brisk, professional good-will, that impersonal charm. Instead, she gazed upon me in a vulnerable, pained manner, her eyes wide, her skin pale.

"Yes?" I sat up, suddenly nervous. "What is it? Something wrong?"

"Yes – there is, but…" She bit her lower lip, glanced back out the open door into the hallway.

"What?" I glanced at the screen that revealed my mother's vitals. I'd come to decipher the numbers and graphs over the previous weeks. It all looked normal. "What's wrong?"

"Chris, this is going to sound really weird, but you have to listen to me." She moved to the door, peered back outside, then carefully closed it.

I stood, that panicky fear giving way to anger. "What's going on here? What's really weird? Who are you?"

"I'm… I'm Lotharia."

I glanced at her uniform. The letters on the name tag were scrambled and illegible. "Who?"

"Damn. I'd hoped… look. We don't have much time. The… ah… hospital director is going to come for me really soon. We need to get out of here."

OK. So not weird, more like crazy. My anger froze as I studied her. "You're not a nurse, are you?"

"No. I'm your friend. You have to trust me."

"Listen, Lotharia, or whoever you are – I'm going to ask you to leave, all right?" I tried to sound firm, to sound calm. "I don't know who you are, but you're not my friend."

"OK, wait." She held out her hands as if I were about to rush at her. "Let me think. You've seen *The Matrix*? You know when

Keanu Reeves gets that cell phone from Morpheus in the beginning, and Morpheus tells him to get the hell out of his office before the agents get him?"

I narrowed my eyes. This, I hadn't expected. "Yeah?"

"OK, well, I'm like Morpheus right now. And this is like the Matrix. You're trapped inside a virtual reality game. Your mother died years ago, Chris. This is just a memory the game has locked you into."

"Oh… right." I tried to smile reassuringly. "Just like the Matrix. Got it."

Lotharia's tentative smile fell away. "That didn't convince you."

"No," I said. "My mother's dying. This is a really, really bad time for you to be playing games here. So leave, or I'm going to call security."

"Shit. Fine. Um – I know about Justin. He's under arrest. And— damn it, most of what I know is from your future. Which makes me sound even more insane. Um."

I reached out for the phone.

"Wait! When you were little, you swam out toward this tree in the center of a flooded lake, and then you dove down and it got really dark and you thought you saw movement and you told yourself it was the devil and you freaked out and nearly drowned, but you got back to shore where your family was having a picnic and never told anybody, and the fact that they didn't even notice you were upset made you so depressed you didn't talk for three weeks!"

I froze and stared at her. "How the hell do you know that?"

"You told me," she said. "You told me in the game. Chris. You have to believe me. This isn't real. This is a trap. Your mother died five years ago. You're trapped in a memory."

"No, for real." My hands were shaking and my temple pulsed with pain. "How do you know that? Because you're right. I've never told that memory to anyone."

"I'll tell you everything, I promise," said Lotharia. "But if we don't get out of here now, it'll be too late."

"Too late?" I felt like I was drowning. Like I was back in that flooded lake. Lost and thrashing and with an unnamed evil rising to confront me. "Too late for what?"

The lights flickered and the ground shivered. A series of emergency beeps immediately sounded from the computer panel and Lotharia's eyes widened.

"Xylagothoth," she whispered. "He's coming."

18

"XYLAGO-WHO?" I MOVED to stand protectively over my mother, one hand reaching for the bed's sideguard. "The hospital director? That's his name?"

Lotharia cracked open the door and peered into the hallway. The lights flickered again, and this time a klaxon began to wail from deep within the hospital. It was pretty damn creepy, and suddenly I remembered why so many zombie movies were set in hospitals with power outage problems.

"Sure, the director. We have to go." She looked back at me. "Now."

I was torn, hovering in a state of agonized disbelief. This was just like the freaking Matrix, but—

Beads of sweat had broken out across my mother's brow. A deep, rational part of me wanted to simply refuse to believe this madness.

"Chris," said Lotharia, moving over to the other side of the bed. "Listen. We go now, or it's too late. The lake, remember?

You told me about that layer of cold water you dove into, said it was as sharply divided from the warm water of the surface as if cut with a razor?"

Cut with a razor. That's exactly how I'd thought of it, my paddling feet punching down into the icy water as I swam in the warm. I stared at Lotharia, unable to breathe. How did she know that?

The lights flickered again, went out and were briefly replaced by a red, emergency glow before coming back on.

"Think," said Lotharia. "Why aren't people shouting? Where are the nurses? The other patients? Can you hear anybody else reacting to this?"

She was right. I should have heard something from out in the hallway, but only that lonesome klaxon wailed on, along with the frantic beeping of the bedside monitors.

Lotharia moved back to the door and held out her hand to me. "I've got to go. Chris. Please. Trust me. Trust your instincts. Break free of this trap. Come with me."

Madness. Pain cut through me as if my soul were being torn out by the roots. I took a step away from my mother's bed. A second step. My body fought me. I reached out for Lotharia's hand and my mother suddenly groaned, twisting beneath the sheets in pain.

Lotharia grabbed my hand and pulled. I stumbled after her, out into the deserted hallway. The lights were doing that horror movie flickering thing and the nurse's station was abandoned. Coffee cups and pens and everything lay as if dropped moments ago, like the *Mary Celeste*. I darted looks into the rooms beside my mother's but they were all empty, sheets mussed as if patients had leapt up and ran away.

"What's going on?" I hated how scared I sounded, but I was getting pretty close to panicked. "My mother—"

"Come on!" Lotharia broke into a run, racing down the broad hallway toward the distant double doors that led out to the elevators. I held tightly to her hand and ran after, half turning back to gaze at my mother's doorway.

Lotharia skidded to a stop. A shadow had appeared in the frosted windows of the double doors. Large enough that it had to be a trick of the light.

"Back," whispered Lotharia. "Back!"

I ran after her. The double doors behind us crashed open. Again, I looked over my shoulder. Shadows flooded the end of the corridor, moving like ink in water, tendrils snaking out as if hungry for us, covering the doors and whomever had just come through them.

"That's—that's not real," I gasped. "Not possible!"

"Anything's possible in here," said Lotharia grimly. She put on speed and I was forced to look ahead as we sprinted back around the nurse's station. My mother's room was empty when we passed it, and that hit me like a punch to the gut. A flash of the empty bed and I nearly tripped, the strength going from my legs, the need to find her, protect her, be by her side overwhelming me.

Lotharia hauled on my arm and got me going again. "No time! Come on!"

Down another hallway. Lights flickering, drowning us in shadow. That wailing klaxon, right out of *Silent Hill*. Something about the darkness. Something familiar. As if, instead of scaring me, it was welcoming. Something I'd normally embrace.

We'd almost reached the next set of double doors when Lotharia fell. Her hand tore from mine, and I turned to see a snake of shadow had curled around her ankle and was dragging her back toward the seething darkness filling the hallway behind us.

"Run!" Her scream cut through my daze. "Chris! Run!"

In the movies – in Golden Dawn, even – it was easy to be a hero. To react with immediate decisiveness. Yet in real life? This shit wasn't supposed to happen. *Couldn't* be happening. I stood, frozen, as Lotharia was pulled inexorably toward the frenzied shadows advancing down the hallway toward us like a tidal wave.

"Chris!" There was anger mixed in with her terror. "Wake up! Run!"

No. I couldn't run. Couldn't abandon her. Just like I'd never wanted to leave my mother's side. Or Justin's.

Justin's? Why had I thought of him?

I blinked. Lotharia jerked another yard closer to the shadows. What could I do? This was a game, she'd said? Then where was the fucking UI, the controls, my inventory? Nonsense! I searched for a weapon, even a terminal on wheels with which to attack the shadows, and found nothing.

My whole body was shaking with adrenaline, my vision narrowing, a roaring filling my mind. Lotharia was almost inside the wall of shadows; any moment now. Run. I should run, flee the darkness—

No.

Embrace the darkness.

The darkness is mine.

I was holding something. A sword. I looked down at it in stupefied wonder. Its blade drank the light. It was sharp down one length, the side that ultimately curved up, and this sharpened slope glimmered black-blue, like the depths of the ocean. What the…?

Void Blade, a voice whispered from the depths of my mind. A shiver ran through me. *Use it.*

I yelled and dashed forward, raising the blade overhead, and brought it slicing down upon the rope of shadow that held Lotharia's ankle. It parted easily, and the blade cut several inches into the linoleum.

"Chris?" Lotharia's eyes couldn't have been any wider.

I took her hand and helped her up. "Come on!"

We backed away as a figure emerged from the shadows. For a moment it looked like a dozen shadows flickering over each other, a score of silhouettes, but then it resolved itself into a figure I'd come to loathe toward the end of my mother's life: Dr. Avisham.

Professional, disinterested, clinical, with a thin veneer of warmth and concern, the doctor had guided us through my mother's treatments right up until her final hospitalization, upon which he'd simply disappeared, refused to return our calls, and left us to wrangle the final details with the staff doctor and the hospice people.

His high brow, his distinguished beard, his eyes glittering behind his austere glasses. He'd once been so incredibly reassuring and inspiring. A figure of hope. But as my mother's condition had worsened he'd lost interest, or perhaps simply stepped away, knowing there was nothing he could do. Either way, he'd abandoned us, and so much of my anger had fixated upon him.

I'd vowed to go to his offices, after, and confront him. Demand to know where he'd been. But to my shame, there had always been a reason not to, and then I'd moved to Seattle and done my best to forget.

"Christopher," said Dr. Avisham, pushing his glasses up the bridge of his nose. "I'm surprised to see you here."

My throat dried up. A flood of emotions choked me. My old anger warred with my desire to be polite, to not alienate this man who held the secrets of life and death in his palm.

"It's not him," whispered Lotharia. "Don't be fooled."

"Lotharia," said Dr. Avisham. "You stray. Come here. Now."

Sharp, short words, and each of them caused Lotharia to flinch. To my surprise, she took a half step toward him, her face wild with fear and loathing. I grabbed her hand, and this time it was my turn to pull her back.

"I don't know what's going on here," I said. "This is some fucked up shit. But you're not Dr. Avisham. And this isn't real. So, no. Lotharia's coming with me. We're getting the hell out of here."

"Are you, now?" Dr. Avisham smiled, that cold, supercilious expression that cut me like a knife. "How amusing. Step away from her this instant, young man. Do you hear me? Return to your mother's room. That's your place. By her side! What are you doing out here? Abandoning her? What kind of son are you? Weak? I always knew you were weak. Too weak."

He advanced on us, swelling as he approached, his words punching me in the gut. "You never believed she would pull through, did you? I could tell. Read it in your eyes. Your noble fatalism. You gave up on her. And now you're doing it again. Leaving her alone to die."

"No," I croaked. The sword was gone from my hand. His words hurt more than blows, because on some level I couldn't deny them. I hadn't thought she had a chance.

"Did you do everything you could? No. Did you research, look for every experimental treatment available across the country, the globe?" His smile grew wider, colder. "No. You were passive. Pathetic. Putting all the responsibility on my shoulders. Even now you blame me, when in truth it was you who failed her. Failed to explore every avenue, every possibility."

"No," I croaked again. My shoulders were rising defensively about my neck. I couldn't breathe. My pulse pounded in my ears. "I talked with my friend. He's a doctor at Mass Central, he said—"

"It doesn't matter what he said. You gave up. Right from the beginning." He shook his head in amusement. "And to think. You thought yourself noble to sit by her side like a block of wood. When a true son, a loving son, would have been out there, moving heaven and earth to save her—"

"No!" My scream was torn from my depths, my hands twisted into claws, but my anger was shot through with horror and self-loathing. I fought to stay on my feet. Dr. Avisham loomed over me, filled my field of vision.

"Chris!" Lotharia's voice came as if from far, far away. "Don't listen to him, he's—"

Shadows swamped her and she was gone, swallowed whole like a pebble dropped into a black pond. I blinked, dumbfounded, and staggered back.

"Now is your chance for redemption," said Dr. Avisham. His tone was kindly. "Prove yourself the son you could have been. Return to her room. Take her hand. Let her know you're there for her, even now." His voice was low, relentless. "She'll recognize you. Take comfort from you. Go on, Christopher. Return to your post."

"I…" I couldn't breathe. Couldn't think. Had I been holding a sword? Hadn't there been a girl here moments ago? What had happened? I passed my hand over my face, and when I looked back up the lights shone brightly in the hallway. Nurses chattered at their stations. One pushed her cart past us, giving me a pitying smile as she went.

"Come, Christopher." Dr. Avisham reached out for my elbow. "You're under a lot of pressure. It's natural to have an episode like this. I was about to visit your mother. Let's go check on her together."

"Yes," I whispered. I let him guide me down the hallway. Something had been stolen from me. But he was right. I took a deep breath and stood straighter. Dr. Avisham had finally returned. I wanted to ask him about the painkillers, about raising the dosage so my mother could sleep better.

I went to run my hand through my hair and then stopped as I saw a small, star-shaped scar in the middle of my palm. I frowned at it. Where had that come from?

I stopped.

Dr. Avisham took a few more steps, then turned back to me. "Christopher?"

I rubbed my thumb over the scar. Where had it come from? A memory flashed through me. A knife punching down through the top of my hand, pinning it to a white tablecloth. The rattle of plates. A face snarling at me, eyes wild, a girl, a woman I was seeing – Brianna?

"Christopher?" The doctor raised an eyebrow. "What is it?"

I closed my hand into a fist. Brianna. Like a Japanese tea flower unfurling in a pot of hot water, my memories unfurled in the depths of my mind.

I shook as they rolled through me. Brianna. Our break-up. Seattle. Championships. Justin's phone call. The flight home. Applying to be a teacher. Euphoria.

Euphoria.

"Christopher?" Avisham raised an eyebrow. "Is there a problem?"

I extended my hand and the Void Blade materialized within it once more. A moment's concentration and my jeans and shirt were replaced by tunic and breeches, my Stone Cloak settling over my shoulders, my shadow belt snarling around my waist.

I smiled at him, and he took a step back.

"No problem," I said. "Just getting my bearings. All good now."

His patrician's face settled into a severe frown. "Now, this—"

A quick check. My mana had gone up while I'd been under the delusion. Had it served as some kind of twisted meditation? No matter. I was back up to twenty mana. It would have to do.

I dropped a Shroud and immediately Double Stepped behind Avisham. A moment of sweet, perfect embrace as I passed through the shadows, and then I was behind him, Void Blade swinging. I hit and he exploded with a roar into a mass of darkness even more impenetrable than my Shroud; it was as if I'd smashed a hammer into a great chimney filled with bats, which suddenly exploded out with a shattering roar.

I leapt back and the darkness coalesced into a massive figure before me, back arching just under the ceiling, huge arms with multiple joints reaching for me, each finger a Ginsu blade.

I completed my Double Step and appeared high above and behind Xylagothoth, activating Stunning Backstab as I hacked at his head. Somehow, he twisted around, reached up and caught hold of my Void Blade mid-swing, moving so fast I could barely follow. The Void Blade, insubstantial, should have passed right through his palm, but instead he stopped it cold, and where he held it the sword spat and hissed like water poured into a pan of hot oil.

Its maw curled into a grin as I fell back down to the ground, then a fist came barreling at me out of nowhere. I barely had the wit to pull the Stone Cloak around me and activate it before it hit. The world shook as if I'd been hit by a battering ram, and my cloak shattered as I was lifted off the ground and sent flying out of my Shroud back into the bright hospital light to land and skid then roll perhaps ten yards along the shiny linoleum.

I coughed, unable to breathe. My head spun and the wind had been completely knocked out of me. With effort, I rose to all fours. Xylagothoth emerged from the darkness. He was horrific. His head was part wasp, part liquid shadow, his mouth behind the mandibles impossibly wide like a serpent's and filled with fangs. His body was Protean, shifting in shape as he approached, swelling with muscle one moment before growing slender and serpentine the next. No lower half to speak of; he trailed off into shadow below the waist.

"Such a pity," he said, Dr. Avisham's voice impossibly incongruous as it issued from his maw. "I'd hoped to keep this neat and tidy. Still. Violence is its own reward."

I grunted and rose to my feet. The periapt's warmth was flooding me, and with a grunt I summoned another Shroud around the monster and followed it up with Grasping Shadows and a set of Ebon Tendrils.

A horde of arms reached up from the ground to grasp at Xylagothoth, clasping at his shadowy extremities and snarling him in their grip like wisps of hair, while the great shadowy tentacles wrapped around his waist, overlapping each other like the coils of massive anacondas.

I sprinted forward. Xylagothoth was ready for me, unperturbed by my bindings, and he spread his arms as if to welcome me into an embrace. I activated Expert Leaper and jumped up onto the corridor wall, where I then activated Ledge Runner so that my feet found purchase on the railing that ran along the wall's length. Not losing speed, I sprinted at a forty-five-degree angle along the wall

This at least took the bastard by surprise. He tried to turn, but my tentacles tightened their grasp; in annoyance, he shredded them with his claws, but by then I'd reached him. A burst of will and my old friend the Death Dagger materialized in my hand. I leapt across the hallway right before him and slammed the Dagger into one faceted eye.

Xylagothoth screamed and reared back, but I was past him, leaping into a somersault and hitting the ground where I turned on a dime and pulled my Death Dagger from his eye socket back into my hand. I activated Uncanny Aim, locked my silver thread on the wrist of the hand that held my Void Blade, and hurled the dagger.

It flew straight and true and lodged itself into the monster's flesh. His hand spasmed open and dropped my sword. I was right there, sliding forward on my knees to snatch it out of the air and then spinning as I passed under his arm to cut straight through his torso.

Xylagothoth roared and his entire form shifted, losing coherence only to reform as a massive black octopoid thing, looking half like a kraken from those old woodcuts and half like an ogre. Three tentacles wrapped around me with terrifying speed, lifted me up off the ground and slammed me so hard into the wall that I crunched into it, sinking through drywall and breaking a wooden stud.

He wasn't done. Even as my armor ring caused a nimbus of blue light to flare around me, Xylagothoth extended his tentacles, ramming me along the wall, shattering through studs and doorframes, splintering the drywall in an explosive roar. I closed my eyes as the pain began to overwhelm me, the periapt burning hot upon my chest. *Shadow belt*, I realized. *Just enough juice left—*

I activated it and immediately became insubstantial, falling through Xylagothoth's tentacles and the wall itself into an empty hospital room. My sense of self stopped my fall at ground level, but then I took a deep breath and dove down. A flash of pipes, darkness, concrete and rebar and then I was one floor down, popping out into a new hospital room. My belt ran out of power and I collapsed to the floor, gasping in pain and shock.

This room was barely formed. The walls were bland and uniform beige. A gray panel was affixed in the upper right corner, meant perhaps to be a TV but without any features whatsoever. A large rectangle held the position of the bed, and recesses along the far wall indicated where the windows should have gone.

A work in progress, perhaps. A stand-in.

The ceiling exploded as a dozen tentacles surged down toward me, and I dove out through the doorway into the hall beyond. The tentacles were like heat-seeking missiles, curving around and shooting out through the door in my direction. I hacked and parried with the Void Blade, chopping the suckered heads off the tentacles, giving ground, but they were too fast, too many: one curled around my ankle, another snagged my left arm, a third wrapped around my thigh.

A hail of icy shards burst down from the ceiling, each the size of a playing card and wickedly sharp; they scored deep lesions into the tentacles, shattered against the floor, and in a matter of moments dozens of wicked cuts had stalled Xylagothoth's momentum. His tentacles loosened their grip, perhaps in something akin to shock, and I screamed and swept the Void Blade through them all, severing them in one fell stroke.

The tentacles collapsed to the ground and the stumps withdrew. Lotharia arose from behind the nurse's station, eyes wide.

"Hell, yes!" I leapt over the counter, wrapped an arm around her shoulders and pulled her into a kiss. Her eyes widened even further and for a moment all the insanity and tumult seemed to freeze, my heart rising as if it would burst, the sensation of her lips against mine indescribably delicious - and then I broke away, grabbing her hand and sprinting down the hall, hauling her after me. "Where to? How do we get the hell out of here?"

"Outside," she yelled. "I think – if we can make it—"

The ceiling before us caved in with a pulverizing roar, dust and wiring and panels raining down as Xylagothoth fell through into a crouch, having changed now into something like an Alien xenomorph, all wickedly-oiled carapace and with a dozen kraken tentacles whipping around him.

"Lotharia…." His hiss was like nails down a chalkboard.

Her answer was to cause ice to sheathe her torso, crackling and spreading down her thighs and across her upper arms.

I backed up, trying not to cough from the dust. "We're not making much headway here. Got any ideas?"

Xylagothoth prowled toward us, using its thick tentacles to keep its body off the ground, plaster and cement crunching beneath each broad sucker.

"We need to get out," said Lotharia. "Out of the hospital."

"All right," I said. "Head to one of the rooms. Weaken the wall so we can punch our way out."

"Done." She backed away a half-dozen steps, then turned and ran.

"All right," I said, slashing at the air a couple of times with the Void Blade. "Just you and me. I can do this. No problem. No sweat."

Xylagothoth screamed and burst forward, springing off its tentacles. I leapt back, dropped a Shroud and summoned a Ebon Tendrils which arrested its passage. Down to three mana. Xylagothoth crouched, ready to throw itself forward, and I dug deep: I summoned another set of Ebon Tendrils so that four tentacles intertwined with its own, holding it fast.

The monster hurled itself forward, but it was like punching at a rubber mat – the Tendrils stretched, then hauled it back into place. It did this a couple of times, then stilled. I continued to back away. Was it giving up? Some new trick?

Its body was blacker than my Shroud's shadows, and I could make out wisps of black steam coming off its carapace. My Tendrils writhed as if in pain.

"Lotharia?" I didn't dare take my eyes away from Xylagothoth. "You ready?"

"Almost!"

Xylagothoth deepened its crouch, then let loose a horrific roar that resonated more in my chest than I heard with my ears. It surged forward, tearing through all four of my Tendrils and exploding toward me in a torrent of slavering shadow. It was like being hit by a subway train. I was bowled right off my feet, engulfed as if by a wave of oil, carried with punishing speed down the rest of the hallway and into the hospital room.

I caught a flash of Lotharia turning toward me, flinging out her hand. I reached, stretched, and managed to snag her wrist a second before Xylagothoth slammed me into the wall with such force I should have been crushed into jelly.

Instead, the wall gave way, blowing out in a mass of sandy blocks, and Lotharia and I flew out into the void.

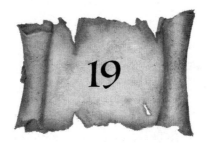

19

WE ROLLED OUT onto one of the massive silver strands, our momentum arrested by its stickiness so that we came to an abrupt stop, entangled with each other, gasping for air and struggling to rise to our feet.

"Wait, wait," said Lotharia as I fought to break free. "It's gone. Look."

The silver strand behind us extended perhaps sixty yards and then forked. There was no sign of the hospital; of a shattered wall; of Xylagothoth in hot pursuit.

"What? Where did—where did everything go?"

Lotharia blew her hair out of her face and scooted out from under me. I obligingly rolled off, and we sat there, facing each other on an impossible strand of webbing suspended in infinite darkness.

"It was never really there," she said. Her tone was careful, as if she were working out the intricacies for herself even as she spoke. "Xyla created that trap in your mind. He lulled you into it and then tried to use your own memories and weakness to hold you. Once you broke free? The trap simply stopped existing."

I pressed a hand to my temple. "Wait. Then how did you get inside my memories? How did he...?"

Lotharia gave me an apologetic shrug. "I don't understand most of this. But it was only through your memories that I could escape. I was trapped, like, three layers deeper than we are now. Really close to him, almost at the core of this place. When he rose up to enter your mind, I was able to ride along with him and enter the trap as an independent agent."

"This is some weird shit," I said. "And before? When we spoke to you, and you were all weird and cryptic?"

Lotharia grimaced. "That was the best I could do to communicate directly with you. That was... not enjoyable. It felt like a really bad trip. Half the time I couldn't even tell if you were there." She shuddered and hugged herself. "How long have I been here?"

"A couple of days now," I said. "I'm sorry. I did everything I could to come as quickly as possible. But this team of high-level mercenaries showed up, and the keep itself..."

She scooted forward and reached out to touch my cheek. "I know. I know you did. I don't blame you."

My throat grew tight. Her face was right before mine. Had I really given her a kiss in the middle of that fight? Why had I been so bold then, and now felt all locked up? "Lotharia..."

"Thank you, Chris. I don't know how much more of that nightmare I could have taken. Being in there with Xyla. Having my thoughts twisted, my perceptions warped..." She trailed off and dropped her hand. "I think he was trying to infuse me into the keep. Spread my consciousness into the walls. And it was working. I was becoming... I don't know how to put it. Like, you know how we all have a sense that tells us where our body is? An awareness of where our hands and feet are at all times? That sense was taking in the keep. I was spreading through the walls, growing ever thinner…" She shuddered and looked away.

Resolve hardened within me. "It's over now."

"We're still in here."

"Then let's get the hell out. Lagash was… where'd she go?" I rose to my knees. There was no sign of the orc. For that matter, I was back in my own body. Which meant… I didn't know what that meant. "How do we find Xyla? You said we have to go three levels deeper?"

"No. You broke free of his trap, which means you have the greatest clarity right now of any time since you entered the keep. Now's the time to strike him. He's helpless if you can avoid his snares. Come on."

We rose to our feet and hand in hand marched down the silver branch. Lotharia was right: the web did look different. Instead of endlessly splitting and fading away into the void, I saw a pattern now that had eluded me before, a circularity that homed in on what had to be the center of the web.

"What is he? Xyla, I mean?"

Lotharia gave an uneasy one-shouldered shrug. "He's… he's not a boss. I thought he was at first. But this – all of this – isn't a quest. It's one big trap. And Xyla is the keep's… consciousness, maybe?" She walked a little closer to me. "When I think of my time with him, it's like a fever dream. I can remember impressions, random images, but there's no coherency to it. I remember being awed at Xyla's complexity. And sad for him, weird as that was. I think he's been going mad in here without someone to work on. Someone to trap. The solitude's been driving him crazy."

"Is that why he took you into his core?"

"I think so. He could have just bound me here on his web, but… something about the necrotic energy I was infused with, or my personality – I don't know. He brought me down to his center of awareness and… I can't describe it. Read me? Absorbed me? I was starting to meld with him, or parts of me were, or parts of me were breaking off and entering him, leaving me…" She broke off.

I squeezed her hand. "You hung in there. You fought him off."

"No," she said. "I was defeated immediately. It was like trying to hold back a tidal wave with my hands. Impossible. But he didn't kill me, or erase me. He wanted me alive, and that's the part that reached out to you. That's… me, I suppose." She looked down at herself, then stopped. "But what if this isn't all of me? What if I lost parts of myself to him and I don't even know it?"

I turned her around and took her by the shoulders. "You're here, Lotharia. I know you well enough to tell you you're here."

She gave me a frightened smile and ran her hands through her hair. "Right. OK. This isn't another dream."

"No, it's not. We're going to get to the center of that web and we're going to kill Xyla and we're going to get the hell out of here. Got it?"

"Got it," she said, and gave me a decisive nod. "We'd best hurry, though. The longer we take, the more likely he is to trick us into another trap."

"Then let's go." I pulled her into a run, and we jogged ever closer to the center of the web, taking different forks, our up and down shifting as we did so, but moving ever closer to the nexus, the point where all the strands converged.

A cube that extruded from the center of the webbing itself, about chest high and as broad as the span of my arms. There was nothing else in the center. Glowing of runes appeared across its surface, scrolling over it and then disappearing from view around its edges.

"There," she said. "That's him."

"Huh," I said. "Like, some kind of rune computer?"

"I've no idea," she said. "But that's his physical form, if that even means anything in this game."

I drew the Void Blade. "Then let's take him apart." We stepped off the final strand onto the circular plane of webbing on which Xyla stood. The air thrummed with power, and the white runes – fuzzy as if projected from within the cube onto its inner surface – scrolled with greater speed in every direction across its exterior.

A wave of drowsiness hit me. I cracked a yawn, squeezing my eyes shut as I did so, and for a moment I saw Justin lying in a small, dark cell, staring out a window at the rain coming down on Miami, tears running down his cheeks. My heart lurched, but then I shook myself and I was back on the web.

"Enough of this," I said. I strode up to the cube and my mother appeared before me, standing on the webbing in her hospital gown, eyes sunken, hair greasy, skin ashen.

I yelled and fell back, but when she reached for me I screamed and cut through her with my blade. She faded away, trailing like mist after my blow.

"How dare you?" I stepped up to the cube. "How dare—"

Lotharia stepped between me and Xyla. "Don't do it," she said. "Please, Chris, you don't understand what's at stake. You don't understand what Albertus is trying to do. If—"

"That's not me," said Lotharia, voice cracking with panic. "Chris? That's not me!"

I looked over my shoulder at where she stood, then back to the Lotharia between me and the cube. "Sorry, Xyla. Nice try."

"Chris. Please." The Lotharia before me dropped to her knees, hands pressed together in supplication. "You think Albertus created me for frivolous reasons? You know the magnitude of his task. How the hopes of the world rest on his shoulders. If you destroy me, you attack part of his plan to save humanity. Don't do this. You don't have the understanding, the context—"

I drew back, my mind racing. "So, what exactly are you saying? I should just let you bind me to your web so you can keep lurking in this keep, catching people?"

Lotharia's features flowed and became Justin's. It was his voice that spoke: "Yes. You are one against the weight of eleven billion souls. You've strayed too far outside your own realm. Lower your blade."

"Lotharia?" I turned back to her. She was staring off into space, unseeing, tears running down her cheeks. He'd captured her. "Damn it!" I wheeled back, but Justin was gone. Instead, my mother stood before me. My mother as I remembered her from my youth, healthy and beautiful, elegantly dressed and exuding warmth and compassion.

"Lay down your sword, Chris. You've fought well, but—"

I stepped through her image and speared my blade into the heart of the cube. My mother shrieked behind me, a sound that caused my skin to crawl, but I twisted the blade, cutting a circle deeper into the rune computer, leaning in with all my strength.

A dozen different people appeared around me, flickering into existence and disappearing just as quickly. They hollered, bellowed, screamed and vanished. Stabbing pain pierced my mind and I saw flashes of my past, a torrent of memories without rhyme or reason.

I gritted my teeth, closed my eyes, and shoved harder. The Void Blade sank in to the hilt. The screams around me rose to a crescendo, a roar, like standing beneath a massive waterfall, and then it all stopped.

I stood in the keep's grand hall. Or, at least, a version of it. Much smaller, the decorations mundane, the light coming in from tall, narrow windows along the left wall causing motes of dust to catch fire and illuminating the war banners and tapestries.

Lagash sat at one of the long tables, head pillowed on her crossed arms. Scores of weapons, suits of armor, rings, amulets, and other gear was strewn across the table tops as well. Lotharia stumbled beside me, eyelids fluttering, reaching out for my arm. I caught her, pulled her in close.

"Chris? Did you—oh." She pressed the heel of her palm to her brow, then straightened. "It's over." There was wonder and disbelief in her voice. "It's—it's really over."

Lagash stirred, uncoiling from her rest like a great serpent, eyes narrowing as she lifted her head and stared around her. "What... where...?"

My mother's scream still echoed in my mind. I felt soiled, corrupted. Used. I shivered, then gave Lotharia a squeeze. "We're out, Lagash. Xylagothoth is dead. The keep is ours."

My XP chime sounded, then again and in a flurry, so many chimes overlapping that I couldn't make out a single note.

"The others?" Lagash rose to her feet, hands rising to touch the hilts of her falchions crossed behind her back. "Vanatos, Balthus...?"

"If they died," said Lotharia, "then their souls are finally released. They'll be respawning now, along with everyone else who was caught in here."

Lagash nodded slowly. "So we're the last ones left."

"Yep." I didn't like the way she was standing. The tension in her frame. "Come on. Let's go check the way into the dungeons below."

Lagash gave another slow nod and stood a little straighter. "Good idea. Follow me."

Lotharia shot me a questioning glance as we fell in behind the orc, but I simply shook my head. I knew just how acute Lagash's senses were. We descended the stairs to the entrance hall, passed through the empty kitchen, and then into the pantry that featured a large trapdoor in its center.

Lagash snorted. "The magic barrier's gone." She crouched by the trapdoor, grasped the large iron ring, and with a grunt lifted the door a couple of inches before releasing it and letting it crash back down. "Looks like the way to the treasure is now open."

"Good," I said. Falkon would be respawning even now in the highland meadow. Michaela? I'd no idea. She'd been in Death March mode but had never actually died. Wherever she was, she was too far to be of any help. Lagash turned to face us both full on. I checked my mana surreptitiously: zero out of thirty-three.

"It's been a pleasure working with you, Chris," said the orc.

"You sound like our friendship's coming to an end," I said. My mind was racing. If Lagash decided to kill us, there was absolutely nothing I could do. My stone cloak was tapped out. My shadow belt was used up. My Ring of the Bull was still recharging. I had my Void Blade, but I wasn't even going to pretend that I could stand toe-to-toe with Lagash in straight combat for more time than it took her to cut off my head.

"I'm the last of the Beggars, which means it's up to me to fulfill our contract." Was that reluctance I heard in her voice?

"By yourself?" Lotharia tried for scorn and almost managed. "In the dungeon below? No matter how tough you are, you'll be slaughtered."

"No, not by myself. I'll hold the castle till the others rejoin me."

"All their gear is on these tables," I said. "It'll be a sight more difficult for them to travel here a second time."

Lagash's eyes were flat. Emotionless. "They can call in debts, get a teleportation spell cast."

"Well, damn," I said. That nixed that line of argument. "So, what's that mean, then? You plan to kill us? After all we've been through?"

"Not if I don't have to," said Lagash. "I'd rather not. But I'll ask you to leave Castle Winter and not come back. Our friendship ends when you walk out the gate."

"Fine," I said. Easy to agree to an offer in which you have no choice. "I take it you mean to escort us out?"

Lagash inclined her head.

We left the storage room and marched through the kitchen. Sunlight made everything appear quaint, almost banal. No creeping shadows, no atmosphere of dread. Just dust and old pots and ashen fireplaces.

We'd team up with Falkon and Michaela. Retreat to Barry's cave and plan a way to take out Lagash before the rest of the Beggars could return. Even if all of us moved against Lagash, I didn't think we had a good chance. She was just that damn powerful.

We stepped into the narrow hallway. Lagash was as smart and competent a player as I was, and worse, had a killer avatar to work with. That meant she'd expect our attack. She'd probably hole up in the keep and force us into a frontal assault. Our best bet would be for me to sneak people in with my powers, but she now knew my character sheet in intimate detail. It'd be really hard to surprise her.

"Chris," said Lagash from behind, and I turned, expecting a blade to the chest. Instead, Lagash had her arms crossed, chin lowered. "If you come back, I'll target you first. Any attempt to remove me will depend on your darkblade abilities. But I know exactly what you're capable of, and I know you're in Death March mode."

I stared at her in silence.

"Don't come back, Chris. Just like I know your sheet, you know mine. You know what I'm capable of. Don't make me kill you."

I didn't respond. I simply held her flat gaze and then turned back to the door. I shoved it open with more force then was perhaps strictly necessary, took a few steps out into the sunshine and staggered to a halt.

Some seventy or eighty orcs stood arrayed before us in the bright sunlight. While unarmored and bearing crude weapons, they were impressively muscled, their dark green skin marked with white war paint. A ripple ran through their ranks at the sight of us, and a low growl filled the air like a hundred junkyard dogs deciding we'd taken one step too far into their territory.

The bottom dropped out of my stomach. We were surrounded by feral, furious gazes, bared fangs, heavily muscled shoulders hunched in anger, knuckles whitening around the grips of clubs and spears.

"Chris!" A young woman made her way to the front, orcs stepping aside with deference and bowed heads. "You made it! Awesome!"

I did a double take. "Brianna?"

She'd donned primitive garb, a leather wrap pulled tight around her generous chest, a bikini bottom and knee-high boots completing her outfit, crossed bandoliers of daggers and her blade at her hip. She wore streaks of the same white paint across her cheeks and bare shoulders, and her infectious grin was utterly incongruous with her savage company.

Her gaze slid over to Lotharia, and her grinned thinned out, but then she moved to stand beside what had to be the orc leader, a hulking mass of dusky muscle and yellowed tusks, and gave him a hug.

"You've just got meet our new friends! This here's Shaman Lickit – he's the spiritual leader of the Big Burpie tribe. Wacky names, right?"

"Shaman... Lickit?" I stared at the monster by Brianna's side. He stood almost seven feet tall, and his massive chest was covered in endless ropes of shiny trash, like fragments of broken mirrors, bent silver coins, and shards of metal. "Holy crap. It really is him."

Shaman Lickit growled so deeply it felt like the rocks beneath our feet were shifting. "Chris is friend of Queen Brianna. That makes him friend of Big Burpie tribe."

"I... great." I walked forward, Lotharia by my side, and then it dawned on me. I turned around to stare at where Lagash stood all by herself in the keep's doorway, eyes wide, both her falchions hanging limply from her hands.

"That's really great to hear," I said, voice growing more confident. I couldn't help but grin. "Hey, Lagash. Look. More orcs. Want to come out and meet them?"

"Shit," said Lagash.

Shaman Lickit let out another growl, and this one seemed much more.... appreciative.

"Brianna," I called out, not taking my eyes from where Lagash stood. "If you asked Shaman Lickit to remove Lagash from the castle, would he be willing to do so?"

Brianna's voice was a trifle more focused now, her tone a little more concerned. "Sure. Right, Lickit?"

An assenting rumble came from behind me.

"Sorry, Lagash. Looks like your luck's run out."

Her eyes flicked from side to side. She half turned to consider the keep, eyed the thickness of the door. I could imagine what she was envisioning. How she'd bolt inside, slam it closed and bar it. Trying to imagine how long it would take the orcs to batter it down. The hellish combat that would ensue as she fought off an endless wave of berserking orcs, retreating until she was cornered. She was probably trying to gauge how many she could kill before she'd be overrun. Twenty? Forty? Sixty?

Whatever the figure, it wasn't enough.

She reached up and sheathed her falchions over her shoulders, and to my surprise gave me a grin. "Ah, well. Looks like I've got no choice. Castle's yours, Chris."

"Just like that?" My character sheet chimed. "You don't even seem mad about it."

"I'm not. As long as I have absolutely no chance of holding the castle, Vanatos can't punish me. Which means I can stick it to him by giving it to you, and then watch him rage. Fair warning, though: he won't give up easily, and even eighty orcs will have trouble keeping all five of us from taking back the castle."

"Yeah, sure. And, um, why exactly are you working for Vanatos if you're not a big fan? Anything we could offer you to make you switch sides?"

Lagash's smile faded away. "I wish. I really do. But my cards have been dealt. The next time we meet…"

"Yeah," I said. "I know."

"Well, then." She straightened. "It was an honor fighting alongside you. See you soon." And with that, she marched directly toward the gate. I turned to watch her go, at once impressed and sobered by her attitude, her capacity, her sheer lethality that made the orcs part before her as if she radiated a killer heat.

Nobody spoke till she was gone, and then Brianna let out a cry of joy. "Success! I knew you could do it!" She ran up and hugged me tightly, leaping into my arms so she could kick up both legs behind her. I staggered, forced to hug her back so as to not drop her, then carefully set her down.

"Brianna? This is Lotharia."

Brianna turned to her with a glittering smile and narrowed eyes. "I thought you'd be prettier."

"I – excuse me?" Lotharia looked bewildered. "I—weren't you…?"

"I'll catch you up," I said. "A lot happened while you were away." I didn't like how Brianna was staring at Lotharia, but when I raised my hand to rub at the back of my neck I caught sight of that star of scar tissue again. Brianna was part of my life. In a way, she'd saved me in there. And she'd saved us out here, right now, again.

"I'm glad to see you, Brianna." I realized I meant it, though probably not in the way she wanted. "Thank you."

She cocked her head to one side and gave me a superficial smile. "Any time, Chris. You know I'd do anything for you."

"Great, thanks." I didn't like the way she was staring at me at all. Time to change the subject. "But, um, how did you get in so tight with Shaman Lickit?"

Brianna glanced down at her nails. "Oh, so folks don't find my company nearly so tiresome as you do. I came in here and found them all climbing to their feet, the poor darlings. I thought I'd have to fight my way through them but then I saw how Lickit was looking at me, and, well." She turned on her smile. "Some men are easier than others to wrap around your finger."

"Especially when you're rocking a charisma over nine thousand," I said. "Awesome. But for now, I think we'd best get some Big Burpies up on the walls and in the main gate. I don't think Lagash will come storming back in, but if we don't post any guards she might feel obliged. Then we've got to hit the highland meadow to meet up with Falkon, then head down to Feldgrau to see if Michaela's down there and give Guthorios the good news."

"We're not safe yet, are we?" asked Lotharia. "Lagash and her friends are coming back. And the dungeons below the keep… I dreamt of them while I was under. They're much worse than anything we've yet faced."

"No," said Lotharia. "You're not safe yet."

I ignored Brianna's tone. "But despite the odds, we're still standing. We cleared the keep and we've got possession of Castle Winter. If that's not a miracle, I don't know what is." I couldn't help but grin, a rich, stirring, deep satisfaction suffusing me, making me feel more alive then I'd ever been before. "And whatever comes, I know we can face it. I know we can win."

"He's cute when he gets excited, isn't he?" Brianna asked Lotharia, who simply blushed.

I laughed and, on impulse, opened my character sheet.

You have gained 832 experience. You have 869 unused XP. Your total XP is 2044.

```
        Congratulations! You are Level 14!
        Congratulations! You are Level 15!
        Congratulations! You are Level 16!
```

```
Congratulations! You are Level 17!
Congratulations! You are Level 18!
Congratulations! You are Level 19!
Congratulations! You are Level 20!
Congratulations! You are Level 21!
```

I stared, wide-eyed.

"Chris?" Lotharia touched my arm. "Chris? What's wrong?"

I gave a shout of exhilaration and then swept her up in my arms, spinning her around in a circle. "Wrong? Absolutely nothing. We're just getting started."

She smiled back at me in confusion and amusement, and I couldn't help myself. I leaned in and kissed her, kissed her truly, kissed her deeply, and when all eighty orcs let out an appreciative roar we laughed and hugged each other tight.

BOOK 3 OF EUPHORIA ONLINE

KILLER DUNGEON

PHIL TUCKER

About the Author

PHIL TUCKER IS a Brazilian/Brit that currently resides in Asheville, NC, where he resists the siren call of the forests and mountains to sit inside and hammer away at his laptop. He is currently working on the epic fantasy series, Chronicles of the Black Gate, launched in May 2016. Connect with him at www.authorphiltucker.com or drop him a line at pwtucker@gmail.com

Sign up for his mailing list here:

WWW.AUTHORPHILTUCKER.COM

Kickstarter Backers

ON May 1st, 2018, I launched a Kickstarter to fund the creation of interior art and the release of the Euphoria Online trilogy in hardcover format.

When the dust settled my Euphoria Online Kickstarter had attracted the support of 385 backers and raised almost $20,000. The project funded in less than twelve hours, and for much of the project's duration was the most popular publishing project across all of Kickstarter's categories.

To say I was stunned is to put it mildly.

Because of the generous support and enthusiasm of my readers and backers, I was able to commission the stunning interior artwork you saw in this novel, and release the books in gorgeous hardcover. I can't sufficiently express my thanks for the folks who chose to support me in this endeavor, and who are listed below with all my gratitude.

—phil tucker

Aaron M

Abel Orlando Garcia II

Abigail Keller

Abraham Lincoln

Adam Derda

Adam Weller

Adrian Collins

Aerronn Carr

Ahinahina

Aisha Laury

Alex Raubach

Alex Schwartz

Alex Tabor

Alexander X Rodriguez

Alexandra Askew

Alexey Vasyukov

Alfredo R. Carella

Alvin Lo

Amanda Longo

André Laude

Andrea Orjuela

Andres Zanzani

Andrew M.

Andrew M. Lyons

Andrey Lukyanenko aka Artgor

Angus Frean

Anita Harsjoeen

anon

Anonymous

Armando V.

Arook

Ashley Niels

Ashli Tingle

Aurelia Smith

Austin Brown

Autumn PeLata

Axel Nackaerts

Barbara Pitman

Ben

Ben

Ben Galley

Ben Heywood

Ben Trehet

Bernie S.

Bracht

Brandon S.

Brannigan Cheney

Brewmasster ov däss

Brian Becker

Brian Griffin

Brijwhiz

Brittany Hay

Brooke

Bryan Geddes

Bryan H.

Bryan Shang

Bryce O'Connor

Bryce Vollmer

C Forry

C. Scudder Mead

Caitlin Krueger

Cameron Brunton-Hales

Cameron Johnston

Captain Dray MacGregor

Carl Armstrong

Carlee Sims

Carole-Ann Warburton
Caroline Kruger
Cat H
Cedric Gasser
Charli Maxwell
Chris B.
Chris Black
Chris Jiang
Chris Roberts
Chris Torrence
Chris Vinson
Christina Bryant
Christina Gale
Christoffer Sevaldsen
Christopher Goetting
Christopher Huddleston
Clay Sawyer
Clementine and Rosemary
Cody Wheeler
Connal
Corey Fake
Cory Crowe
Daefea
Dale A. Russell
Dan
Daniel
Daniel K
Daniel Sgranfetto
Darrius Taylor
Dave & Christy Quigley
Dave Snowdon
Dave Upton
David Andre

David Kitching
David Queen
Dayvd D
Dean McQuay
Derek J Roberts
Derrek Kyzar
Derrick Eaves
Dianne Munro
Dion F. Graybeal
Do not include a name
dogmadude
Don Reiter
DRJ
Dustin Cramer
e
E. Mac
Ed McCutchan
Ed Wallace
Edwin, Eli and Ender Hunt
Eric miller
Eric Terrell
Erik Jarvi
Erik Nielsen
Errel Braude
Esko Lakso
Ethan Michael Thompson
Gabe and Nicholas
Gavin Claxton Mahaley
GhostBob
Glenn Curry
Goran Zadravec
Greg Tausch
Grendelfly

Hannah Tanner
Haunar
Heather Q
hidsnake
HiuGregg
I do not need my name listed.
Ian Mitchell
Iliyan Iliev
Inga
Iquito
Ivan Majstorovic
J Ford
J Goode
J Lance Miller
j wright
J. Eged
Jack Ankeny
Jackie Standaert
Jacob "Iocabus" Jones
Jacob Matthews
Jaime gilbert
Jake Whipple
Jakob Ingi Vidirsson
James H.
James O.
James Poe
James Rowland
James Yeary
Jamie Danielle Woods
Jamil
Jan Thomas Jensen
Janet Young
Jason Campbell, MD

Jason Coleman (BX)
Jason Rippentrop
Jason Sickmeier
Jay Peterson
JC Kang
Jeffrey Berry
Jeffrey Hurcomb
Jeffrey Munro
Jennifer L. Pierce
Jer
Jeramy Goble
Jesper Pettersen
Joe Dorrian
Joe White
Joe Williams
Joel Roath
Joel Wright
John Couchman
John Iadanza
John Idlor
John Woosley
Jonathan Garcia
Jonathan Haas
Jonathan Johnson
Jordan Hoddinett
Jordan Jones
Jose Javier Soriano Sempere
Joseph Born
Joshua Anderson
Joshua Basham
Joshua Stewart
Joshua Thornton
JP Pinsonneault

Justin B. Ellis
Justine Bergman
Juts
Keanu Bellamy
Kelly Bowen
Kelvin Neely
Kenneth Kalchik
Kepi
Khyreerusydi
Kimberly Kunker
Kopratic
Kristen McDowell
Kristen Roskob
Kristian Handberg
Kristy Wang
Kyle Pike
Kyle Swank
Landrovan
Larry J Couch
Lawrence Preijers
Leah White
Leila Ghaznavi
letoze
Loeki
Luke Challen
Lynn Worton
Madison Treat
Making adventures more like
    life. - Joh
Marc
Marc Rasp
Marcos Ramirez
Martina

Matt Klawiter
Maureen Bacon
Max Dosser
Maz
MC Abajian
Micbri
Michael D. Taylor
Michael Downey
Michael Fazio
Michael Hodgman
Michael J. Sullivan
Michael Leaich
Michael Q Anderson
Michelle Findlay-Olynyk
Michelle P. Dunaway
Mike Tabacchi
Mike Weber
Misko
Mitchel Geer
Mitchell Hostiadi
Nate Cutler
Nathan
Nathan Anderson
Nathan Nabeta
Nathan Turner
Negative Red
Nick Human
Nick Ryckbosch
Nicolas
Nimrod Daniel
Norman Rechlin
Not necessary.
nothing

Old Grey Haired woman
Oliver Knight
Orliv
P carvalho
Pam Wickert
Paolo Jackson
Pat Walsh
Paulo
Penny Evans
Pery R
Peter Badurek
Pobin
Pornokitsch
Przemek Iskra
Psiwizard
Rama Lex
Rebecca Mc
Reuben
Rev. Kevin Muyskens
Rhcoll
Rhel ná DecVandé
Riccardo Maderna
Richa
Ridian Jale
Rob Henschen
Rob Holland
Robert F Towell
Robert Karalash
Robert Q
Roger Stone
Rory Thrasher
Rosie Vincent
Roxanne Lingenfelter
Ryan Leduc

Ryan Porter
S Gelgoot
Saad Hasan Syed
sal1n
Sally Qwill Janin
Sara G.
Sarah Merrill
Scott Dell'Osso
Scott Foster
Scott Frederick
Scott M. Williams
Sean Anderson
Sean L
Sean McCune
Shadowcodex
Sharon Wells
Shawn Polka
Shawna J. Traver
Simon Julian
Sir Aaron of Clan Shaefer
Stephanie Au
Stephanie Carl
Stephanie Meier
Sterrin
Steve Brenneman
Steve Thompson
Steven Lank
Stubbs
Succotash
Susan Contreras
Susanne Porter
SwordFire
Sylvia L. Foil
Tam

Tanner McVey

Tarasa Escoubas

Tavis W.

Thank you Andrew

ThatAnimeSnob

Thomas Pettersson

Thomas Stratton

Tim

Tim Harron

Todd L Ross

Tomas Bowers

Tomer Bar-Shlomo

Tommye Hart

Tony

Tony Muzi

Tony Nguyen

Trae Watkins

Travis G

Travis Horner

Tyler Chadwick Rabren

Victoria Johnsen

vikyle

Walter Schirmacher

Wayne Mathers

Will Pomerantz

William C. Tracy

William Robbins

Wolfram Pfeifer

Zach Slade

Zack McFarland

ZAK

Zathras do Urdenz

PHIL TUCKER

The PATH OF FLAMES

The Path of Flames

Book 1 of the
CHRONICLES OF THE BLACK FLAME
Is available now.

The first book in the epic fantasy series readers are comparing to David Gemmell and Raymond E. Feist.

A WAR FUELED BY the dark powers of forbidden sorcery is about to engulf the Ascendant Empire. Agerastian heretics, armed with black fire and fueled by bitter hatred, seek to sever the ancient portals that unite the empire - and in so doing destroy it.

Asho—a squire with a reviled past—sees his liege, the Lady Kyferin, and her meager forces banished to an infamous ruin. Beset by tragedy and betrayal, demons and an approaching army, the fate of the Kyferins hangs by the slenderest of threads. Asho realizes that their sole hope of survival may lie hidden within the depths of his scarred soul—a secret that could reverse their fortunes and reveal the truth behind the war that wracks their empire.

Unpredictable, fast paced, and packed with unforgettable characters, The Path of Flames is the first installment in a gripping new epic fantasy series. Grab your copy today!